When Time Stands Still

Sara Furlong Burr

CHAPTER ONE

"It's Luke," she said, her voice flat. She spoke his name with care, handling it as though it were an egg balancing precariously on the edge of a spoon. Her trepidation, so raw and apparent, had inherently transferred itself into me the moment I heard her voice on the end of the line, forcing me to soak up every tear she must have shed over the last few weeks like a sponge. And despite the care she took, at some point, the egg she was balancing fell from the spoon and exploded on the ground, leaving nothing but a hollow shell in its wake. All emotion had been sucked out of her, rendering her so fragile that even the slightest jostling threatened to shatter what remained of her into a million pieces. "Something's happened, Elle."

The very second my synapses transmitted her voice from the receiver to my brain, resurrecting memories I had long ago laid to rest deep within the recesses of my mind, I'd grown numb. I'd grown so numb, in fact, that I hardly heard the words she spoke, except for bits and pieces; for my mind had been racing almost as fast as my heart, and it had been all I could do to keep my composure and not fall to the floor in despair in the cramped confines of my cubicle.

Not usually an eager telephone conversationalist outside of work, I had nonetheless been thankful that we hadn't been having this conversation in person, so she couldn't see just how much my hands were shaking or how pale I knew my face had become. I suspected she, too, was thankful for this, as every so often, a slight tremble in her voice presented itself, betraying the strong-willed woman she had always presented herself to be. Broken, she had somehow managed to assemble some of the pieces together again and was doing everything in her power to keep them in place.

"I know this is going to sound crazy," she'd continued, the defeat so strongly evident in her delivery I had begun to believe that she was feeling just as awkward speaking to me as I was with her, especially with all the time that had passed between us, "and I'm sorry for the imposition of my request, but you see, we're desperate. We've tried to avoid it coming to this, but he's been so demanding, bordering on the point of hysterical and, you see, we can't think of any other option. His doctors ... well, some of them, are hesitant, but others feel like this may help him, like—"

"I'll come," I'd said without hesitation, taking even myself aback.

The other end of the line fell silent, so silent in fact that I wondered briefly whether we'd been disconnected, even going so far as to remove the phone from my ear to check the screen before her voice returned at the other end. "Really?" she'd asked, overcome with disbelief. "Thank you, Elle. I can't express to you how grateful I am— how grateful we all are."

"Of course," I'd said, holding back the tremble in own my voice while trying to make myself sound like I, too, wasn't about to crumble right then and there. At my desk in a cubicle surrounded by a sea of my fellow call center co-workers, I'd had to keep my voice low and my emotions in check to keep from drawing attention to myself. Not to mention the fact that personal calls were understandably frowned upon, as well as enabling the busy function on our desk phones to take them. "Hey listen, Candy, I have to get back to work. Text the address to me, and I'll make all the arrangements I need to make to arrive tomorrow evening."

* * * * *

2

That conversation, now almost twenty-four hours ago, replayed over and over again in my head, like it was actually taking place in the present. Candy's voice, the sound of my past, drowned out the grinding sound of the road underneath my tires, the horns of disgruntled motorists, and the roar of vehicles in desperate need of a muffler repair. In contrast, it was deathly silent in my small, black Camry, yet the commotion going on within me was so loud it was deafening, and it wasn't until I pulled over to the side of the road and took in a series of deep breaths to calm my frazzled nerves that I realized I'd neglected to turn the radio on. Whether in the car for five minutes or five hours, I always had music playing. And its unnoticed absence was a testament to the jumbled mess going on inside of my brain.

Fingers shaking, I pressed the audio switch on the stereo touch screen, selecting the icon for my iPod over the option for satellite radio—all while thinking that if Eric were in the car with me, his irritation would have come in the form of a sigh, comically loud and drawn out to make his point. "Why pay for satellite radio if you never listen to it?" he'd ask.

"Because I like having the option to listen to it or not listen to it," I'd say, throwing in a, "Besides, you know I don't understand how to work the damn thing anyway," to exasperate him all the more.

Eric.

My left hand loosened its grasp on the steering wheel as my eyes trailed downward to the sizable princess cut diamond engagement ring and gold wedding band around the fourth finger of my left hand. I detested gold, always believing it to be the more pretentious of the precious metals. It had been bought in haste. The consequence of my having been late one month and of Eric's chivalrous need to make an honest woman out of me.

We'd married three months after he'd proposed, a month after any necessity for a shotgun wedding had dissipated in the form of a miscarriage, and only six months after we'd first met. A one-night stand that turned into a three-year-next-month marriage. Eric had taken

3

the news of my unexpected telephone call well. Much better than I had been expecting; much better still than I would have had the roles been reversed.

* * * * *

"So, your ex-boyfriend was in an accident?" Eric asked, repeating everything I had just told him, only at a much slower pace than my barely coherent blubbering had been. I'd found him standing over the stove in our kitchen, browning hamburger to use in the goulash I had planned on making that evening.

"Yes, a car accident," I answered him, attempting to recall the fuzzy bits of the conversation I'd had with Candy, praying that the shock to my system hadn't prevented me from having absorbed any pertinent information.

"And he woke up in the hospital after a month-long coma with amnesia?" Eric shut off the stove, removing the frying pan from the burner. Turning around to give me his undivided attention, he braced his body against the island directly across from where I stood.

"Yes, retrograde amnesia," I answered him, doing my best to sound like I actually understood the ramifications of Luke's diagnosis. Unable to make eye contact with him, I kept my eyes downcast, focusing instead on the scuff that had appeared across the toe box of my brand new pump.

"And because of this retrograde amnesia, he believes …"

"That he and I are still in a relationship. H-he can't remember anything that happened since 2008, or so his neurologist has been able to ascertain." Sensing his gaze on me, I looked up from the offensive mark on my otherwise perfect shoe and locked eyes with him. Even irritated, his face never portrayed a hint of malice. The only clue that something was wrong was the slight deepening of his usually sea foam green eyes to a hue resembling the turbulent waters of an ocean during a hurricane.

"And so when your ex-boyfriend's mother calls you and asks you

4

whether you will come and see him in the hospital seven hours away, you immediately acquiesce and agree to put your entire life—your job, your husband, your commitments—on hold at a moment's notice on the off chance you can somehow provide the miracle cure even his doctors cannot?"

"Something like that," I meekly squeaked out, realizing just how ridiculous it all sounded when read back to me. He said nothing further, instead staring at me from across the kitchen as though expecting me to spring a belated "Gotcha" on him at any moment. A seasoned trial attorney, he was waiting for my rebuttal, some well-versed prose that would cement my argument for making this trip with the jury he'd assembled in that analytical mind of his. "Look, Eric, I know how it sounds. I know I'm absolutely insane, but a part of me feels like I owe this to Luke for the way things ended between us."

"It's been what, seven or eight years since you broke up with him—"

"Nine years," I interrupted him. "Ten years this May."

"Okay." Laughing, he rolled his eyes. "It's been nearly ten years since you left him high and dry. If he isn't over that yet, that's his problem."

"That's just it, he doesn't know there's anything he has to be over yet."

"So you're going to make him relive the break up all over again?"

"I don't know, I haven't gotten that far," I confessed. Eric remained slouched over the island's granite surface, uncharacteristically quiet. Most likely, he knew that any attempt to change my mind would only prove futile. "Come with me?"

His expression softened, and a smile creased his face for the first time since I arrived home that evening. "As much as I'd like to spend the next week hanging out in a hospital waiting room while you time travel back to 2008 with another man, I have client meetings scheduled throughout the week, a brief due on Wednesday, and a trial that starts on Friday for a case involving a pretty important client of the firm's."

"So that's a maybe, then?"

He laughed, rubbing his temples, something he always did

whenever he was ready to concede a losing battle. I'd often wondered whether he broke that tic out while in the courtroom, too.

"On the contrary, that's a hard no, Elle Bell."

"Oh god, this being an adult crap blows the big one, doesn't it?"

"Speaking of being an adult, what on earth did you tell your supervisor?"

"That my favorite aunt from out of state passed away in a tragic boating accident."

"Oh, so a lie, then?" Eric leaned in closer across the counter, resting his hand on my own. "I must say, though, the use of a boat in your aunt's untimely demise was a nice touch, really authenticates things."

"If you're going to fib, you'd better not half ass it."

"Trust me, nothing about you is half-assed." Lifting my hand, he pressed his lips against the smooth skin of my fingers and sighed.

"Are you upset with me?"

Seconds passed—a few too many for comfort, in fact—before he answered me.

"No." His eyes looked down into mine, the fiery intensity of his irises having dissipated into their natural lighter shade of green. "It's hard for me to be mad at someone for just wanting to do what they feel is right. I mean, come on, what do you think I am, a dick or something?"

I laughed in spite of myself and joined him on his side of the island. "No, but I'm certain there are quite a few former opponents who would agree with that sentiment."

"Which means I'm doing my job." Wrapping his arms around my waist, he drew me in closer to him. "So, exactly how incapacitated is he, anyway? I'm not going to have to make an impromptu trip down to the intensive care unit to kick his ass for getting too handsy, am I?"

"He has two broken legs and several broken ribs to go along with his head injury."

"He's a man, that's not incapacitated enough."

"What do you think I'm going to do, completely forget I'm married and jump his bones in his hospital bed?"

"You're right, I'm being foolish. Besides, he probably wouldn't remember it, anyway."

"Eric Bell, you're positively horrible." I attempted to push him away, but his grip on me was resolute and my combativeness only served to make him tighten his grasp.

He kissed me lightly, his lips lingering on my own as he spoke. "Why don't we go upstairs so that I can give you something to remember me by?"

* * * * *

The early spring sun swiftly set on the horizon behind the splendor of the Allegheny Mountains, a welcome change from the relatively flat lands of southern Indiana, where a long drive was bound to put you to sleep. Seeing them in all their splendor, the remaining ghosts from my past came rushing back to haunt me, reminding me of the drives Luke and I used to take at my insistence. He'd grown up here, while I had only been in town long enough to attend—and eventually drop out of—Cogsworth University after two years. He'd chuckle to himself as I'd gazed awestruck at the emerald expanses towering around us as far as my eyes could see. Never condescending of my obviously sheltered life prior to arriving in Roanoke, he'd just smile whenever I would comment on how his growing up surrounded by such beauty must have been comparable to waking up in a fairy tale every morning.

And it was here in Roanoke where he was awaiting my arrival, completely unaware that his heart was destined to be broken by me once again.

CHAPTER TWO

2006

"He's been staring at you since we sat down. He's trying not to be obvious about it, but I see him. I've got his number," Mena spoke softly from across our table. Her eyes had been just as glued to the screen of her laptop, as mine had been to my own. It was beyond me how in the world she could have noticed anything outside of the Word document on the screen in front of her.

"Are you sure it's me he's looking at? You haven't turned your head once since we've been here, not even when giving the waiter your order ... which was kind of rude, I may add."

"I have a paper due tomorrow and no time for pleasantries, and I don't have to turn my head to see anything; my screen may as well double as a mirror with the way it's reflecting everything in this horrendous lighting."

"It beats sitting in our dorm room, listening to Bruce Springsteen on your iPod all evening," I muttered. Curious, I tried to see over Mena's chestnut brown hair, casually craning my head upward and then quickly looking back down again for fear of being caught.

"Keep that up and he'll think you're having a seizure," she quipped. "Give me a second and I'll bend down and act like I'm tying my shoe. You'll get an unobstructed view of him, then."

"Mena, for god's sake, you're wearing boots."

"He doesn't know that."

"How do you know he's looking at me? It could be you he fancies."

"Fancy? I thought we were in some dive coffee shop on the east side, not in a quaint café in some storybook English parish."

"Blow me."

"That's more like it."

Mena's finger made a final swipe across the touch pad on her keyboard, as she saved the paper she'd been feverishly working on for the better part of the last three days. Paper safely tucked away on her hard drive, her big, brown eyes glanced up at me for the first time since we'd been seated. "I know it's you he's interested in because, as you'll recall, I was walking behind you when we came in. Elle, when he saw you, it was like one of those scenes out of every corny ass romantic comedy I've ever seen ... you know, the one where time stands still the moment the love interest walks into the room in slow motion to the tune of some even cheesier eighties song playing in the background. That's how he was looking at *you*, not me. As far as I'm concerned, he's probably cursing my mother for my conception right now, since I'm the only thing standing in his way of getting an unobstructed view of you." She took a sip of her frappuccino, pursing her lips and narrowing her eyes in disgust as she set the cup back down. "The next time you want to drag me out of our dorm, I'm choosing the venue."

"At least I'll have until when hell freezes over before I have to worry about that."

Mena rolled her eyes, backing her stool away from the table. "Show time," she said as she bent down to inspect her lace-less boot.

I waited a few seconds before I allowed myself to look, trying not to appear overeager or make what we were really doing all too obvious to whomever it was I was trying to see. Truth be told, I hadn't noticed much when we walked in, instead keeping my eyes focused on the small table in the corner of the shop where we were now sitting; the perfect spot to be alone, yet among the Roanoke social scene at the same time. After the passing of a respectable amount of time, and finding myself unable to hold back any longer, I allowed my eyes to wander to the table situated twenty feet behind Mena.

"Well?" she asked.

"There's like a half dozen guys, all staring at either textbooks or laptops sitting at that table. Which one am I supposed to be noticing ogling me?"

"The blond one, third one from the end, closest to the door. Hurry up, I'm starting to get a neck cramp."

I glanced back up at the table full of our college-aged peers again, a little more obvious about it this time than before. If I'd had any doubts about the identity of the blond Mena had wanted me to find, they were quickly erased when, the second I found him, he found me, too. Everything told me to divert my attention elsewhere, not to make it obvious that I was staring back at him, but once my eyes caught a glimpse of his face, there was no turning away, despite my better judgment.

His blond hair was thick, bordering on shaggy, even though it was obvious from the way he was dressed and seemed to carry himself that he probably had painstakingly attempted to groom it before going out. It reminded me of my own unruly locks before I cut them to their length just above my shoulders, making them easier to maintain. Even more striking, though, were his eyes. Set in a round, cherubic, face were two azure orbs that stood out so vividly they couldn't help but take your breath away. Eyes that commanded your attention, that begged you not to look at anything else. I didn't look away, and neither did he. His blue eyes met my hazel eyes and they remained locked in a shameless tryst that wouldn't—perhaps, couldn't—be broken by either of us.

"For Christ's sake, Elle, how hard is it to find the only blond guy at—" Mena sat back up, breaking the connection. "Oh balls, he saw you, didn't he?"

"Something like that."

"And you just stared at him like a deer in the headlights, didn't you?"

I nodded, my face suddenly flush. "Is it possible to have sex with someone without actually touching them?"

Mena stared at me, transfixed, trying to decide whether my question was serious or rhetorical. "Well, I hope so, because that's the only way I'm ever going to do it with Professor Dietrich."

"We need to go. Now." I closed my laptop, grabbing the straps of its case from the hook underneath our table.

"Go?" Mena asked, confused. "You aren't going to introduce yourself to him, first? I think that's only common courtesy, considering you just eye-fucked the hell out of him."

"I chose Cogsworth University, a school comprised predominately of women, to avoid situations like this. I-I can't get into a relationship. I'm not putting myself through the same thing I went through before."

"Wait, are you talking about the high school boyfriend? That was three years ago, Elle. I know he was an asshole, but I think you can move on now." Mena grabbed her coat, hurriedly shoving her arms into it out of frustration.

"An asshole?" I zipped my laptop up inside of its case and slung the strap over my shoulder. "The last time I saw him, he beat me over the head with a coffee mug until it shattered and then assaulted me as I laid on the floor half conscious in a pool of my own blood. Yet, I still came out of the whole ordeal feeling sorry for *him*. He wasn't an asshole, Mena, he was a sadist."

"But you left," Mena offered, her voice softening considerably. "You managed to get away from him."

"And I'm not breaking that cycle now." I reached into my pocket and fished out a ten dollar bill, enough to pay for both of our drinks with a reasonable tip, and threw it on the table as I breezed past Mena, making it a point not to look anywhere but straight ahead. Behind me,

Mena's footsteps frantically struck the floor. Considerably shorter than me, her legs had to work overtime to catch up to my strides. Farther behind us, a noise resembling a chair scooting across the shop's tile floor provided an ear-splitting screech that slaughtered the otherwise library-like silence.

Was that him? Is he coming after me?

Like an errant top, my mind spun with contradictions. My heart, sensing the absolute connection that had undeniably been made between two strangers in a coffee shop, beat erratically. All the while, my brain made flashbacks of my past come to life, aiding to speed up my legs even more in a somewhat fight or flight scenario.

"Dammit, woman, slow down." Mena, now close to a jog, managed to catch up to me. Her coat was unbuttoned and had swiftly begun falling off one of her shoulders during our hasty retreat, and she struggled to finish zipping her half-open laptop case closed. "You know there are some good ones out there, right? And unless you want to make the news when you die at the age of eighty and your body is found in your apartment, partially consumed by your two dozen cats, I suggest you at least take a leap of faith."

We'd made it out of the shop and to the parking lot, where my head was becoming clear again with the sting of the cool fall breeze against my skin. "It's not just that ..." I paused, leaning my body against a lamppost, "my entire life has been comprised of a series of letdowns, perpetrated by pretty much everyone I've allowed to get close to me. That last relationship with Kyle—"

"Asshole," Mena corrected me. "Don't give him a name; he doesn't deserve one."

"Okay, during my relationship with Asshole, I completely lost myself, who I was, what I stood for. It's like I didn't exist anymore. I was nothing, which was exactly how I'd been made to feel my whole life, until I left home. I've found myself since I've been in Roanoke, and I don't want to lose me again."

"Man, I really need to get you laid," Mena said, buttoning up her coat.

"Nice, really nice, Mena. That's so the opposite of what I need. What do I have to do to make you understand the poin—" A sudden movement in my field of vision commanded my attention, simultaneously causing me to forget what I had been saying mid-sentence.

The contradictions returned even before I allowed myself to look up at him, exhilaration and fear waging a war on my digestive tract. My body knew it was him even before I could visually confirm it.

Eyes wide, Mena turned and then quickly spun back around again to face me with a smile on her face that could rival the width of the Grand Canyon.

"I'm sorry," the blond boy spoke. His voice gave me pause; deep, yet just soft enough not to come across as threatening. And my eyes found his again, where they remained locked just as they had only moments prior. He was tall, towering over me. No small feat considering I was pushing six feet myself. "I meant to introduce myself in there," he said, needlessly pointing in the direction of the coffee shop, "but you left so fast, this was my only option. Now I probably look really desperate."

"That's a coincidence," Mena said, patting me on the back, "because Elle's middle name is desperate."

I was thankful then for the poor lighting from the lamps in the parking lot and the steadily approaching nightfall, because I knew my face had probably turned about thirty shades of red. 'Bitch,' I mouthed at Mena, hoping she was the only one who saw it.

"I'm Luke," he continued, ignoring Mena's comment. "Luke Hutchins. Your name is Elle? Is that short for Eleanor?"

Mena discretely elbowed me in the back, forcing me to speak after I'd taken too long to respond to his inquiry. "Ellen, actually, and my middle name isn't Desperate, it's Rae."

Behind me Mena muttered, "Oh Jesus Tapdancing Christ, Elle," under her breath. I took a few steps forward, putting some distance between myself and her commentary.

"Do you live in Roanoke, Luke?" I asked.

13

"Only my whole life." With the way he answered the question, it seemed that fact irritated him. Perhaps, more than anything else. "I'm a student at Roanoke Community College."

"Cogsworth," I said. "I attend Cogsworth University."

"Cogsworth … impressive. I know a couple girls who go there. You have to be pretty amazing to get in there."

"Oh, and exactly how many girls do you know, Luke?" Mena asked, prompting me to turn around and cast her a warning glance, which she just shrugged off.

Thankfully, Luke found some humor in it. "Not very many at all." He chuckled, somewhat embarrassed by that fact. "I think that must be pretty obvious, what with my complete lack of game."

"That's okay, Elle doesn't know too many people here, either," Mena offered again. "In fact, I was planning on taking her on a tour around town on Friday night, but something has suddenly come up. Perhaps you'd like to take my place, Luke?"

I couldn't be certain, but I was fairly confident that my jaw had fallen and was now but mere inches from scraping across the asphalt. Shock had overcome me to the point where all I could do was stand there like an idiot, speechless aside from the thought that I was going to kill Mena when we returned to our dorm. "Yo-you don't have to. Really, don't let my frien—"

"Of course," he said before I could argue any further. His posture had relaxed a bit, a sign he was becoming more comfortable, which should have conceivably transferred itself onto me, too. Instead, my hands became clammy, and my stomach twisted itself into knots. "I'd love to show you around. I know Roanoke like the back of my hand."

"And the palm, surely," Mena quipped just audible enough for me to hear her.

"What time should I pick you up and where?"

"Wha— Uh, I …"

"What my friend here is trying to say is that she'll meet you downtown at Magillicutty's at six o'clock sharp, where you can have

SARA FURLONG BURR

the honor of buying her dinner while you both come up with a game plan for the rest of the night."

"Mena!"

"Well, I guess I don't have to introduce myself to him now."

"Actually, that sounds like a plan to me." Luke smiled sheepishly in my direction, as he slid his own laptop case off his shoulder and opened one of the side pockets, where he removed a pen.

"Here," Mena said, digging in her purse. She pulled a crumpled envelope out and tore it in half, handing it to Luke, who took it with a smile and a nod. "And now you." She handed the other half of the envelope to me, along with a tube of bright crimson lipstick, labeled Hearts On Fire. I glanced up at her, prompting her to shrug as, with a sigh, I opened the tube and began carefully gliding the ruby hue across the paper to form the ten digits of my cell phone number. It reminded me a bit of the pastel art I used to do when I was a child while my mother lay passed out on the couch surrounded by a cluster of pills and beer bottles.

"Don't worry, it's my real number," I said, exchanging my paper for his. A slapping sound erupted behind me, most likely the result of Mena having struck her forehead with the palm of her hand.

"That's a relief, because I was a little worried," he replied with a chuckle, as he inspected the slip of paper I'd handed to him. "Where's the eight-one-two area code?"

"Indiana. Jasper, Indiana, to be exact."

"Of which you can learn all about this Friday night." Mena plucked the lipstick tube out of my hand, threw it back inside of her purse, and locked her arm around mine. "But now, Elle and I have to get going back, as I have a paper due in the morning and at the rate you guys are going, we're going to be here all night."

"Yeah, I actually have an assignment due myself," he spoke. "Not to mention a table full of confused, abandoned classmates I probably should get back to." He smiled at me, a crooked smile with perfectly straight teeth. "It was a pleasure meeting you, Elle, and I'm looking forward to getting to know each other a little better on Friday."

15

"Totally," I said. "It's a date."

"Yeah, I suppose it is."

"Well, this has been fun, but we best be on our way," Mena interceded, steering me in the direction of her car. "Ciao, coffee shop boy."

I wanted to look back, to see whether he was watching us leave, to get one final view of his face so that I could to commit it to memory, but with astounding restraint, I kept my eyes glued to Mena's Ford Focus as the beating in my chest subsided.

"What the hell just happened?" I asked once we were both seated inside of her car.

"I just landed you a date with a tall, dark, and handsome—"

"Stranger."

"You're welcome. Besides, we're all strangers to each other at one time or another."

"What's wrong with you? Even better, what's wrong with me for not stopping you?"

"You didn't want to stop me—that's your answer. Come on, Elle, I saw the way you were looking at him, and the way he was looking at you, too. That's not something you can just walk away from, because if you did, you'd spend the rest of your life wondering what if, and that's no way to live your life."

"What if he's crazy … like certifiable? I don't want to end up on an episode of *Dateline*." I studied the numbers scrawled on the paper. His handwriting was unremarkable, with the typical harsh, masculine edges synonymous with male penmanship. For some crazy reason, it relieved me to see that, as though the credibility of his sanity would have been questionable otherwise.

"Which is why I'll hang out around town. You know, stay close in case he gets all freaky deaky on you."

"Mena, I know my way around Roanoke better than you do, and that's not saying much, considering neither of us know our way around Roanoke. I actually nearly lost it when you broke out that whole taking me on a tour bullshit."

"Yes, but wasn't it genius? At least it accomplished what I hoped it would: Him asking you out on a date. We just have two days to work out the logistics."

"Or back out."

"You'd better not!" She hit the brake so suddenly it made the back of my head smack against my seat, as though her foot was protesting my statement right along with the rest of her. Thankfully, the traffic was light and there were no cars directly behind us. "Seriously, are *you* the crazy one? Because I'm really beginning to wonder."

"Am *I* the crazy one? With all due respect, I'm not the one sitting in the middle of the road right now."

Frustrated, she returned her foot to the gas pedal. We rode in silence for what was in reality probably only close to a minute, but at the time felt like a whole political science lecture, before Mena spoke to me again. "Look, I'm sorry. Call him and cancel it if you want. It's just that I saw a light in you that I hadn't seen before. Ever. You always seem so sad all the time, even though you try to hide it. I know a fake smile when I see one. The smile on your face tonight, it wasn't fake; it was beautiful. So, I reacted by doing what I thought may keep it there."

"Dammit, Mena," I said, my eyes watering. "Okay, you win. I'll go."

"What is it that has you so afraid? Is it happiness? Rejection? All of the above?"

"No, it's none of those things." I paused, thinking about what it was that actually did frighten me. "It's love. I'm afraid of falling in love."

2018

Mena, I need you now more than ever.

I sat in my car parked in the parking structure at Orion Medical Center, remembering the night I met him. My head rested on the steering wheel as I attempted to summon the strength Mena had tried to impart in me over the years. Having been born and raised in Ohio, she'd moved to New York shortly after graduating from Cogsworth, where she'd accepted a position at a publishing firm in Queens. We'd kept in touch over the years, more so in the earlier part, and less often after Eric and I were married. She never cared for Eric much.

I'd called her shortly after I'd left earlier today, leaving a message when, as usual, her phone rang straight into her voice mail.

The butterflies I'd experienced the night I first met Luke had steadily begun to migrate back into my stomach with each mile closer I came to Roanoke. There was currently a swarm in there, all vying to be the one to make me vomit, faint, or all of the above.

You can do this, Elle. It's just Luke. You know Luke. Just do what you told Candy you would do and then leave. In a few days, this will all be over.

Raising my head from the steering wheel, I took a handful of short breaths, willed my hand to reach for the door handle, and before my anxiety could direct me otherwise, forced myself to step out of my car. Taking more deep breaths, I began to make the walk toward the catwalk that would take me inside of the hospital. I'd purposely parked as far away as I could to allow myself the time to digest everything that was about to happen. Unfortunately, it also had the adverse affect and forced me to think of everything that may yet happen, both pleasant and not so pleasant.

My wedding ring weighed heavy on my left hand, like a load of bricks had been tied to my finger with string. It both reminded me that I needed to remove it from my finger before Luke could see it and question its existence, and also that Eric would be coming home right about now to an empty house and his ring still firmly around his own finger. *I'm so sorry, Eric.* Overcome with guilt, I placed the bands into a pocket in my purse. I'd make it up to him someway, somehow.

The catwalk was still remarkably bright, despite it being dusk, so much so that the fluorescent lighting mounted to it had yet to flicker to life. While making my way down the lengthy tunnel, I caught myself

18

stealing a glance at everyone I passed as they left the hospital. Did they know Luke? Were they briefed on my pending arrival? How long had they known Luke? None of the faces seemed familiar to me, but over nine years had gone by and people had a tendency to change.

People change.

Strangely, the thought hadn't occurred to me just how much I may have changed in a decade. I was just shy of twenty-two the last time I saw Luke and practically thirty-two now. Surely, I must have changed. Any childlike physical attributes that had remained present into my early twenties must have been exchanged for a more adult exterior by now. Had I gained weight? What about my hair? My face? It would be a dead giveaway the moment he saw me.

God, what the hell was I thinking? This isn't going to work at all.

I'd entered the hospital without realizing that I had done so. My mind was in another place, swirling like a whirlpool. In the foyer to the right, were the set of elevators Candy described on the phone. As instructed, once inside, I pressed the button for the fourth floor, suffering through the stops it made on the second and third floors to let others riding in the car with me in and out. I used this time to primp as best as I could, smoothing my hair from what I could see of it in my refection in the car's steel exterior.

When my stop came, it seemed like the doors were opening in slow motion. And as they did, they creaked and groaned with such ferocity I wondered whether they were trying to communicate to me to turn back, that all my fears were valid. But not unlike many other pieces of sound advice I'd received in the past, I chose not to listen.

Closing my eyes, I exhaled as I stepped out of the elevator and into the hallway.

CHAPTER THREE

2006

"I'll be around if you need me," Mena called out to me from the parking lot behind Magillicutty's.

"Gotcha," I called back to her.

"Just send a text."

"Yup."

"If I don't hear from you by eleven, I'll assume you're either going home with him or tied up in his trunk."

"Okay."

Passersby in the crowded parking lot chuckled, further egging her on. "Did you bring protection?"

"Oh, Jesus H. Christ, Mena!" I whirled around, bumping into a tall, solidly built man who had been walking behind me. Although plowing into me barely fazed him, I came a stone's throw away from crashing down on my rear to the asphalt. "You know I'm not having sex with him, and that's really none of your business, anyway."

"I was talking about mace. Geez, get your head out of the gutter." Though she maintained a straight face, I knew she was having the time of her life at my expense.

"I'll see you tonight."

"Love you, honey. Behave yourself! Don't stay out too late!"

"Go to hell."

To my extreme relief, the ladies restroom in Magillicutty's was directly inside the back door. Even more miraculous, it wasn't nearly as congested as I would have expected. Already, I could sense my pulse quickening from a trot to a leisurely jog. My forehead and cheeks were flushed. I had never been good at meeting new people, preferring the companionship of my own thoughts, instead. When it came to dating, I'd been even worse.

A reflection in the mirror took me by surprise at first. The young woman reflected in front of me looked positively terrified, and it wasn't until I'd taken a couple steps farther that I realized the person I was staring at was myself. Hands shaking, I reached inside of my purse and pulled out the bottle of anxiety pills I kept in there for occasions such as this. I may not have mace, but I had prescription sedatives, and they were almost as effective.

I popped one of the ridiculously small pills into my mouth, turned on the cold water in one of the bathroom faucets, and filled my hands with water, which I used to wash it down. Hands still dripping wet, I used the excess water to smooth my hair back behind my ears. A slight improvement made to the otherwise hot mess that stood before me.

Okay, Elle, it's now or never. You can't hide in this bathroom. Wait, can I? No. No, Elle, you can't. Now get out there and quit stalling.

From the outside, Magillicutty's looked pretty nondescript and quite cramped, hardly the weekend mecca for the Roanoke college scene, but flocked to it, people did. On the inside, Magillicutty's was pleasantly spacious, with a modern open floor plan that allowed far more people to fit into the space than what I was sure the fire marshal would deem acceptable. Craning my neck, I stood on the tips of my toes to look around the crowded room. In the middle sat the bar, and around that stood what appeared to be every single college student in the greater Roanoke area. At least it seemed that way from my perspective.

Wonderful idea, Mena.

My eyes scanned each face and head, not finding any familiarity among any of them. Maybe he wasn't coming? Perhaps, he'd been the one with the change of heart. It was either that or he had been swallowed by the sea of people before me, never to resurface again.

"It's a living hell in here, isn't it?" a guy's voice spoke behind me. Startled, I turned around to find myself face-to-face with Luke.

Just as we had done two days prior, we stood staring at each other for several seconds, only this time it was me who interrupted the silent conversation our eyes were having with each other. "I thought you were lost at sea." The sheer amount of people in the building forced me to raise my voice several octaves.

"It felt like I was for a bit, but luckily it spat me out next to you." His hand brushed my arm, sending a momentary shock wave through my body. "I'm not usually a personal space invader, but as you can see, no one else in here cares about that too much."

Behind Luke, more and more weekend revelers had poured in, packing us sardines in even tighter. The atmosphere had become positively stifling, bringing about beads of sweat across my forehead. If we stood here any longer, I feared that whatever latent claustrophobia I may have would present itself with embarrassing results, namely me hitting the floor after blacking out. Passing out wasn't that far-fetched. The vertigo had already begun to set in.

"Do you want to get out of here?" Luke asked, probably sensing that circumstances were about to become dire.

"Very much so."

He nodded, reaching his hand out to me like a life preserver, which I took without hesitation. Being big in stature worked to Luke's advantage. The crowd naturally parted for him as though he were Moses himself and God would smite them down had they done otherwise. In no time, we'd made our way to the front of Magillicutty's and were heading outside.

"There's a small Italian place a couple blocks down—that is, if you like Italian."

"Yeah, actually, that would be great. Anything's better than that rave we just left back there."

"It's funny, because the second your friend mentioned Magillicutty's, I wanted to start laughing."

"Why's that?"

"Because either she was exaggerating and she really doesn't know as much about Roanoke as she wanted me to believe, or she really hates you."

"Is all of the above an option?"

Luke laughed. He had an infectious laugh, one that couldn't help but make you feel happy, if not because of the sincerity behind it, then because of the way his face contorted when he did it. His eyes, normally wide, shrunk into slits; the dimple on his cheek came out of hiding, and the cleft in his chin became markedly more pronounced.

"If you suspected she was full of it, then why did you agree to Magillicutty's? Why not suggest somewhere else?"

"Well, that's just it, I wasn't certain, and I didn't want to take my chances by completely shooting down her idea with the only justification for doing so being because I didn't want to share you with half the town. I couldn't say, 'Gee, it sure would be nice to take your friend somewhere quiet and secluded.' Serial killer alarms would have gone off in her head."

"Well, there's been too many witnesses tonight, so don't get any ideas." I blurted it out before my brain could stop me. In the short space between my utterance and Luke's laughter, a burning sensation rushed through my face and neck.

"I guess it's a good thing I kept the receipt for the zip ties, duct tape, and shovel I bought this afternoon, then?"

With wide eyes, I glanced up at him, catching a hint of the smile he was trying to suppress in his profile, all while a smirk overtook my own face. "Zip ties and duct tape, eh? I must say, I'm pretty disappointed."

"Why's that?"

"It's so unoriginal and expected. I pegged you for an innovator, an arsenic and succinylcholine kind of guy."

23

"I'm not sure whether I should be terrified of you or completely intrigued right now."

"I get that a lot." I realized then that he hadn't let go of my hand in the two blocks we'd walked, and I was even more surprised by the thought that I didn't want him to. "Are you regretting sort of asking me out yet?"

"Sort of asking you out? What do you mean by that?"

"Well, you know, Mena kind of did the work."

"Trust me, Elle, had Mena not been there, I still would have managed to ask you myself. We may still be standing in the parking lot right now, but it would have eventually happened."

* * * * *

"You honestly believe that *Return of the Jedi* was better than *The Empire Strikes Back*?" His face projected sheer contempt and consternation, but his eyes revealed the laughter he was working overtime to hide. "No, I refuse to accept it, Sloan. I refuse to believe that my ears are hearing what my mind says they just heard."

"Oh, so now we're on a last name basis? Okay then, Hutchins, yeah, I most certainly said that. I said it, and I refuse to retract my statement." I gave him the same faux look of disgust, squinting my eyes and pursing my lips so blatantly that I feared it translated into more of a look of someone plagued by a week's worth of constipation than anger.

"Then I fear we may have reached an impasse here," he stated with a raised eyebrow and the smirk returning to his face. Strumming his fingers on the table, he projected an air of being deep in thought. "This changes everything. I mean, if I would have known you felt this way, I never would have considered asking you out. Now this is all just so … awkward."

"Would you like me to leave, Hutchins? Because I can totally get this fettuccine boxed up and take off, leaving you free to scour the town in search of more like-minded women." I motioned toward the steadily emptying streets with my hand, trying my best to remain serious.

He liked making me laugh. It was evident all over his face, like he'd accomplished some incredible feat anytime so much as a giggle resonated from me. We'd been so engrossed in conversation with each other since we sat down that neither of us had touched the plates of food in front of us in the half hour, or more, since our waiter had brought them. Relenting to the appetizing smell of Alfredo sauce, I grabbed my fork and stabbed one of the rubbery noodles, twirling it around the utensil.

"No, I'm not ready to give up on you just yet. I think you can be turned. I sense some good in you, young padawan." Following my lead, he began cutting into the likely lukewarm veal on his plate.

"Nope, sorry, there's nothing but the dark side over on this side of the table."

He studied me with his large turquoise pools for eyes. "Okay then, since I can't convince you to be reasonable about this, would you at least humor me and explain your reasoning … if any such reasoning exists."

"Well, Hutchins," I said between bites, "as you can probably tell, I am a woman."

"You don't say? I hadn't noticed."

Ignoring him, I continued, "And being a woman, I rather enjoy a movie with a happy ending from time to time. *Return of the Jedi* had it all, a father saving his son, a son figuratively saving his father, good triumphing over evil, and a bunch of dancing teddy bears, not to mention that Luke finally stopped being a whiny little bitch."

"I can't argue with the latter."

"So, did your parents name you after Luke Skywalker, then?"

"No, actually, I was named after my great, great, great, great, great Grandfather Hutchins. He was held as a prisoner of war in the Revolutionary War. The name has been somewhat of a family tradition, passed down from generation to generation."

"Oh wow, geez, I'm so sorry. I guess I shouldn't have assumed—"

"I'm just screwing with you." He snickered, the gleam returning to his eyes. "Yes, my parents, namely my father, named me after the prolific Jedi of lore. If my mom had been able to have more of a say, though, I probably would have been named after a famous historical war hero. She's a history teacher."

"And your father?"

"He's a mechanic at a BMW dealership in Salem. My father's a regular blue-collar kind of guy, something of which—I think—he's always been somewhat ashamed. Ever since I can remember, he's always pushed me to be more than him, to be better. What he doesn't realize is, I could try my entire life, but I will never be better than him. I won't even come close."

"You sound like you're very close with your father."

"He's my best friend, and the reason I'm in nursing school right now."

"Oh, so you're going to be a doctor? That's amazing, Luke."

"No, no," he responded, chuckling a little. "I'm not going to medical school."

"Oh." The thought that I may have just offended him brought out a sickness from deep within the pit of my stomach. "I'm ... I'm sorry, I shouldn't have assumed."

"It's okay, really. I've gotten the same reaction thousands of times from just as many people. My dad, he was recently diagnosed with Parkinson's disease. His symptoms are fairly manageable now, but in time, they won't be. And when they're not, I want to be able to help in in any way I can."

Struggling to fight back the tears, I turned my attention to the barely-touched meal on my plate. One of the first memories I had of my mother was of her telling me never to let anyone see you cry. To cry was to show weakness, and to show weakness made you vulnerable. Vulnerable was never something you wanted to be. My mother had always been something of a sage.

"What about your family?" he asked, returning my attention back to him.

"We're having such a good night, let's not ruin it now."

"That bad, huh?" he asked, beginning to laugh, but stopping short when he must have seen how serious my face looked.

"I like you, Luke, and I will tell you anything you want to know. I will. Just not now."

"So you like me?" He smiled, revealing teeth so brilliant and perfectly pearly white they looked like something straight out of a Colgate commercial.

"That was your takeaway from all of that?"

"Do you want to get out of here?"

"Uh, sure. Yeah."

He nodded. "Okay. I'm going to run to the restroom quick and then we'll head on out."

I nodded, watching as he plunked money down on the table to cover our tab before walking toward the back of the restaurant, where a sign indicated the restrooms were located. When he was out of sight, I grabbed my cell phone out of my purse. I'd silenced it after receiving the first text from Mena, much to her chagrin, apparently, as several more had followed the first.

So is he creepy?

Elle?

Are you still at Magillicutty's?

Please don't tell me you're in the trunk of his car.

Are you dead?!

Elle!!!

Dammit, you're too old for an Amber Alert!

Holy shit, Mena. Rolling my eyes, I typed a reply message to her to ease her anxiety.

I'm fine. See you later tonight.

She must have been sitting near her phone, as her response came just as soon as I sent my message.

Don't do anything I wouldn't do. Actually, retract that, please do. You need to get laid.

"Are you ready?" Luke asked, startling me.

"As I'll ever be." Hoping he hadn't stolen a glance at my phone, I threw it back inside of my purse and joined him, leaving the restaurant and our practically full plates behind.

2018

His room was down the hall, on the left, ten doors past the nurse's station, an eternity to most other visitors, except for me. I hadn't had a lot of time to mentally prepare for what may happen next. Perhaps, all the time in the world wouldn't even have been enough. Still, I felt like I needed every last second I could get. Luke had been moved to a regular patient room from the ICU the day Candy called me, three days after he'd awoken from his coma.

One, I counted the first room I came to after the nurse's station. *Two. Three.* Legs turning to rubber, I could feel the beating of my heart in my eardrums. *Is it too late to turn back? Yes, of course it is. Grow a pair, Elle.* Room number four came and went just as my gelatin legs went numb and I couldn't feel myself walking anymore. What would he look like? What would I even say to him? Should I just walk into his room? Maybe I should knock first? Was it proper protocol to knock?

Fortunately, I wouldn't have to wait too long, as the answers literally came to me when I passed the fifth room.

28

She was close to how I remembered. The last decade showed on her face, as time so often does, and I was certain, the last month had only served to advance the aging process that much more. Wrinkles had carved themselves deeper into her pale skin. Strips of gray streaked her light brown hair. Underneath that, though, were echoes of the woman I had known. Petite, she was positively sprite-like, never ceasing to leave me perplexed as to how in the world her body could have ever created the six foot, three inch man who had sprung forth from her womb. Seeing her gave me pause, stopping me dead in my tracks in the middle of the hallway.

She didn't notice me at first, too preoccupied by her own thoughts and her son in the room behind her. *Should I say something to let her know I'm here, or just leave her be to work out the internal conversation I sense she's having with herself?* Instead of speaking, I took a step forward, proving that actions indeed spoke louder than words, as my movement drew her attention. Upon seeing me, her face lit up with a smile, something of which I sensed hadn't been present there in at least a good month.

She brought her hands up to her mouth in conjunction with taking her first step toward me, and as hard as I tried to keep my composure, I couldn't suppress the tears from cascading down my cheeks.

"Elle," she said, walking slowly over to me as though I were a feral animal and she was afraid that I would take off if she were to make any sudden movements. "Oh my goodness, Elle. It's really you?"

"Hello, Candy," I was able to eke out, while wiping tears from my face with the back of my hand.

"You … you look exactly the same. Your hair, your face, you." She gestured at me in my entirety with both hands. "In all these years, you haven't changed a bit."

"What, Candy? Were you afraid I had gotten fat?" I asked, nervously laughing as I spoke.

"Honestly, yeah, a little bit." She chuckled, despite the tears that were forming in her own eyes. "In the back of my mind, I knew you probably looked just as beautiful as I remembered, but I couldn't help but worry that you'd somehow changed too much and that this whole thing would implode the moment Luke saw you, but geez, Elle, you're perfect."

She wrapped her arms around me in an unexpected embrace. Our difference in height forced me to bend down to reciprocate, and I held onto her shaking body just as tightly as she held onto mine until I felt her grip loosen. After I'd broken up with Luke, I just assumed that she must have harbored a sort of deep-seated hatred for me for tearing out her son's heart. Any ill-feelings she must have once harbored obviously had been buried for Luke's sake and whatever the goal was for me being here right now.

"You look amazing as always, too, Candy."

"Oh, honey, you don't have to be nice. I know I look like a hot mess—one that has been stomped on by an elephant, run over by a train, and then shit on by life." Up close, I noticed she wasn't nearly as put together as she had appeared from a distance. Eyeliner was smeared around one eye, the remnants of it having been rubbed away either from stress or from pure exhaustion. With the bags that had formed under each eye, I assumed it was the latter. Though impeccably dressed as always, her clothes were disheveled in appearance, with half her blouse having come untucked and a noticeable dark brown stain on the right thigh of her trousers in the shape of a ring, which appeared to have been from a coffee mug. In essence, she was a far cry from the polished woman I had known so many years ago.

"Why don't we take a walk down to the waiting room?" she suggested, guiding me back down the hallway in the same direction from whence I had just come. "There's much we need to discuss before you go in there."

* * * * *

"So how have you been? Well, I hope."

"I can't complain," I answered, purposely not offering up any of the details of my personal life to avoid reopening old wounds. "Pretty much just work and home. I lead a boring life."

"A boring life can be the best life to lead," Candy replied, staring blankly out the window in the fourth floor waiting area. "It was certainly understanding of your employer to allow you the time off work on such short notice."

I blushed a bit, thinking of the lie I had told my boss to get me here. "Yeah, well, when you hardly ever take any time off as it is, they're a little more accommodating when it comes to emergencies."

She nodded. "And your husband?"

I couldn't remember having mentioned Eric over the phone, but of course, in the age of social media, it wasn't a shock she would have found out that I was married, and probably also knew that I didn't have any children.

"Eric took it well, better than I would have. He thinks that my being here is important, and he supports it. I asked him to tag along, but he has a trial coming up in the next week and is busy preparing for it."

"An attorney? Good for you, eh?" She nudged me playfully with her elbow.

"I suppose," I said, looking for a way to divert the conversation. "How's Tom doing? Is he here?"

"Tom's hanging in there, like the rest of us. His Parkinson's has been stable for the last couple of years in that his symptoms haven't gone beyond stage three, but they're still much worse than they were ten years ago. That was actually one of the first instances where we began to realize the extent of Luke's amnesia. When he saw his father and how much worse his tremors were now compared to what they were then—and in not just one, but both of his hands—he completely lost it." Candy wiped her eyes with a tissue she pulled out of her purse. With the month she'd had, she was probably single-handedly supporting the Kleenex corporation. "Luke thought the stress of his accident had caused Tom's condition to progress. Tom hasn't been by to visit much since then. It's too painful for him to see the expression on Luke's face. The fear, the guilt, it's all been too much to bear."

"Luke and his father were always so close. It has to be torture, them being apart."

"He's been through worse." With the inflection present in her voice when she made that statement, I wasn't certain whether the 'he' she was referring to was Luke or Tom.

"How did the accident happen?" I asked, instantly wishing I could take it back when a new wave of pain washed over Candy's face. "You ... you don't have to talk about it, if you don't want to."

"No, no it's okay." She readjusted herself in her chair to make her body comfortable to compensate for the torture her mind was reliving. "It was at night and Luke was driving home from an evening out with the guys. He was traveling down the interstate, less than two minutes from his exit, when a car came barreling through the median, striking him head-on. The driver had been texting and admitted to police that he had taken his eyes off the roadway for ten whole seconds before he finally looked back up again. And when he did, he saw the brake lights of the car in front of him. There was no time for him to stop, so he reacted by swerving."

I closed my eyes, imagining the horror that Luke must have gone through in the final precious seconds he'd had before waking up again over a month later. Shuddering at the thought, I listened as Candy continued to recount the night that had ultimately brought the two of us together again.

"Ironically, the boy who hit Luke was the age Luke was in the year he thinks it is now. He walked away without a scratch, that boy, while Luke had to be extricated from his car. It was touch and go for a while; there were times when we didn't think he would make it. Luke had been on the verge of dying and the boy who hit him got to walk away and sleep in his own bed that night. Hardly seems fair, does it? I wouldn't wish all the suffering Luke went through on anyone, but the least he could have done was suffer a broken pinky toe to add some weight to the other end of the scale." She paused. At no time did I sense any malice from her toward the young man who'd hit Luke, indicating that she must have made peace with any hatred she may have initially held. Knowing Candy, that wasn't surprising. "You must think I'm a terrible person."

"No, no of course not," I replied, turning to Candy. "Heck, while you were talking, I couldn't help but think about how much I'd love to get my hands on that idiot and shake the stupid out of him."

Candy laughed, a welcomed sound in an otherwise dismal conversation. I hoped to hear more of it during the next week.

"When Luke woke up after a month of being in limbo, we thought the nightmare was over and that we could finally begin to heal right along with him. And then when he couldn't remember the accident or why he was in the hospital, his doctors assured us that it was normal. It was a coping mechanism. His body's way of dealing with the trauma. But when he started asking for you, demanding to know where you were, we realized the nightmare had followed him straight to consciousness."

"What did you say to him when he started asking for me?" It was one of the many questions that had been burning a hole in my brain.

"At first, nothing. We didn't know what to say, so we acted like the question wasn't being asked. We'd hoped it was temporary—his amnesia. But it kept persisting, and so did he. And after everything he'd been through, none of us had the heart to tell him that you weren't coming." Her voice broke a bit as she spoke that last sentence, threatening to break me, too.

I exhaled a breath I hadn't known I'd inhaled and had been holding in the first place. Candy and Tom had been the family I'd never really had, parents straight from a family sitcom. They were the Seavers, the Bradys, the Winslows. Everything I ever wanted and none of what I deserved. Her pain—all of their pain—was so palpable, it tore through me like a bullet shot from close range.

Candy spoke when the silence that had grown between us began to feel uncomfortable. "Usually visiting hours would have ended by now, but the hospital is making an exception for us."

33

"I wondered why there was no one else in here," I responded, taking a sip from my cup of fresh-twelve-hours-ago coffee I'd gotten at the wet bar adjacent to the waiting area.

"His neurologist doesn't believe this is a good idea. Some of the other doctors do, but not him. He thinks we should come right out and tell Luke everything now, that doing so may speed along the recovery process, or somehow make him remember the last decade of his life. Like flipping a switch, he called it."

"Why aren't you following the doctor's recommendations?"

"We are—or we will, rather. Just not quite yet. I need ... I need to see my son happy again, if only for a few hours. It's been a while since I've seen that, probably just as long for him since he's felt it. I know it's selfish of me, but I can't understand how a few moments of joy could damage him anymore."

I looked away, squinting my eyes to keep my composure. "And you," I began, stopping to clear my throat when the quiver in my voice threatened to destroy the unflappable image I was trying to project. "And you think I can make him happy?"

"I don't think. I know you can."

I nodded, gazing out the same window Candy had been fixated upon. Any trace of light that had been present outside had since vanished. Now all there was to stare at were our own reflections in the glass. It was through these images that we continued speaking to each other. "Is there something I should know before I see him?"

She smiled awkwardly, like her face had completely forgotten how to make that expression. "There isn't enough time in the day to brief you on all the idiosyncrasies of this place, or the way Luke is now, for that matter. Aside from the amnesia, the brain injury left him with some cognitive deficits that he's going to have to work hard to recover in therapy. He has debilitating headaches that his neurologist, Dr. Reid, is attempting to control with small doses of narcotics, but the medications make him groggy most of the time and he sleeps a lot. He becomes overstimulated easily, which prompted Dr. Reid to ban him from watching television. A good move for us, because if he were to watch pretty much anything on it, the jig would be up quite quickly."

"So I should lay off on the pop culture references. That shouldn't be too hard, considering my idea of entertainment consists of flipping through pages instead of channels."

"You're going to have to jump inside your time machine and forget everything about the last decade. It's not easy. Gosh knows I came close to slipping up a few times. My father—Luke's grandfather—passed away three years ago, and I made the mistake of making a statement on how he used to like canning his own tomatoes, speaking of him in the past tense. That took quite a bit of backtracking on my part. And even then, I don't think Luke believed me."

"When, approximately, in 2008 do you think his amnesia begins?"

"Sometime in the late winter or early spring, we believe based on some comments he's made about attending his cousin Dave's wedding in February."

"I remember going to that with him. It was a Valentine's Day-themed wedding, a lot of reds and pinks, if I remember correctly."

She nodded. "That's the one."

"Well, at least it wasn't summer or fall," I offered. "If that had been the case, then he wouldn't even be able to look out the window right now without becoming suspicious."

If the time frame Candy specified was correct, then that would put Luke at a point in time roughly two to three months before our breakup. I tried to think back to that point and the events that had transpired around then. The bottom had completely fallen out on my life around May, about a month prior to the end of our relationship. But before then, in February and March of that year, things had been good, downright wonderful, in fact. If I could have had any say in it, I would have chosen to have been transported back to that point in my life, too.

Candy stood up and stretched. "Luke has been chomping at the bit all day to see you, so before it gets too late, why don't we have you go in for a few minutes. If you're comfortable with that, of course?"

"Yes, of course," I answered her, my heart sinking back down into my stomach. "That's why I'm here, to see him."

I followed her as she began the walk back to Luke's room, practicing the deep breathing technique I was taught by my mother to help counter the anxiety attacks from which I'd been prone to suffering since my teen years. It was by far the most useful thing she'd ever taught me. A trashcan stood at the edge of the waiting room near the adjacent hallway and quickly became home for the stale coffee in my hand.

"I fixed up the spare bedroom for your stay tonight. If you want, you can leave your car here and ride home with me."

"Oh, Candy, I couldn't possibly impose upon you like that. I'll stop in at one of the hotels nearby and book a room."

"It's no trouble whatsoever, dear. Trust me, if anyone is imposing on anyone, it's us on your life. The least we could do is provide lodging while you're in town. Besides, what with the music festival taking place and the gaggle of parent open houses at the local universities, you're probably not going to be able to get a room anywhere close by."

I mulled over Candy's offer. Already, fatigue from traveling and the emotional toll this day had taken on me was beginning to set in, and I really didn't have it in me to drive around town to various hotels on the off chance one of them may have available accommodations from a sudden cancellation.

"I'll stay tonight," I offered. "But tomorrow I'm going to call around to some of the hotels to check on a room."

"Sounds like a plan." Candy stopped in front of the door to Luke's room, turning her body partially around to face me. "This is it, Elle, he's in there waiting for you. Are you ready?"

2006

"Are you ready?" Luke asked me.

"I should say yes, but no … no, I'm not even close to being ready yet." My head had come to rest on his shoulder. When it found its way there and how, I did not know. And it didn't matter.

"Me neither," he said almost in a whisper.

I glanced up at the clock on the dashboard of his sedan. Ten minutes after one o'clock in the morning. We had been sitting in his car, parked in the parking lot of my residence hall at Cogsworth, for over two hours, talking, laughing, not saying anything at all, and it never once felt awkward. Everything had been so natural.

"I have to work tomorrow morning," I moaned.

"Tell them you got car sick and then stay here with me. They'll understand." His body shook a bit as he chuckled at the thought.

"As tempting as that sounds, my books aren't going to pay for themselves."

"Yeah, tuition is downright brutal."

"Thankfully, that's one thing I don't have to worry about."

"My parents are paying for mine, too. It's my goal to pay them back someday, even if it's little by little."

"Oh, trust me, my tuition isn't being paid by my mother. I actually won a scholarship for an essay I wrote on the changing roles of women in literature, all expenses paid, except my books. Apparently, Cogsworth thinks I know the words good enough without them."

"So you're telling me you're beautiful, charismatic, witty, *and* smart. I didn't think it was possible, but I'm even more intimidated than I was before."

"Trust me, Hutchins, there is nothing intimidating about me."

"I beg to differ, Sloan."

I reluctantly lifted my head from his shoulder, sighing.

"Where do you work? Wherever it is, I already hate it."

37

"At Christenberry's Books," I said, laughing.

"Christenberry's? No way! I've been going there since I was a kid. It was like a second home to me. What do you do there? I don't remember ever seeing you there before, and I'm pretty certain I would have remembered you."

"Acquisitions, which is a fancy word for rummaging through the bins of donated books in the backroom and placing the ones in acceptable condition on the shelves in the used section of the store. I also run the front counter when they have me close."

"Maybe I'll just have to go home and do some rummaging for books to donate to Christenberry's Books' acquisition department tomorrow."

I smiled. "Maybe I'll just have to go and meet you out front to accept your donations."

"Now that you've fallen for my diabolical plan to see you again, do you mind if I walk you to your door? I hear that's what gentlemen are supposed to do, not to mention your roommate scares me a little. I think she'd track me down and break my legs, otherwise."

"Nah," I said, opening the door and stepping out of the car, "Mena's not quite prone to violent tendencies. If anything, she'd just slash your tires first, and leave the maiming for your second infraction."

He met me at the front of his car and reached for my hand, which I gave to him as we began our walk to my home away from home. Luke's hands, like the rest of him, were large, and completely engulfed my own.

"What are you studying?" he asked me as we stepped up onto the sidewalk.

"English, more or less. I'm majoring in creative writing and minoring in language arts. You know, so I don't feel like I'm completely throwing away my scholarship."

"Who would think you're throwing away your scholarship?"

"My mother, for one. Let's face it, the odds of me being able to make a living as a writer probably aren't all that great, so I figured I'd humor her and protect my future by minoring in something somewhat useful in the real world."

"If you want the opinion of a man you just met, I think that as long as you're happy doing whatever it is you end up doing, then it doesn't matter what your salary is or whether you end up writing novels or blurbs for the back of cereal boxes. Your life will have been a success, regardless."

"Would you mind telling that to my mother?"

"Certainly. When can I meet her?"

"For your sake, I would prefer never," I answered, only slightly joking.

"That bad, huh?"

"Like I said earlier, that's a conversation for another night."

"I'm looking forward to that night and, I hope, others."

We'd reached the walkway leading up to the residence hall. Most of the lights were out, including the dorm Mena and I shared. Never one to be a night owl, she'd probably been asleep the entire time Luke and I had been sitting in his car.

Luke squeezed my hand, returning my attention to him. "I've been dreading this moment the entire night, doing everything I can to prolong it from happening."

"Me too," I said, turning my body to face his. "At one point, I found myself staring at the clock in your car, willing the minutes to turn backwards. You know, trying to use my Jedi mind tricks and all."

Luke's other hand reached for my face, hesitantly at first, until he mustered up enough courage to allow his fingertips to brush my cheek before opening his hand to hold the side of my face in his palm. His thumb rested on my cheekbone just below my eye. His hand was warm and comforting, like a blanket I wanted to drape over my body. Closing my eyes, I took in the sensation of his touch.

"May I kiss you, Elle?" he asked softly.

"Yes," I answered him.

Heart racing, I stood, waiting in anticipation to feel his lips brush against mine, only to find myself somewhat disappointed when I felt them on my cheek, instead.

"No," I said, opening my eyes. "You don't need to ask permission to do that." Rising up on the very tips of my toes, I reached for Luke's face. "You ask for permission to do this." Without hesitation, I took his lips in mine. Clearly stunned, Luke's body stiffened at first before readily giving in. He wrapped his arm around my waist while still cupping my face with his hand, pulling my mouth back against his after I began to pull away. Like the rest of the night, it was a moment I wished wouldn't end, and apparently neither did he, as neither one of us was too eager to break the bond forming between our bodies.

"Don't make me get the hose, you two," Mena called out from the balcony.

Luke's and my lips parted slowly, but his grip around me remained unwavering. By this time, my toes were starting to grow numb from bearing my weight, and despite my best efforts to stay up, my feet planted themselves back down on the ground. The sudden loss in my height forced Luke to bend down, where he rested his forehead against my own. My heart remained beating faster than normal, but had slowed down exponentially from where it had been just a moment ago, though my breathing was nowhere close to being settled. Thankfully, neither was his.

"I trust you brought her back with her virtue still intact. She's worth nothing to me if she's not pure," Mena said in her best East Coast mobster impersonation.

I let go of Luke long enough to present my middle finger to Mena. Luke laughed, as he lifted his forehead from mine and loosened his hold from around me.

"Now is that any way to treat your friend, who's been up all night worried sick while you've been out besmirching your name around town?"

"Rest assured," Luke began, "nothing went on to prompt said besmirching."

"What? Is my friend not good enough for you? I fully expected her to come back defiled. You both ought to be ashamed of yourselves."

"Goodnight, Mena. I'll be up in a minute," I called up to her, my cheeks beginning to burn.

"That's right, and when you get up here, you're going to have some explaining to do." Mena wagged her finger at me, turned back around on her heels, and walked inside our room.

"This night just got shot to hell," I muttered, much to Luke's amusement.

"I'll see you tomorrow, then?" he asked, more hopeful than expectant.

"You'll see me tomorrow." I squeezed his hand and walked up the sidewalk toward Mena and the spirited interrogation she would soon inflict upon me.

2018

I heard voices even before I stepped inside of the room. They were soft, but one by one, I was able to discern who was speaking. The first voice struck me like a freight train, catapulting me further back in time with each word he spoke. The second one made my heart skip a beat.

As I walked farther into the room, I saw another vision of my past sitting next to the hospital bed. His attention, at first, was entirely focused on the occupant in the bed, until movement from me diverted his attention to me. He locked eyes with me, surprise on his face quickly turning to an odd combination of contradiction. Anger, excitement, and suspicion all appeared to be waging war and were enough to give me whiplash just looking at him. Peter Monroe—or just Monroe, as he preferred to be called—had been Luke's best friend since pretty much the dawn of each other's existence. He'd aged. His boyish good looks had hardened into a man who would have been difficult to recognize to me, save for the same square chin, overly large nose, and mischievous eyes I had remembered so fondly.

Another step inside the room revealed a sight I had fought valiantly to keep from infiltrating my dreams for the last several years. Like Monroe, he didn't notice my arrival at first, and I was grateful for that because the shock I was feeling at that moment would have undoubtedly transferred onto him. His head was turned, his eyes, from what I could see of them, were closed. Most of his features were facing Monroe, but from what little I could make out of them, he looked exactly how I remembered him. The rest of his body, however, was a different story.

His hair had begun to grow back after having obviously been recently shaved to prep him for surgery. On the side of his head that was visible to me, a bandage was secured to his scalp just above his ear and was wrapped around his head. Both of his legs had been broken and were secured with immobilizers, resembling large boots. He'd been through hell and back physically, and I feared he'd soon go through the same emotionally, all because of me.

Tears fell down my face before I even had the chance to realize they had formed. Not wanting Luke to see me upset, I dabbed my eyes with my sleeve and did my best to maintain my composure before he realized I was there. With a lump in my throat, I took a step closer to the bed, approaching it on the opposite side of Monroe. There another chair sat, which I was grateful for in the event my legs felt like they were going to give out on me. Monroe sat watching me expectantly, silently screaming at me to announce my presence and put an end to the torment Luke must have been going through since regaining consciousness.

Closing my eyes, I took a breath and spoke. "Luke."

CHAPTER FOUR

His breath hitched in his throat the moment I spoke his name, but I wasn't quite certain whether it was from him hearing my voice or from the fatigue the simple act of breathing inflicted upon him. Just being in close proximity to him again, I felt myself trembling, more internally than outwardly … at least, I hoped it was more internally.

Keep your shit together, Elle.

As he turned, I noticed a large bandage across his neck. My eyes immediately fixated on the former tracheostomy site, until I couldn't see it anymore behind the water clouding my vision. He'd been injured—severely. I'd known that coming here, but it didn't hit me for some reason until now. Until I was forced to face it head-on. His life could have ended a month ago. A month ago, when I was home in bed by myself while Eric was pulling yet another late night. I was in a warm, safe bed while Luke was fighting for his life. But by some miracle, he'd survived. Luke was a living miracle.

I sniffed back the moisture that threatened to come pouring out of my nose and blinked back the rest of my tears just as his face came into view. His bright blue eyes hadn't lost their luster. The curvature of his face was just as I remembered, except a little more unkempt than he usually kept it. Whether it looked that way from age, infirmary, or lack of proper maintenance, I wasn't certain, but it was a nice look on him. It made him seem dignified, less like a boy and more like the man he couldn't remember he was.

Our eyes met, the same way they used to, and no matter how hard I tried to fight it, the signature electric shock sensation I'd always felt whenever I looked at him made its way down my spine. He'd ingrained himself in me, down to the very marrow of my bones.

I wasn't sure which one of us would speak first, whether it would be me who had years' worth of things stored in my head to say to him, or Luke, who had whatever his last memory of me was—or what he thought it was, anyway. Without knowing what that last memory was, it was hard to tell what he may say when he did speak. Needless to say, nothing could have prepared me for what it turned out to be.

"I'm sorry, but who … who are you?"

My jaw went slack. If I weren't so tall, it probably would have hit the floor. Physically, I went numb from head to toe, even my brain, so often swimming in thought, ground to a screeching halt. I was un-equivocally paralyzed, unable to respond to his question or run back out the door and return to Indiana.

"For god's sake, Luke," Monroe scoffed. "Stop screwing around. Look at her, she looks like she's stroking out over there."

Luke's expression softened; his lips formed a smile, the mere act of which seemed painful.

"You're a sight for sore eyes, Sloan." His voice came out in a rasp, a reminder of the tracheotomy he'd so recently had.

I could do nothing but stand there, staring at him. At any moment, I figured I would wake up, and I suppose I was waiting for that, because this couldn't possibly be real.

Luke laughed. "Elle, you look like you've seen a ghost. Do I really look that horrible?"

"No," I blubbered, "you're perfect."

"Oh crap, have you hit your head, too?"

"No … I mean, I don't know."

"Come here." He lifted his arms up and motioned for me to come to him. I complied with his request and sat down next to him on the bed, where his arms quickly and unexpectedly, considering his level of infirmary, engulfed me in an embrace that was just a step down from qualifying as a death grip. Although he tried to hide it, a grunt of pain clearly escaped his lips.

Beginning to crumble, I threw my arms around him, holding him with more care so as not to aggravate his injuries.

"It feels like it's been years since I last saw you," he said, his voice cracking.

"I know exactly what you mean."

"I'm going to leave now, buddy." Monroe now stood at the foot of the bed. I looked up to find him glaring down at me as though giving me a silent warning.

"See you tomorrow?" Luke asked him, expectantly.

"Of course, man. After class, as always."

With a nod at Luke, he stole another glance at me before he walked through the door. I was fairly positive that Monroe was no longer in class and wondered how he felt about having to lie to his best friend.

"Did you get your hair cut?" Luke asked me, running his fingers through my hair.

"Wha— Oh, yes, I did. Right before I came here."

"It looks good, but of course, you'd look beautiful with a shaved head and dressed in a burlap sack."

"Has your head doctor been in here lately? Because I think he needs to do some more scans or something," I replied, circling my finger around his head.

Luke grabbed my hand and held it, entwining his fingers with mine. "Even unconscious, you were all I could think about. It was like one big, beautiful, messed up dream with just the two of us. No school, no jobs, no crazy family drama. In a strange, equally messed up way, I didn't want to wake up, because then I'd have to face reality."

"And that is?"

"That our separation is inevitable, and I have to share you with

45

the rest of the world. I think that's why, when I woke up and you weren't here, I freaked out as badly as I did. I knew you were visiting your mother, and that you were doing what you needed to do. I knew I shouldn't be so selfish, because you're dealing with a lot right now, but it was like you had disappeared, and the dream had been nothing but a big lie."

"I'm here now, Luke," I whispered, "and I'm not going anywhere for a while. I promise." I wanted him to tell me more about the dreams he'd had during his coma. I'd always enjoyed listening to him and the detailed stories he told, no matter how long-winded they ended up being in the end.

Luke pulled away from me, taking in the features of my face, perhaps trying to recollect the memories that eluded him. I did the same, though more to take in the subtle differences between the face staring back at me and the one I had left behind so many years ago. He'd begun to develop crow's feet in the corners of his eyes. Around each socket, a yellowish hue signified bruising that was in the final stages of healing, the remnants of raccoon eyes—a telltale sign of an injury to the brain.

"There's something different about you," he said, rousing me from my ruminations.

Hesitantly, I asked, "How do you mean?"

"It's like you matured a bit, almost like I was out for longer than a month."

"Trust me, I looked exactly the same a month ago. And are you implying that I look old, sir?" I asked, trying to divert his attention.

"Let's face it, Sloan, you aren't the spring chicken I met almost two years ago." He smirked as he always did whenever he was able to get a rise out of me. "You've been through a lot these last thirty days, huh?"

"*I've* been through a lot?" I asked, incredulously. "It never fails, even after having just awoken from a coma with two broken legs, fractured ribs, and one hell of a bump on the head, you're still more concerned about how your accident has affected the lives of everyone other than yourself. You're unbelievable, Hutchins."

"That's why you love me."

I averted my eyes away from his face, unable to look at him. He was right, his selflessness had played a big role in my having fallen in love with him. It had been a trait I hadn't been used to seeing in the people around me before he came along—or after, for that matter.

"Are you okay?" he asked. "You looked so forlorn there for a second."

"I'm fine," I assured him, painting a smile on my face.

"Oh, geez, Elle, I'm sorry. I completely forgot to ask you about your mom. How is she fairing?"

It was an understatement to say that Luke hadn't been a big fan of my mother and not thorough enough to say that he'd positively detested her. Their first and only meeting had not gone off without a hitch, and as far as he knew right now, my mother's health was on the verge of declining, a fact of which she'd only had herself to blame. What Luke didn't know, however, was that my mother had passed away a mere six months after our break-up, still clutching a drink in her hand until the bitter end.

"Same old mom," I answered him. "Some things never change."

He shook his head, disgusted. "I'll never be able to understand how someone would willingly choose to give up on life when they so clearly have so much to live for." He rested his fingertips on my cheek, allowing them to linger there.

I closed my eyes, remembering all the times he used to cradle my face in his hands. He had a sixth sense, Luke, at least when it came to me. Somehow, he always knew when I was feeling the most vulnerable, when even my soul needed comforting.

"She's sick," I said, opening my eyes to find him gazing upon me. "Alcoholism is a disease, a mental illness, just like depression or anxiety. Unlike those afflictions, though, its repercussions are far reaching. It's not just the alcoholic who suffers, their families do as well—sometimes worse because they're completely sober and aware of what's taking place. What's painful is knowing that, at one point, she could

47

have gotten better, that she didn't have terminal cancer where there was nothing medically that could have been done to save her. She could have been saved had she been strong enough, or maybe even if I would have done just a little bit more."

"You're talking about her like she's already dead, Elle," Luke remarked. "Maybe you should sit her down and tell her everything you've just told me. I mean, there's still time, right?"

"There's still time," I answered him, quickly trying to conceal my near flub. "There's always time as long as one grain of sand remains in the hour glass."

"That's my Elle." His thumb traced my cheekbone, moving from side to side as far as it could stretch, mimicking the motions of a pendulum. It drew my attention away from the emptiness in which I was staring and back to him. He hadn't taken his eyes away from me the entire time, and the intensity contained within them was so over-powering, I found myself captivated by them once more. "What are you thinking?" he asked out of the blue.

"A bunch of things and nothing at all," I answered quite truthfully. "It seems like my mind has been going a mile a minute for a while now. No matter what I do, I can't get it to shut down."

"It's because of me, isn't it? I'm so sorry, Elle. I know you have a lot to juggle at the moment."

"Don't you dare try to apologize for being in the hospital, Hutchins. It's not your fault. None of this is."

"If I could only remember the accident … But it's probably better that I don't. Still, I don't like having a chunk of my life unaccounted for, you know?"

I did the only thing I could do and nodded my head in agreement, my eyes still searching his for any signs of recognition of his past.

"I can't even remember what I was doing the night it happened. Mom keeps telling me not to dwell on it and to move forward, but for some reason, I feel like if I move forward, I would lose so much more. Does that sound crazy to you?"

48

I wanted to cry, but I held it together, knowing darn well that his intuitions were leading him to the truth the rest of his mind struggled to keep buried away. "Of course not," I answered him. "You want closure. There's nothing wrong with that. Everyone should have closure."

Really, Elle? Because you never afforded him that luxury.

He smiled, still caressing the contours of my face. "How is it that you always know what to say to me, Sloan?"

"I guess my wisdom precedes me."

"It does in more ways than you realize. If there's one silver-lining to this whole thing, it's that I didn't lose any memories of you. God, Elle, I don't know how I could go on without ever having known you. It wouldn't be a life worth living."

He leaned in closer to me, and as he did, his eyes reflected an unforgettable look—one I had seen every time we were together, beginning outside my residence hall on the night of our first date. I froze then and there, not knowing what else to do.

"I told you this countless times in my dreams, when I was unconscious, trying to claw my way back to the real you. And it's almost unfathomable to me that I came within a breath away of never being able to tell you it again." My stomach tightened as he moved in closer to me. "Now that I'm awake, I promise you that not a day will go by where I don't tell you how much I love you, Elle. Oh lord, how I love you."

Though my body remained frozen, my mind raced into action, attempting to find a way to prevent what was about to happen from happening, all while maintaining my integrity. It all happened in slow motion, Luke drawing steadily nearer, closing the gap between him and I, that when my brain was finally forced to settle on an acceptable solution, it shot through my body like lightning. Before the rest of me knew what was I happening, I had jumped up to my feet from the bed, clutching my calf a respectable distance away.

"Ah!" I feigned a scream, straightened out my leg and then limped around the room.

49

"Are you okay?" Luke asked, concerned.

Doing my best to sound like I was legitimately in pain without being overly dramatic, I answered, "Leg cramp," as I continued to hobble around the room. "I probably just need to eat a banana or something."

"Or drink more water, like I'm always telling you to do."

I remembered my younger days when water was a dirty word to me, and I would literally have to force myself to drink it. In recent years, I'd grown more accustomed to it, mainly because Eric despised drinking anything carbonated and refused to keep soft drinks in the house.

"I thought I heard a commotion in here. Is everything all right?"

I glanced up to see Candy entering the room, and discretely shot her a look as if to say, *Where the hell have you been?*

"Leg cramp," I said, rubbing my calf again for good measure.

"Oh my, I have some Tylenol in my purse, if that will help with the pain at all."

"I think it's okay now." I caught her watching me with a knowing expression.

"It's time Elle and I called it a night here," she said to Luke. "We've overstayed the extra time the hospital has given us for Elle's arrival, and after the long drive she's had, I'm sure she would like to get some sleep."

Before she mentioned how tired I must have become, my body hadn't betrayed the slightest presence of fatigue. It wasn't until it was spoken out loud that it presented itself in the form of a noticeable yawn from me, really driving Candy's argument home to Luke.

"I'm sorry, babe. You should have been able to have gotten some sleep when you got back into town, and not have had to rush straight over here."

I grabbed his hand, which had been resting at his side. "Don't be silly, Hutchins. Nothing could have kept me from coming to see you the second I got back."

He smiled as I squeezed his hand and set it back down on the bed next to him. His eyelids were growing heavy, a sign his recent dose of morphine was kicking in. A losing battle was being fought by him to keep his eyes open. Watching him, I searched through the recesses of my mind to unearth all the subtle quirks that made our relationship what it had been—every touch, every look, every aspect of our ver-nacular—and found that I was able to recall them with surprising ease. We never said good-bye, Luke and I ... well, except for once. There was only one time where I had spoken that word, using it as more of a tool to drive home the finality of what I was trying to convey. No, we never said good-bye.

Knowing it was time to leave, I told him what we always used to say when we parted. "See you soon."

Even ninety percent asleep, Luke's mouth curved upward into a smile before his voice cracked as he spoke the words, "Not soon enough, Sloan."

* * * * *

The smell of vanilla, mixed with freshly baked sugar cookies, catapult-ed me back through time as Candy and I entered through the door of the Hutchins' split-level home. Déjà vu, the likes of which I hadn't ex-perienced with such intensity before, struck me, transporting me back to the day Luke first brought me here to meet his parents. A decade later, the house still smelled the same.

"Tom must have gone to bed already," Candy observed, turning on the light to the kitchen.

The once red room had been updated to a more neutral hue, for which my tired eyes were thankful. I stole a glance at the clock on the microwave—ten minutes to ten o'clock. Eric would have gotten home long before now, probably working on a last-minute project before calling it a night. He spent more time in our home office than he did in bed with me, or so it seemed.

"Would you like some tea?" Candy asked, picking the kettle up from the stove.

"No, thank you." I yawned involuntarily, setting my suitcase down on the tile floor. Taking a seat on one of the stools surrounding the island in the middle of the room, I rested my head in my hands.

"Oh, I'm sorry, dear. Do you want me to show you to your room? It has undergone some renovation, but it may still look familiar to you, seeing as it's Luke's old room." She hesitated a moment, casting a glance in my direction as she filled the kettle with water. "That is, if that's okay. The other spare bedroom is being used for storage at the moment, but I can clear some of the boxes out of there if it would make you feel more comfortable."

"No, no that's fine."

She nodded, once again returning her attentions to the tea kettle. I smiled to myself when her back was turned to me. Luke's room was associated with nothing but fond memories for me.

What are you doing, Elle? Stop it. Just stop it right now.

"Are you okay, honey?" Candy asked, taking a seat across from me while waiting for her water to boil. "You look a little flustered."

"I'm fine," I said, embarrassed by the route my thoughts had taken me. "Just a hot flash, I think." I grasped the collar of my shirt and pulled it away from my neck.

"You're way too young for those, darling." Candy chuckled a bit. "If you think you have it bad now, just wait. It gets better."

"I can't wait." I laughed, my cheeks beginning to cool down.

"I must say, I missed that laugh of yours." Candy scooted off her stool and crouched down on the floor, searching through the cabinet for something housed underneath the island. She emerged seconds later, holding a bone china teapot, vintage in appearance and adorned with intricate rose decals. Candy had always meant business when it came to making a proper cup of tea. I'd found it fascinating just to watch her. And I watched now as she poured some of the boiling water from the tea kettle into the teapot, and then as she set the kettle back down onto the burner. She was warming the pot, a procedure I remembered her explaining to me when I inquired about it while trying to make conversation with her shortly after we first met.

"Your laugh is so spirited and full of life. We could use more of that around here," she continued her thought, taking me aback a bit.

She and Tom had seemed like such a happy couple, energetic and completely devoted to one another and to Luke. It was a tough pill to swallow thinking that somehow that may have changed. Although I hadn't wanted to think about it, it was difficult for me to believe that Luke hadn't moved on at all since our breakup. No matter how painful it was to imagine him being with another woman, I had always wanted him to find happiness, and the thought that he hadn't bothered me more than the prospect that he had. Clearly, there was no one in the picture now, or I wouldn't be here and Candy wouldn't have been prompted to make that comment.

"I remember when I used to watch you make tea whenever Luke and I would come to visit," I said, satisfied to see that the teabags were still housed on the third shelf to the right of the refrigerator. Whenever everything else in my life was going to shit, at least I could count on my memory.

"What's funny is that I was just thinking about that myself. You used to watch me so intently, like you were taking notes for a final exam." She laughed, grabbing the box from the shelf. "It was so cute. I know Tom used to get a kick out of it, too." Still chuckling, she walked her perfect cup of tea back to her stool, where she sat back down. "That hits the spot after tonight." She'd taken a sip and closed her eyes, allowing the flavor to strike her palate. "So, if I may ask without getting too personal, did I almost walk into what I think I may have almost walked into tonight?"

"Yes," I answered, the memory of Luke leaning in to kiss me still fresh on my mind. "It took some creative maneuvering on my part, but I managed to pull off a leg cramp with ease. I think."

"Yeah, except you changed legs a time or two."

Oh, crap.

She took another sip of tea and smiled. "Luke didn't notice, though. He was pretty whipped before we left and will probably be out like a light until morning. For the life of me, I can't understand how anyone could get a good night's rest in a hospital, what with nurses coming in every five minutes to check your vitals and IVs, but Luke manages most nights."

Candy wasn't kidding. I remembered how Luke slept, how just the slightest noise would arouse me from a deep sleep, yet not even God himself could get that man's eyelids to open until he was darn well good and ready. I'd envied his innate ability, like it was a super-power he'd been blessed with. Screw flying or walking through walls, I wanted to be able to sleep a full eight hours without waking up once.

"I know this can't be easy for you," Candy continued. "And despite us being exceptionally grateful to have you here, just know that if you get too uncomfortable, none of us would blame you for leaving."

"No," I said more defiantly than even I expected. Candy's eyes widened in surprise as she paused mid-sip. "I mean, I couldn't even think of doing such a thing. I'm here to help, and that's what I intend to do, until you kick me out."

Setting down her cup in its matching saucer, Candy reached one of her hands out to grasp mine. "Thank you." She drew her hand back to swat away a tear, felt but not yet visible to the naked eye. "If it would make you more comfortable, I can make sure someone is in the room with the two of you at all times."

I must have gaped at her like she was an alien with three heads, as I couldn't imagine how anyone couldn't be comfortable around Luke. He had always been one to show considerable respect and restraint. At times, irritatingly so. Still, I knew what she meant. Though Luke wouldn't be able to do much beyond a peck on the lips, it was still crossing a line he couldn't know existed, and there was only so much I could deflect before he would begin to grow suspicious. Yet in spite of all of that, the thought of being under constant surveillance, of never getting to have a heart-to-heart conversation with him while I was here, didn't set well with me.

"That won't be necessary," I answered Candy. "I'm a big girl who can handle herself."

"That's the understatement of the century," Candy said, setting her now-empty cup down. "Well, if you change your mind ..."

"You'll be the first to know," I reassured her.

"Let me show you to your room. I'm sure you're just as beat as I am, and we have an early day tomorrow."

She crouched down to pick up my suitcase, thwarting my attempts to take it from her with the stealth moves that only a mother knew how to make, which were made all the more impressive by my knowledge of the weight of the bag she carried. Eric would lament on how I couldn't travel light if my life depended on it. That fact was further illustrated by the obvious imbalance in Candy's shoulders, like one side of her was carrying a feather and the other, an elephant.

As I followed her deeper into the house, I was overcome by nostalgia, struck senselessly by my brain awakening to the sights and smells it once knew so fondly. Candy rounded a corner in the living room, taking the final set of stairs to the upper level of the home where the bedrooms were located. Luke's bedroom had been the first door on the left as soon as you ascended the stairs. And it was toward that door that Candy turned and paused.

Nervous, I followed her into Luke's room. Overcome by mixed emotions, a part of me—the smaller part—was relieved that the room had been dramatically altered. Once blue walls had been painted a shade of beige. Carpet had been replaced by more sophisticated bamboo flooring. Overall, the feminine quotient of the room had been raised by several notches. Still, I was happy to see it remained reasonably recognizable as once having been Luke's room.

"There are empty hangers in the closet if you want to hang up your clothes," Candy said, setting my suitcase down inside the barren walk-in. "The remote for the television is on the bureau, and— Oh, darn it, Tom." She paused, staring at the pile of sheets laid out on the striped mattress. "I asked the man to do one thing," she sighed, lifting up a sheet.

"I can get that, Candy," I said. "You've had a long day. Why don't you go ahead and get ready for bed?"

"Nonsense, dear. This will only take a minute."

By then, Candy had already secured the fitted sheet neatly over the mattress pad, and I figured I'd be more of a hindrance than a help to her. As she made the bed, I found myself looking around Luke's former room, trying to remember where each of his things had once been. A chess set used to sit on top of his dresser in the corner, various basketball and academic trophies had been displayed on a bookshelf adjacent to the bed, a guitar belonging to his grandfather, of which he hadn't the slightest idea how to play, had sat in the corner next to the closet. In that corner now sat a potted plant, which I quickly identified as being a Peace Lilly—my favorite flower.

I bent down to inspect the delicate white flowers, which felt like silk in my hand. "You still like those, don't you?" Candy asked, much to my surprise.

"Oh, my gosh, yes," I answered her. "You ... you remembered that I loved Peace lilies?"

"How could I forget?" Candy asked with a chuckle. "Luke always insisted on our having them in the house whenever you and he stayed over for the weekend, so when it was confirmed that you would be making the trip out here, I figured I wouldn't break tradition. Besides, I hear they're natural air purifiers, those plants. Every little bit helps in that area, eh?"

Taken aback, I stood up to find Candy finished with making the bed and, before I knew what I was doing, I threw my arms around her in an embrace. Stunned, she kept her arms down at her side for just a moment before I felt them wrapping tightly around my body, too.

"Thank you," I said, willing myself not to cry.

"No, thank you," she replied, attempting to do the same.

I loosened my grip from around her body and sat down on the bed. "What time are we leaving tomorrow?" I asked, removing my cell phone from my purse situated on the floor at the foot of the bed.

She half-yawned the answer. "Around seven thirty."

"Okay. I'll go ahead and set the alarm on my phone, then."

"Do you remember where the bathroom is up here?"

"Down the hall and to the right?" My question was in more of the form of a statement than an inquiry.

"If only I could have half your memory." She smiled, turning around to walk back to the door. "If you need anything, don't hesitate to knock on our door."

"Goodnight, Candy."

"Goodnight, Elle."

As the door closed behind her, I checked my phone, realizing I had missed a call from Mena while I was inside of the hospital and the ringer had been muted. I checked the time—ten thirty. With her hectic schedule, Mena may still be awake and was probably confused by the message I had left for her, but there was another person I needed to call tonight.

"Yeah?" Eric answered, groggy and mildly irritated.

"It's me," I said needlessly. "I just wanted to call to let you know I made it. I'm sorry, but I thought you would still be up. You never go to bed this early."

"I told you I have a lot going on this week." He paused for a moment before adding, "But I know your mind has been preoccupied by other things."

"Eric, if you don't want me here, just say it. You could have said it before I left."

"It's fine, Elle. I'm just exhausted and stressed out."

"Well, I'll let you get back to sleep, then."

"No, it's okay." His voice made him seem more awake and alert, but there were still undertones of a struggle. "So, how's lover boy doing?"

"Seriously, Eric?" His irritation was beginning to rub off on me. "He's not okay. Actually, he's in pretty poor shape, if that makes you feel any better."

"Oh, geez. Of course it doesn't. Listen, I'm sorry. That came out a lot worse than I meant it to."

Did it though, Eric?

"It's okay," I responded. "I know this isn't an ideal situation for either one of us."

"So where did you end up staying?"

Oh, shit.

Hesitating, I knew I couldn't—and shouldn't—keep anything from him, but that doesn't mean my brain wasn't teaming with alternative answers. "By the time we left the hospital, it was late, so Candy insisted that I come back to their house for the night."

"Your BFF Candy insisted, eh? Then what other option did you have?" The snark was strong in his tone. Had it fallen under any other scenario, I probably would have taken some offense, but considering the circumstances, I tried to let it slide off my shoulders.

"Next you'll tell me you're sleeping in his bed in his old room."

He was expecting me to shoot back, to quickly dispel his statement as nothing more than foolishness, but my silence was all the validation he needed.

"Seriously? Jesus, Elle."

"I'm not in his bed," I retorted, "and the room is unrecognizable as ever having been his."

"Because that's so much better? It's too damn late for this."

"Which is why I'll let you get back to sleep. I'm sorry I woke you up only to piss you off. I guess I thought you may actually want to know that your wife was fine and that she wished to talk to you to tell you goodnight."

"Of course I wanted to know that you were fine. It's just ..."

"You're tired, stressed, and I'm utterly exasperating. I know, Eric, which is why I'm saying I love you and goodnight. I'll call you earlier tomorrow ... or, you can call me, whichever. Sound good?"

"I love you, too, Elle. Talk to you tomorrow?"

"Sounds good."

CHAPTER FIVE

2006

I watched the clock on the wall across from the cash register at Christenberry's Books intently, willing the minute hand to move as quickly as the second hand. It reminded me of every clock that had been in every classroom I had ever attended in the public school system while growing up. Basic white with large black numbers, it was the bane of my existence on what had already been a slow night. Rodney, the store owner, had left hours ago, only slightly before the last customer. In Rodney's absence, the fort had been left to me to guard.

Outside, the early darkness indicative of a late fall evening had begun to take over, making it seem like it was later than it really was. Our new inventory had been cataloged, then placed on their appropriate shelves; the drawer had been counted and the deposit bag prepared. I'd even swept the floor, taken out the trash, and occupied myself with other busy work to pass the time, and I still had a half hour left. Either I was exceptionally efficient or time had literally begun to move slower since my shift began—my money was more on the latter than the former. If only I would have brought my study guide for my British Literature test next week, I could have killed two birds with one stone.

As I was about to close my eyes to nap away the remainder of my time, I heard the jingling of the bell affixed to the top of the door, used to alert the store's employees of a customer's arrival. Slightly annoyed, yet relieved that I would have something to do to pass the last few minutes, I looked up to see the same gawky, just-a-smidgen-older-than-me gentlemen who'd perused our aisles earlier today and at various times during the last week. Strange that he would come back now. He must be as bored as I was.

I smiled as he came into view, asking him whether there was anything I could help him find.

"No," he answered, unusually short. "I'll let you know if there is."
Well, okay then.

I nodded, stealing another glance at the clock. Ten more minutes. If he wasn't done by then, he could come back tomorrow. Near the back of the store, his footsteps thundered against the wooden floor, intensified by the lack of white noise created by other customers and the usual sounds of business operations. *Thump, thump, thump,* they persisted, never slowing down or stopping to take a moment to look at the books on any of the shelves.

Odd, I thought, wondering exactly what it was that had brought him back here. His footsteps only grew heavier as he continued his unrelenting walk up and down each aisle. He was looking for something in particular—he had to be. That was the only explanation for it. Still, the hairs on the back of my neck stood on end, triggering alarm bells in my brain.

Don't be silly, Elle. He's a customer—a regular, even.

His footsteps turned back and began heading to the front of the store. Relieved, I glanced up at the clock to see less than five minutes remaining before it was time to close shop. I watched as he walked up the aisle directly in front of the cash register where I sat. The intensity he projected in his stare bored a hole right through me, sending a shiver down my spine. I'd never had anyone look at me the way he was right now, and if I had any say in the matter, I never would again. Confusion, self-loathing, conflict, his expression ran the gamut, skipping over any of the more positive emotions. Averting my eyes, I returned my attention to the computer screen in front of me to quell my racing heart.

I'd expected him to walk out the front door, defeated by his inability to find whatever it was he'd been searching for. I expected to hear the jingle of the bell that would both herald my blood pressure's return to normal and bring the night back to it's uneventful state. Reality, as it so often does, scoffed at my expectations.

His footsteps stopped abruptly in front of me, commanding my attention back to those eyes that had made my blood turn to ice and my breath seek refuge in the crevices of my lungs.

"M-May I help you, sir?" I asked, clearing my throat to make it seem as though my stammering had been as a result of a tickle rather than pure fear.

"I need a book," he said in a voice so flat it would give a pancake a run for its money.

"Well, you've come to the right place," I joked, hoping to elicit a smile that would perhaps serve to pacify my paranoia. No such luck.

Without so much as a smirk, he jumped right into his request. "Does this store carry any copies of *Of Mice and Men*?"

"A Steinbeck man, eh? Yeah, we carry it. Our books are all arranged alphabetically by the author's last name. The S's begin on the fifth shelf from the left."

"I looked through that shelf, but didn't see it. Would you mind helping me?"

No. No. No. No. Hell no.

I knew he was lying. His footsteps never wavered and had been nothing but consistent the entire time he'd been back there. There was no way he allowed himself a fair amount of time to really find anything.

"Um, sure," I said, every ounce of my body protesting the words my mouth had produced.

Stupid, stupid, stupid.

Reluctantly, I walked around the front desk and made my way to the back of the store, listening once again to the man's footsteps, which were following closely behind me. In my head, I began trying to commit a mental picture of him to memory. Besides being tall and awkward, he had a large, bulbous nose with stringy, dark hair that hung just an inch above his shoulders. Pock marks covered his cheeks where acne once had been. But above all, his eyes were what stood out the most. Dark, black even, so murky it was hard to make out his pupils. Yet another feature to haunt my nightmares.

As we rounded the corner to the shelf containing the book he was looking for, I began to search my mind for anything I may have on my person to protect myself if the need arose, quickly coming up short when I remembered that anything I had that could remotely be used as a weapon was in my purse at the front of the store.

Shit.

My eyes surveyed the shelves, trying to decipher whether they could be capable of being toppled over onto any would-be assailants. That idea was put to bed when I remembered each unit had been bolted together and subsequently secured to the wall for safety purposes.

Double shit.

"Here it is," I said, using my finger to pull the book back by its spine, exposing enough of the rest of its jacket for me to grab. "If you want to head back up front, I'll ring you u—"

Cut short mid-speech, my body became paralyzed when his hand came to rest on my arm and gently started caressing it. I realized then, all too late, that this particular set of shelves had been chosen deliberately, as due to the presence of a load-bearing wall at the far end of it, there was only one way in and one way out, and the only way out was being blocked by the body of a man who probably had five inches in height and a good forty pounds on me. Unable to speak, let alone scream, all I could feel through the overwhelming numbness overtaking my body was the burning sensation in my eyes.

"I've been watching you," he said in the same flat affect he had spoken earlier. His hand moved up the length of my arm to my shirt collar, where his fingers traced the exposed skin of my clavicle. "I couldn't help but notice how smooth your skin is, so pale, so pure. Are you just as pure and as flawless?" His hand slid down from my clavicle to the space between my breasts, where, using two fingers, he began to unbutton my flannel shirt.

"I'll scream," I said, an ounce of nerve returning on the cusp of an adrenaline rush. "The door is unlocked, someone will hear me."

He laughed, a cocky, demented laugh that preceded his retort. "You know there's no one out there this time in the evening. And I know, too, because I've been observing this store for a couple weeks now. I've been watching you."

Tears falling down my cheek, I screamed at the top of my lungs, "Help! Someone, please, help me!" Instinctively and in self-preservation, I backed up, hoping by some miracle that the wall I knew stood behind me would suddenly vanish, or suck me into its depths to shield me from harm. My heart sank when the back of my heels struck the bricks, effectively trapping me, instead.

"Now is that any way to treat a paying customer?" he asked, wagging his finger back and forth like a stern parent. Scolding complete, he took his hand and placed it over my mouth. "I've never been one for idle chatter, so why don't you say we just get on with it, huh? Don't worry, I'll make it quick."

Heart pounding, every part of me knew that he had no intention of letting me go after he was done doing whatever god awful things he was planning to do to me. I had to fight. I had to try to get away. Adrenaline kicking in, I drew back my fist and, with all I had in me, I struck him in the side of the face. The blow I dealt served only one purpose: to anger him all the more.

"You stupid bitch!" he yelled before drawing back his hand and slapping me across the face. The force of his slap was enough to send me stumbling backwards into the wall, where he pinned me with his body, the swelling in his pants pronounced against my thigh. With

63

both hands, he commenced unbuttoning my shirt, ripping it the rest of the way open when it wasn't going as quickly as he'd hoped. My bra exposed, he cupped my breasts in his hands. "All that little stunt did was make me want to take my time with you," he cooed in my ear. "Instead of feeling very little, you'll feel everything." To drive his point home, he sank his teeth into my earlobe, causing me to shriek in pain.

I tried to think of a way, any way to get away from him, but the weight of his body, pressing mine against the wall, coupled with the sheer force of his desire to do what he had set out to do, was too much for me to fight against. All I could do was sob and hope to find a way to remove myself from my body before he did, as a trickle of blood fell from my wounded ear onto my shoulder.

My desire to remove myself consciously from the situation at hand must have worked, as I never heard the bell ring when the front door was opened; neither, apparently, did my assailant. Nor did I hear the heavy, rushed footsteps that followed the sound of my sobs. The only thing I heard clearly was the sound of his voice, followed by the crack of a fist striking my attacker's skull.

"Get off of her!" Luke all but growled. The man, visibly more incapacitated by Luke's blow to the head than he had been by mine, turned in retaliation, only to be cold-cocked by Luke's right hook. The force of this blow threw the man backwards with such force that the back of his head violently struck the bookcase behind him, knocking him out instantly. Paralyzed, I watched his limp body crumple to the floor, buried by an avalanche of books from the shelf he'd struck.

I felt around my waist to make sure my pants were still on and that his violation of my body hadn't extended below the waist. Thankfully, it hadn't. With the adrenaline rush leaving my body just as fast as it had arrived, my legs became less than sturdy. No longer able to support my body, I collapsed, shaking and sobbing the entire way down. If not for Luke, I would have fallen to the floor. He'd saved me for the second time that night.

"It's okay, baby," he said, removing his jacket and wrapping it around my half naked body. "You're safe; he can't hurt you anymore." His voice shook almost as badly as my body.

Still in shock, I wasn't yet able to speak, only stare at the man lying unconscious on the floor, wanting desperately to finish the job Luke had started. To make him yelp in pain; to make him feel fear; to make his life flash before his eyes. But as my brain was actively plotting, the rest of my body remained comatose. And there was nothing I was able to do.

I suddenly felt Luke lifting me up into his arms as he stood up and carried me to the front of the store. My head rested against his chest, near his heart, which beat feverishly the entire way across the store. "I have to set you down for a second," he said softly, putting me down on the front counter. He looked around, confused for a moment, before remembering that what he was looking for was still in the coat I was wearing. With an apologetic smile, he pulled his cell phone out of his coat pocket and called 911.

My eyes returned to the back of the store, waiting for the man to come barreling at us at any moment. Clearly, he'd set out to accomplish one mission tonight, one in which he'd been hellbent to see through to completion. It made me wonder exactly how long he'd been watching me. I'd remembered seeing him in the store only just recently, but I didn't keep a running tally on those who patronized the store and when. Even though my attacker was one of those who would have certainly stood out, even in a crowd of a million. Those eyes alone would have been enough to set him apart from everyone else.

Those eyes. I shuddered, feeling goosebumps rise up on my arms.

"The police are on their way," Luke said. Catching my shudder, he rubbed his hands up and down my arms to warm me. A spark returned to his eyes when he caught sight of the mark left on the side of my face. "It's going to bruise," he observed, moving to inspect my ear next, fuming. "What kind of animal bites another human being?" I flinched when his thumb brushed the sore area on my earlobe. "The bite is deep, but I don't think it'll require stitches, just disinfectant and kept clean."

I nodded. Outside, a squad car had pulled up in front of the store with it's lights on, shining brightly through the window. "I'm so sorry, Elle," Luke murmured, resting his forehead on mine.

"Why are you sorry? This wasn't your fault."

"I'm sorry for men as a whole. I'm sorry that young women aren't able to work by themselves at night without becoming targets. But mostly, I'm sorry that I didn't get here sooner."

I found myself trying to comfort him just as much as he had comforted me. "Don't be silly, there was no way you could have known. Besides, just exactly what are you doing here, anyway?"

"After my shift at the hospital, I figured I'd drop in to see you and ask if you wanted to get a bite to eat, since I knew you'd be getting ready to leave."

I smiled, resting my hand on the bright red knuckles of his right hand. He'd have a bruise of his own to contend with. "I'm sorry, too," I said, rubbing my thumb over the knuckle of his index finger. His skin had split open, sealed only by the blood that had already coagulated.

"I'd do it a thousand times over, if that's what it took to keep you safe." His lips brushed my forehead, lingering there until the bell signaled the arrival of the responding deputies.

Luke broke away from me to address the officers, escorting them to the back of the store. I heard him speaking to them, recounting the events he saw transpire in front of him. One of the deputies remarked on his handiwork, commenting on the restraint he must have had to not have done more damage than he did.

A short time later, the bell on the door signified the appearance of an older man wearing a badge from the Roanoke Police Department, along with a couple EMTs, who greeted Luke. The three of them stood off in the corner, as Luke directed one of them to the back of the store and the other one to check on me.

"I'm okay," I said, my senses beginning to return to me. "Just a little bruised."

He was young, around Luke's age, short in stature, but muscular and broad. It was clear he lifted quite often. "You may not feel it right now," he said, inspecting my face and ear, "but you're going to be sore tomorrow. When you get home, put some ice on it and take it easy. I'd recommend eating soft foods as anything else may exacerbate your pain."

I nodded, more or less having already mentally told myself what he'd just verbalized. "How do you know Luke?" I asked, curious.

"From the hospital," he answered matter-of-factly.

Duh, Elle. You really must have sustained some blow to the head. Luke did patient intake at a local community hospital, so of course he would know them.

"We also have a couple classes together." He opened a kit he'd brought with him, revealing an array of bandages, ointments, and other first aid materials. I watched as he grabbed a bottle of alcohol, which he placed on the counter next to me, allowing him a free hand to open one of the cotton swabs contained in the kit. "I was also at the coffee shop the night he met you."

"Oh?" I asked, unprepared for that bit of information.

"Yeah, I was one of the other geeks sitting around the table. When he saw you, he lost all ability to focus. None of us knew what was up until we saw him chasing after you." He poured a few drops of alcohol onto the cotton swab. My body stiffened in preparation for what was to come, still flinching nonetheless when the alcohol infiltrated the injury to my ear and a burning sensation took over. "Sorry," he said, genuinely apologetic. "You are going to want to keep an antibacterial ointment on that for the next couple of days to prevent infection." He closed up his kit and performed a final inspection of my injuries. "He's a good man, Luke," he stated before returning to assist his fellow technician.

"I know," I replied, watching as the man with the badge made his way over to me next, followed closely by Luke.

"Ms. Sloan, I'm Detective Ross," he introduced himself. "I'm sorry to hear about the events that occurred here tonight. How are you? Are you doing all right? Do you want to be checked out at the hospital?"

"No," I answered. My face and ear were throbbing more and more as each second ticked away and my body relaxed again. "I'll … I'll be fine."

He nodded, removing a small steno pad from his jacket pocket. "My deputy needs to take photographs of your injuries before you leave, but first, and I'm sorry to make you have to relive this, Ms. Sloan, but there was only so much information Mr. Hutchins was able to provide to us."

Luke hopped up on the counter to sit beside me. His long legs stretched nearly to the floor; a comical sight to behold in a situation that was anything but.

"I understand," I said, my fingers searching for and finding Luke's hand.

Detective Ross pulled a pen out of his pocket and clicked it open. "I'm sure you want to get home, so let's get this started. Start from the beginning and leave out no details—even the smallest of them could provide us with useful information."

As the detective scribbled frantically, I described the entire encounter with my attacker, beginning precisely the moment when I heard the bell ring, to his persistent footsteps in the back of the store, to his request that I assist him with finding *Of Mice and Men*, and finally, the attack, including what I considered as verbatim, every word he'd spoken to me that I could remember. Luke cringed the entire time I spoke, an expression that persisted during Detective Ross' follow up questions.

In the corner of my eye, I caught sight of Rodney Christenberry, the store's owner, who'd slipped inside undetected, as my still-unconscious assailant was being wheeled out of the store on a gurney. He leaned against a wall, roughly twenty feet away from where Detective Ross was interviewing me.

"You know, I don't mean to frighten you more than you've already been tonight, but this guy sure sounds like the suspect wanted in two other rapes two counties to the south of here. I've been following it very closely. In at least one of the cases, he had been stalking the woman for a short time before he moved in, figuring out her patterns and waiting for the perfect opportunity to make his move. Physically, he also fits the description she gave, same height and build, from what she could remember, at least. She was interviewed in the hospital after he'd roughed her up pretty badly."

"And what about the other woman?" I asked, knowing in the back of my mind that I probably didn't want to hear what he would tell me.

The expression on his face was all the answer I needed. "Uh, well ..." Detective Ross began, expertly trying to divert this new line of questioning off course. It wouldn't have flown with me, and it certainly wasn't going to fly with him.

"Please, Detective."

He sighed as he clicked his pen to a close and stuck it in his pocket along with his steno pad. "The first victim, a woman a year older than you, was murdered, Ms. Sloan."

If I hadn't already been sitting, I probably would have collapsed to the floor. As it was, I had a hard time staying upright. Luke, sensing my distress, sprang into action, extending his arm around me to keep me upright, both in comfort and out of necessity.

"Someone was certainly watching over you tonight," Detective Ross continued, "and they sent this young man here to protect you."

Rodney, having kept quiet since his arrival, took a step forward and spoke. "Dear god, Elle, I'm so sorry."

Detective Ross, appearing somewhat annoyed to have had someone eavesdropping in on his interview, turned to address him. "And who are you, sir?"

"I'm Rodney Christenberry, Detective. My family owns this store."

"Oh really?" Luke fumed, never letting his anger detach his arm from around my body. Obviously, Rodney hadn't been one of the Christenberry's to whom Luke had been acquainted. "And is it your custom and practice to leave young women by themselves at night? Because from what I remember, your father always had two people working in the store at all times."

69

"Luke, stop!" I chastised him. "I'm sorry, Mr. Christenberry. I know there's no way you could have known a suspected serial killer would be visiting the store tonight."

"And that's exactly why he should have had more than one person here," Luke muttered. I eyed him before turning my attentions back to Mr. Christenberry.

"The young man's right," Mr. Christenberry agreed. "Which is why, from now on, we will always have two people in the store at the same time, even if I have to stay here myself."

"As will I," Luke said.

"Don't be silly, Luke. You have a job, there's—"

"I'll rearrange my schedule, or I'll see if Monroe can stop by."

"Monroe?" I asked.

"Gentlemen, if you don't mind, I'd like to finish my interview of Ms. Sloan without further interruption."

* * * * *

"You're still shaking," Luke remarked as we walked from the book-store to the parking lot. His arm hadn't left its place around me since Officer Ross' interview. Still quaking, my nerves had calmed down a touch. At this point, it was most-likely the sudden, bone-chilling cold that was causing my trembling more than anything else. "How about we go out for a bite to eat. I'm sure you're probably starving. I know this amazing Chinese pla—"

"I'm not hungry," I interrupted him.

Though subtle, I felt his body slump a bit, as though he were a balloon and my words had poked enough of a hole in him. Not to pop him, but to allow him to deflate ever so slowly.

"Okay then, how about I take you back to your dorm?"

Now it was my turn to be deflated. His words cut me in a way I hadn't expected. I didn't want him to leave my side, and his suggestion of such only served to further intensify my trembling. "No," I said more defiantly than necessary.

"Elle, I didn't mean to upset you. I just don't think it's a good idea for you to be driving, is all."

"No, it's not that, I just … I just don't want to go back to my dorm and face Mena and all her Mena-like questions, right now."

"Well, I can't say as I blame you there," Luke muttered. "Then what now? Where do you want to go?"

The answer was much easier to say in my head, much clearer and more dignified than what actually came out of my mouth. "I-I was thinking that … if it's okay with you that, since it's getting late, that I could just go back to your place for the night."

"Oh," Luke said, genuinely surprised by my proposition. "Yeah … yeah, of course. Let me just call Monroe first to make sure he has pants on when we get there. He needs a heads-up when it comes to visitors."

"That's the second time you said that name tonight. Who is this Monroe guy?"

"He's my roommate, and my best friend since grade school."

I was suddenly petrified by the thought of meeting someone who'd known Luke for so long. In a way, it was like our relationship was being taken to another, slightly more advanced level. Luke opened the passenger door for me, as he removed his cell phone from his pants pocket with his free hand. "Don't worry, he's had all his shots."

Luke's apartment was a mere ten minute drive from the bookstore, near the campus of Roanoke Community College. Part of a one hundred unit complex, it was located in the vicinity of the aptly-named student ghetto, ninety percent of its tenants being local students. Other than that, the building was a nondescript brick structure with intermittent rectangles of light from the windows of the tenants who were still awake at this hour. The driveway curved around the building, leading to the tenants' designated parking spaces in the back. Luke drove to almost the very end of the line of cars, pulling into a spot assigned with the number eight.

"What, too cheap to spring for one of the spots underneath the carports?" I teased.

71

Through the light afforded by the lamp post a couple spots away, I was able to discern a smile on his face, highlighting the dimple on his chin. "It was either that or cable, so I made the choice any sane person would make."

"That's called getting your priorities straight," I chided.

"Damn right."

Following his lead, I opened the door and walked with him up the sidewalk. Luke swiped an ID card at the door to his building and plugged in a code to unlock it.

"I just want to apologize in advance," he said, wary as we walked down the hallway.

"For what?" I asked, nervously,

"Monroe. He's not for everyone."

"Oh, is that all?" I laughed, amused by his concern. "Neither is Mena, but I didn't feel the need to provide you with a disclaimer before you met her."

"I didn't exactly give you a chance to, either."

"That is true, too."

Luke stopped in front of a door marked '17B,' all the way at the end of the hallway. "Just know that, deep down—deep, deep, deep, down—beneath all the smart ass commentary and the 'I don't give a shit' attitude, there's a guy who volunteers his time at soup kitchens and mentors at-risk youth at the local YMCA."

"He sounds amazing."

Smirking, Luke glanced at me and said, "Do me a favor, don't ever say that out loud in his presence."

I followed him into his dimly lit apartment, stopping halfway inside to allow my eyes to adjust. My nostrils flared when the smell of pizza struck them, creating a rumble in my stomach that had managed to stay dormant until now. Allowing the door to shut behind me, I took in the cozy space that Luke and Monroe shared, noting, in particular the sparse furnishings. In the modest living room, a recliner and a couple of bean bag chairs sat in a crescent moon shape around a sizable television that took up roughly a quarter of the room. In the small, open kitchen, dishes sat piled in the sink. Empty—at least, I hoped they were empty—takeout containers sat stacked on the counter. Overall, it was every bit the bachelor pad in which I would have envisioned two young college students as cohabiting.

"I would have cleaned, but I didn't want to." His voice startled me at first. Coming from the living room behind where I stood, I hadn't expected it. Turning around, I saw a dark figure entering the apartment through a sliding glass door. Being on the first floor, their apartment had a walkout, leading to a small cement slab rather than a balcony. He'd been out there when we came in, smoking from the smell of it.

As he came into the light, I was taken aback by how striking he was—not at all the image I'd conjured in my head based upon Luke's assessment of his personality. His dark hair was in perfect disarray, not unlike male models I'd seen in ads for the latest blue jeans or cologne. If not for his over-sized nose, he probably could have gotten offers for modeling in print work—maybe he still could. His large blue eyes looked expectantly from me to Luke and back again, as he waited for his friend to remember his manners.

"Elle, this is Peter Monroe; Monroe, this is Elle Sloan."

He rubbed his hand down his pant leg before extending it out to me. Hesitant, I accepted it, second guessing whether that had been a good idea when I withdrew my hand from his and discovered an orange residue on my palm.

"Sorry about that. I just murdered a bag of Cheetos before you guys got here."

Luke sighed, offering to take his coat from me. I shrugged it off and handed it to him, amused. My shirt had been torn but was still wearable in that it covered only what it needed to.

"So, Elle, eh?" Monroe asked. "That's a new one. Luke hasn't brought an Elle home before."

I whirled around to find Luke's face bright red, more from rage than embarrassment, I guessed.

73

"Relax, man, I'm just kidding," Monroe said, slumping down onto one of the beanbag chairs on the floor. "Hell, I think anyone in this building could attest to your never having brought any member of the female persuasion back here. Come to think of it, I don't think you've dated anyone in years, not since Marg—"

"Monroe!" Luke said sternly. It had been a long night for the both of us, and his tolerance for his friend's shenanigans had dried up.

"What has your panties in a wad tonight?" It seemed Monroe was growing just as equally as irritated with Luke.

Luke turned to me, ignoring his friend. "Are you sure you don't want anything to eat?"

"No, I think I just want to go to bed, if you don't mind."

"Are you kidding?" Monroe asked, laughing. "Of course he doesn't mind. He's been waiting his entire life to go to bed."

"Not now, Monroe!" Luke shot his friend a glance containing all the warning he needed.

Perplexed, Monroe opened his mouth to say something, thought better of it, and promptly closed it again.

Luke put his arm around me and guided me down a short hallway to his bedroom at the end. As far as bedrooms were concerned, Luke's was pretty unremarkable. Bare white walls with minimal furniture, which was probably a good call on his part, considering the room wasn't exactly spacious. His bed stood in the center of the room. It was a full bed, and a little too big for the space itself, yet it felt as though it belonged there and any other bed would have been out of place.

"I'll … I'll find something for you to wear," Luke stammered, as the door latched shut behind us.

Nodding, I walked over to the bed and sat down. He'd made it, a fact which shouldn't have surprised me. Not everyone was a slob like I was, or believed that making their bed was a pointless waste of time. I rubbed my hand over the flannel comforter, exhausted and shaken from the events of the day and also oddly nervous about being in Luke's bedroom.

"It's a little too—a lot too big, but I'm pretty sure everything I have would fit that description," Luke said with a nervous laugh.

"I'm sure it will be perfect," I replied, taking the T-shirt from him.

"I'll g-give you a second to get changed." He turned to walk to the door when a thought occurred to me.

"Luke?"

"Yeah?"

"Would you mind doing me favor?"

"Sure, anything. Do you want me to kick Monroe out of the apartment? Because I can do that."

"I'll put that under my hat for the next time." I removed my phone from my purse and handed it to him. "Would you mind calling Mena for me? She should know where I'm at."

"Can't I just kick my best friend out onto the street, instead?"

Undaunted, I kept the arm containing the hand holding the phone extended out to him. With a sigh, Luke took it.

"I owe you like a million," I said, kicking my shoes off.

"You owe me nothing," Luke replied, opening the door. "I'll be back in a couple minutes, I hope." He held up my phone with a dead look in his eyes, closing the door behind him as he left the room.

I held the T-shirt he handed me out in front of me. A basic heather gray with a large bug of sorts on the front, it was about three sizes too large for me. Further unfurling revealed the bug to be a hornet, a high school mascot to be exact. Luke's footsteps disappeared down the hall, replaced by both his and Monroe's voices in a quiet conversation that was still very much audible given the cramped apartment.

"So why was she wearing your coat? Is she just that ill-prepared for the season or are you just that chivalrous?" Monroe clearly asked once Luke returned to the living room. "And what the hell happened to her? She looks like the headlining event at a UFC match."

"Were you born a dick or did society make you that way?" Luke responded, anything but amused.

"What's your problem tonight?"

75

"I figured since we were asking rhetorical questions, I'd get one of my own in." He lowered his voice out of courtesy for me when he began answering Monroe's questions and recounted to him the events of the night that had lead to us all being present in this apartment.

Caught in a mental struggle between wanting to respect their privacy and wanting to listen to him recount the events my mind was already trying to make me forget, I jumped up from the bed as I began to undress. By the time I'd gotten to the door, their voices had already moved from the living room to the porch. I threw my clothes—my ripped button-down shirt, stained with drops of my own blood, and my blue jeans that had come within an inch of being torn—in a pile on the floor. Those clothes weren't something I ever wanted to look at again, let alone wear.

I threw Luke's T-shirt on. As I suspected, it became more of a dress than a shirt, falling just above my knees.

Luke must have walked back inside of the apartment, and his long drawn out sigh followed him with every step. "Oh god, help me," he muttered. A brief pause ensued before he spoke again. "Now isn't that a pretty colorful way to address your friend."

He was on the phone with Mena.

"Yes, I know it's late, but I'm betting you were still awake anyway? ... No, that's exactly my point. ... Listen, Elle asked me to call you. ... She's sleeping. She had a really rough night."

Luke walked back down the hallway, again trying to keep himself out of earshot of me and what would no doubt be the shit show his conversation with Mena was about to become. I probably should have jumped in to save him, probably should have pried the phone out of his hand and took the bullet myself, but I just couldn't bring myself to do it. Not tonight.

Luke's jacket laid on the floor where he'd thrown it down to look for a T-shirt for me. It rested near my pile of clothing. I stared at it, thinking to myself how it didn't belong there. It wasn't damaged goods like the rest of the articles of clothing on the floor. With the sound of

Luke's footsteps walking back in the direction of the bedroom, I picked up the jacket and searched for some place in his room to hang it up.

"Yes, Mena, for the last time, she's fine. She's resting. And, no, I am not going to wake her up. I'll have her call you in the morning. ... For god's sake, I will not send you proof of life. I don't even know what that means. If you want to send a search party, you have my address. For now, goodnight, Mena."

I smirked, knowing exactly what he'd just been through. Finding nothing else more suitable, I resigned myself to hanging his jacket on the handle of his closet door, just as a light tapping on the bedroom door beckoned my attention.

"I'm decent," I said, chuckling a bit as the door opened.

"I'm going to j—" Luke stopped, words apparently failing him when he saw me standing in the middle of his room wearing his shirt-dress, wide-eyed.

"What? Haven't you ever seen a pair of legs before?"

"Uh, what?" He cleared his throat. "Y-yeah, all the time. I mean, not *all* the time, but you know, the appropriate amount of times. I'm just going to grab my pillow." Flustered, he kept his eyes downcast to the floor as he walked over to his bed. In his hand was my cell phone, which he remembered he had when he reached the side of the bed. "I'll put it on the nightstand," he said, holding it up.

"Thank you, Luke. For like the one millionth time tonight, thank you."

His demeanor loosened up, his nerves eased, and he smiled, the sweet smile I'd come to associate with him, as he grabbed a pillow from the bed. "I'll be down the hall if you need anything."

It was my turn to stammer. "Wh-where are you going?"

"The couch," he answered matter-of-factly. "To sleep."

Every bit of me became rigid in protest and with disappointment. Maybe I should have let him leave, maybe I shouldn't have made the request I made, considering everything that had happened to me tonight, but I did, and the desperation in my voice was palpable.

"Stay ... please."

"There is no way I'm going to have you sleep on that ratty old couch that I'm fairly certain Monroe picked up from the side of the road somewhere."

"That's not what I meant."

Confused, he looked up at me with a raised eyebrow before the realization struck him. "Oh, oh, oh," he said, apparently incapable of vocalizing any other word. "Are you sure, Elle?"

I nodded. "I don't want to be alone right now, if that's okay. I just ... it's just, right now, I equate you and your arms that carried me away from the rapist at the bookstore with safety, and I know that may sound strange to you, but I really don't want that feeling to end. It might if I'm left alone in the dark, even if you are only steps away, it still could. So please, please, Luke, stay with me."

He nodded before his mouth could form any words. It reminded me of the way lightning is seen before one hears the rumbles of thunder during a storm. "How could I say no to that?" He smiled.

"It would pretty much make you an asshole."

He laughed. "The king of assholes."

"Your majesty." Doing my best to keep my composure, I curtsied, much to his amusement.

Opening his dresser drawer, Luke pulled out a pair of shorts and a T-shirt. "I'm going to run to the bathroom quick." He gestured out the door with the hand holding the articles of clothing.

I nodded, watching as he left the room before crawling into his bed. He had one sheet aside from his comforter, both of which smelled like him. A mixture of musk and testosterone, if testosterone even had a scent. It wafted from his pillows up my nostrils, so strong and intoxicating that my olfactory system craved more of it, like a drug. Eager to appease my nose, I buried my face in Luke's pillow, just as a knock on the door frame brought me back to my senses. Face burning with embarrassment, I looked up to see an amused Monroe staring at me in the doorway.

"I, um, felt a sneeze coming on," I explained.

Not one to miss a beat, Monroe responded in the same self-assured, if not slightly arrogant, way I'm sure he always did, "Hey, whatever you need to tell yourself."

I patted the pillow, sat up on the bed, and tucked it behind me.

"Luke told me what happened, and I just wanted to say that I'm sorry you had to go through that. Had I known, I would have been a little less like me and a whole lot more like the man whose pillow you were just snorting. He does smell dreamy though, doesn't he?" He smirked, an expression that I would have bet my life's savings was on his face the moment he was born.

"Thank you, Monroe," I said through gritted teeth. At that moment, I wanted to crawl into a hole and bury myself alive.

"No problem." He strummed the door frame with his fingers, punctuating each syllable. "See you in the morning."

"Goodnight."

Luke stepped out of the bathroom right as Monroe walked back down the hall in the direction of the living room. He appeared nervous, averting his gaze whenever his eyes happened to lock with mine. It were as though this was a first for him, having a girl in his bed. Closing the door behind him, Luke turned off the light and slowly shuffled in the dark from the door to the bed. I felt him sit on the mattress before I saw him, as my eyes, too, were adjusting to the abrupt darkness. The pull of the comforter told me that he was laying on top of the covers.

"You can get underneath them. The covers. It won't bother me, Luke."

He was silent for a moment, perhaps mulling my offer over carefully before rejecting it. "I'm fine, Elle. I usually don't sleep with much over me. The blankets are more for show than anything else. I barely use them.

He rolled over onto his side, facing me. Even though I couldn't see his features in the dark, I could feel his smile. It beckoned me to him like a beacon of light, and I rolled onto my side, allowing him to wrap his arm around me.

79

"I told Monroe about what happened," he said, his mouth close to my ear. "I caught him eyeing the bruise forming on the side of your face and decided to fill him in before he started in on his usual inane round of questioning."

"I know, he came over to apologize."

"Dammit, Monroe."

"What?"

"I told him not to say anything. In case you hadn't noticed, he was born without a filter."

"That actually makes him more endearing to me."

"Really? Because endearing and Monroe, I'm pretty certain, have never been said together in the same sentence."

"That may be true, but only because people don't want to hear the truth about themselves. They'd prefer to be lied to if it means they can keep up the charade they conjured up in their heads. They can't face the truth or the fact they have faults. People like Monroe are necessary in this world to maintain balance. You know exactly where you stand with Monroe. I respect that."

"Would you like me to call Monroe in here and I'll go out to the couch?" Luke laughed, holding me tighter like he thought there may be a snowball's chance in hell that I would ever take him up on his offer.

"Don't be silly, there's plenty of room for the three of us." I giggled as I rubbed his hand. Already, I could feel myself drifting off to sleep, despite my efforts to fight it off. As downright horrible as the night had started off, it had turned around substantially, and I didn't want it to end, not yet. I'd take every second I could squeeze out with Luke before having to face reality again.

Next to me, Luke chuckled, which turned into a yawn.

"Not you too," I moaned.

"I'm fighting a losing battle here," he answered, just as frustrated with his body's insubordination as I was with mine.

"Me too. If I close my eyes, I'm done for."

"You know, this doesn't have to be a one time thing. If Mena and

80

Monroe don't make our lives a living hell, you can stay over again."

"This is true, but there will never be another first night again, or another night like this, for that matter."

"And there will never be. I gave my word to you, Elle, and I mean it. You won't be at that store by yourself anymore."

"You saved my life tonight, Luke, like you were my very own personal superhero, but even superheroes can't be everywhere at once."

"Don't start branding me with an 'S' on my chest just yet. That was luck tonight, me coming to the store when I did. I just happened to be in the right place at the right time. Timing by itself won't cut it in the future."

"But you can't beat yourself up trying to make sure something bad never happens to me. It's an impossible promise to keep."

"Try me, Sloan." His voice grew softer as he was on the verge of losing his battle with exhaustion. "As long as you will allow me to be a part of your life, I'll do everything in my power to protect you."

Smiling, I listened as his words trailed away, like leaves blown from a tree, each venturing on a journey of their own. Soon, there was nothing but silence, followed by the rhythmic breaths of sleep near my ear. And as I drifted off, I couldn't help but think that Luke had been wrong about one thing tonight. I did owe him. I owed him my life, my spirit, my very existence; I owed him so much more than I would ever be able to repay him.

CHAPTER SIX

2018

I'd often found myself waking up in a cold sweat after having had the nightmare surrounding that night in the bookstore, now so long ago. With eerie precision, the night always proceeded the same way in my subconscious, except for one important detail. As the months after our breakup progressed, Luke went from appearing later and later in the scenario, until he stopped appearing at all, leaving me completely alone with my assailant. When he disappeared completely, it was up to my body to become my savior, which it did, but not before I had been further violated in ways that thankfully had never actually happened that night. Luke had kept his word. As long as I'd allowed him to be a part of my life, he'd kept me safe. Eric, on the other hand, had grown weary of my nightmares over the years, at first having sympathy for me and my plight, but then doing an about face the seventh or eighth time I'd woken him up screaming on the night before he had an early morning hearing. It was shortly after the last nightmare—about six months ago—that he'd taken to sleeping in our spare bedroom more and more often.

The latest nightmare still fresh on my mind, I shot up out of bed shortly before my alarm sounded, confused as all hell by where I was for the first ten seconds after my eyes opened. Slowly, my senses returned to me, heightened all the more by Candy's voice coming from the room below. I'd slept like death—stiff and totally oblivious to the world around me, as if I were no longer a part of it. It'd been a while since I had been that exhausted.

Yawning, I kicked my legs free from the duvet and sat up, resting my feet on the floor. This was probably a first for me, getting up without having to hit snooze a half dozen times before committing to the day, not to mention the first time in longer than I cared to admit that I had actually been somewhat excited to begin my day. My body, however, didn't share the same sentiment. Half walking, half staggering, I made my way to the door.

As I approached the stairs leading to the main level of the house, I came to a halt. It wasn't so much due to the fact that Candy was still speaking below me as it was due to the tone she was using with whomever it was she was speaking.

"I told you, he's not ready yet. ... Oh, for Pete's sake, he just woke up. Give him some time. Really, have you lost all your compassion, too? ... Yes, he still has a brain injury. You don't just get over that."

I could hear the sound her slippers made as she paced on the carpet. Although I felt bad for eavesdropping, I listed to the end of the conversation.

"I understand you have a deadline, but I honestly don't think he could even do what you need him to do right now, anyway. ... Just give us some more time, okay? Will you at least do that? He'll be ready soon. ... All right, I'll be in touch. Uh-huh, good-bye now."

I didn't know who it was at the other end of that phone call, or what they were saying, but I could sense my blood beginning to boil at the thought of someone speaking to Candy in the manner in which this person obviously had been. Candy had never been anything more than hospitable to me at all times, and I couldn't comprehend what

83

she—or Luke for that matter—could possibly have done to warrant the contentious conversation that had just taken place.

Miffed, I took a step down the stairs, remembering a second too late that these were no ordinary stairs, but the stairs of doom down which I'd had the privilege of slipping and falling on occasions too numerous to count. And slip I did—on my rear end, all the way down, hitting each step along the way.

Sitting at the bottom of the stairs, ego bruised worse than my body, I cursed myself under my breath, hoping Candy hadn't noticed, a notion that went up in flames when I looked up to see a trembling hand reaching down to help me up. My eyes trailed up the frail arm, to the once broad shoulders, and the gaunt face with the sunken eyes. No wonder Luke had freaked out the moment he'd seen his father. The difference between the Tom of my memories and the Tom of today was so profound it was downright jarring.

"I know I must look a fright to you," Tom said so apologetically that it made my heart hurt for having gaped at him the way I'm sure I had.

"Of course not, Tom." I pushed myself up to my feet, only grabbing his hand when I knew he wouldn't have to exert much of an effort to help me up. Once upright again, I gingerly draped my arms around him in what was probably the most careful hug I'd ever given to anyone.

"It's okay, Ms. Ellen," he said, his voice almost as shaky as his hand had been, "you won't break me."

"What was that commotion?" Candy asked, returning to the room. "It sounded like someone fell down the stair …" A brief pause ensued before she invariably burst out into laughter. "I guess some things never change," she said between chuckles.

"I was really hoping to redeem myself, too," I said, rubbing my backside, "or that you'd forgotten about my deficiencies in the area of stair descension."

"Oh dear, no, that's something I'll never forget. How could we?

Luke never forgot, either. Whenever he'd come over to visit, he couldn't help but giggle each time he passed them. That is until ..."

Tom cleared his throat as he eased himself down into a recliner in the corner of the room.

"Until what?" I asked.

"Nothing," Candy continued.

The atmosphere turned awkwardly silent as I desperately searched for something to say to steer the direction of our conversation back into more lighthearted seas.

"Is everything okay with Luke this morning?" I asked.

Eyebrow raised, Candy responded, "Why yes, why do you ask?"

"Please know that I didn't mean to eavesdrop, but I couldn't help but overhear you speaking with someone on the phone. The conversation sounded pretty heated, and you seemed upset, which is why I came downstairs still donned in this lovely attire." I motioned to my flannel pajama pants and gray tank top. "Is everything okay?"

I caught Candy stealing a quick glance at Tom, seeking guidance through telepathic means.

"I don't mean to overstep my boundaries," I said. "You just sounded so upset, so I naturally thought something must have happened with Luke."

"Nothing happened, Elle. It's just that the rest of the world keeps spinning even when yours comes to a grinding halt. Just a few medical bill collectors looking for their money, is all. Nothing I can't handle."

"Isn't the car insurance taking care of those?"

Although trying her best to conceal it, Candy became noticeably ruffled. "It's a little complicated."

"That's just horrible. You would think the debt collectors would be able to wait a few more weeks, out of respect and all."

"You would think, but some people are just born horrible human beings." She shook her head at the thought, motioning for me to follow her into the kitchen. "Don't get dressed yet, I made breakfast."

With my empty stomach guiding my way, I followed her into the

85

kitchen, all while my thoughts stayed preoccupied with the conversation I'd overheard a moment ago, and the overwhelming feeling that there was more to it than Candy had been willing to tell me.

* * * * *

My long legs carried me down the hall at a much faster clip than Candy's did for her. At first, I did my best to slow down and stay with her, but after about the tenth time of doing so, I gave up. As we approached Luke's room, a middle-aged, balding man of average stature walked from the room and out into the hall. The presence of a white lab coat identified him as a doctor.

"Dr. Reid," Candy confirmed my suspicion, "good morning." Her legs picked up the pace, carrying her past me the rest of the way to the room.

"Good morning, Candy," he acknowledged her, looking up from the tablet in his hands. With the casual way he greeted her, they must have gotten to know each other well over the last several weeks. He glanced from Candy to me. For someone who had never met me before, there was a clear recognition in the doctor's eyes when he looked at me. Normally, that may have made me feel uneasy, but considering everything that had happened to me over the last few days, I was beginning to adjust what I considered normal. "And this is?" he asked Candy needlessly, as I was quite certain he already knew who I was.

"Elle," she humored him. "This is Elle Sloan."

"It's Bell, actually," I said, shaking the doctor's outstretched hand.

"Your name is Elle Bell?" he asked, amused.

"Ellen Bell, really. It sounds a little less ridiculous that way. How's Luke doing?"

I asked, trying to peer inside his room. "May I see him?"

"He's resting now," Dr. Reid answered me. "But you can go in if you like. There are a few things I need to discuss out here with Candy, anyway."

Nodding and without further need for an explanation, I entered Luke's room, leaving Candy and Dr. Reid in the hallway. Just as Dr. Reid had said, Luke was sleeping peacefully, though noticeably pallor in appearance, so pale that I felt the necessity to touch his forehead, like a mother tending to her sick child. His skin was damp. Most likely, he'd recently broken a fever. He stirred slightly when I touched him, but shortly fell back into a deep sleep after I withdrew my hand.

I pulled a chair next to his bed and sat down beside him, watching the rise and fall of his stomach, as Candy and Dr. Reid spoke outside his door. They'd moved closer to the room, perhaps so they could look at Luke while they there talking, however, in doing so, it canceled out the white noise that had prevented me from hearing them before their move.

"It's called bacteremia," Dr. Reid said. "A bacterial infection in the blood, most likely from his catheter. A nurse is on the way with an antibiotic for us to begin an infusion." He paused, and although my back was turned to them, I could feel the doctor's eyes on me. "How did he do with her yesterday?" he asked Candy, referring to me. "Has her presence yielded the desired result?"

"If by that you mean has he regained his memory, the answer is no. Not even a glimmer of it. But she just arrived, so we'll see what today brings."

"I know we've been over this a thousand times, but him seeing her isn't going to automatically jog his memory. He suffered a traumatic brain injury and needs time to heal, if he ever truly does. It's very hard to predict how his injury is going to manifest. He could show symptoms he doesn't have now six months from now; his memory may begin to return today, or it may never return to him at all. That's why I think it would be wise to tell him everything sooner rather than later."

"I know, Doctor, and we will. I'd just like a couple more days."

"Okay," he replied, defeated. "But you realize that Ms. Bell's being here could be all for nothing. In fact, it most likely is."

"That's where you and I will have to disagree. Because even if Luke never remembers the part of his life he lost, Elle still managed to perform a miracle."

"Oh? How do you figure that?"

"She made him smile."

They continued their conversation, their words growing fainter and fainter as they walked down the hallway and away from the room. Dr. Reid had been wrong for another reason. Whether Luke remembered anything about his past or not, there was a purpose for my being here. When the time came and Luke still couldn't remember his life after me, and Candy had to tell him everything about the time he'd lost, I would face him in person, instead of hiding behind a cell phone like I had done so many years prior. This time, I would take his pain and make it my own.

Luke shivered in his sleep. His blanket had been kicked to the side of the bed at some point in his feverish state. I grabbed it, straightened it out, and then draped it back over his goosebump-covered body.

"Hey," he said sleepily as he laid a hand on my arm.

"I'm sorry, I didn't mean to wake you." I pulled the chair I had been sitting in closer to the bed and sat down next to him.

"It's me who should be apologizing to you. I'm sure the last thing you wanted to do was watch me sleep."

"That's where you're wrong, because I can think of a half dozen other things that would qualify as the last thing I wanted to do today. This doesn't even crack the top ten."

He smiled, the very act of which must have been painful as evidenced by the grimace that followed.

"Rough night?" I asked sympathetically, taking his hand in mine.

He opened his eyes to look at me. "That's what they tell me. Thankfully, I was too drugged-up to remember most of it."

"And here comes more drugs." I whirled around to see the nurse Dr. Reid had mentioned coming with antibiotics for Luke. A short, dark-haired girl around our age, she was Webster's definition of perky.

Curious to know the identity of the spunky nurse assigned to Luke today, I stole a glance at the white dry erase board at the front of the room and saw the name Hannah written in perfect cursive, complete with a daisy containing a smiley face placed at the end of it.

I looked back to see Hannah hanging the antibiotics on the infusion pole, before turning back to Luke, who, curiously, was watching her intently.

"I brought you something," I said, remembering the book of Sudoku puzzles I'd purchased at a drug store during my trip here. Sudoku puzzles had been Luke's Achilles' heel. He never neglected to finish one he started.

"Oh, yeah?" he asked, only momentarily taking his eyes off Hannah. "Is it a Maserati? Tell me it's a Maserati."

"Better," I replied, removing the book from my purse and setting it down on the bed next to him.

His eyes lit up as he picked the book up and turned the pages. "Well, I'll be damned if you didn't do one better."

"I figured there may be a chance you'd want something to keep you occupied."

"You know me all too well," he said, resting the book on his lap.

I lifted my gaze to see Hannah watching us. Her demeanor had changed from the chipper, yet professionally composed nurse she had been when she first entered the room to a more melancholy presence with a smile that reflected more pain than cheer. There was something in her crystal clear hazel eyes that told me she also knew Luke all too well.

"You're all set," she said, prompting Luke to divert his attention away from me. "You're on this antibiotic for twenty-four hours." Luke inspected the IV skeptically, his eyes squinting as though he were concentrating on extracting something from deep within his brain.

A memory, perhaps? Was he remembering something?

Hannah, also noticing the recognition in Luke's face, perked back up. "I'll be in periodically to check up on you, Luke. Is there anything you need?"

89

"Yeah," Luke said, his confidence in whatever it was that had captivated his attention growing stronger. "I need you to unclasp the rollerball on the antibiotic, so it can infuse."

"Oh?" Hannah asked in an overstated sense of shock, "let me take a look." She feigned an inspection of the IV, quickly spotting the error she'd made. "Would you look at that. Wow, what has gotten into me today?" She unclasped the rollerball, turning back to Luke. "Are you a medical professional? How did you know I had forgotten to do that?"

Luke, looking genuinely perplexed, answered, "I-I don't know. It's just, when I looked at it, something didn't seem right. I'm in nursing school, perhaps it's something we learned in class coming back to me."

"Perhaps." Hannah smiled, casting her eyes up at me just long enough to catch my attention, but too brief for Luke to notice. "The therapist will be in shortly for your morning occupational therapy session," she informed him. As Luke remained staring at the IV in utter concentration, I watched as Hannah left the room with more of a swagger in her step than she'd had when she arrived, making a mental note to myself to try to speak with her later. Alone.

As much as I wanted Luke to make a recovery and regain everything he'd lost, a part of me was nervous about how everything would transpire when and if he did. I'd forgotten how he used to look at me with adoration. Suffice it to say, it had been a while since I'd seen that gleam in anyone's eyes, Eric included. What would happen to this expression if he were to regain his memory? Would hatred and loathing trade places with the love I knew was there now? Only twice before had I seen Luke show any malice toward anyone. The first was toward my attacker in the bookstore; the second, my mother.

"Hey, you're awake," Candy said, entering the room holding a cup of coffee in each hand. I nodded my head in thanks as she handed one of the cups to me. "How are you feeling? Dr. Reid said you have some sort of an infection."

"It's nothing I can't handle," Luke responded. "I was hit by a car and lived to tell about it, so I'm pretty certain I can handle a minute bacterial infection."

"Yeah, you're a regular super hero." I took a sip of my coffee. "Pretty soon you'll be lifting cars with your bare hands and leaping over tall buildings with a single bound."

"Yet, I assure you I will never be faster than a speeding bullet." Luke smirked, as my face began to burn. If he hadn't already been in a hospital bed, I probably would have put him in one myself.

"Okay, son, that's a little too much information for your mother."

"Mom, get your mind out of the gutter. I just meant that you'll never see me winning a marathon, is all."

"Mmmhmm," Candy said, rolling her eyes.

Feeling the need to change the subject, I interceded, "Luke caught a mistake his nurse made while she was setting up his IV."

"Oh?" Candy asked. "What mistake was that?"

I listened to Luke recount his discovery to his mother, discounting it as nothing more than something he must have learned in class and not from personal experience.

"Well, that's wonderful, sweetie," she said after Luke finished the story. Despite trying to project a positive vibe, there was something in the way she spoke that made me almost believe she wasn't as thrilled with Luke's discovery as I thought she would have been—or should have been, for that matter. Did she have something to fear by his re-membering his past, too, or was she, like me, worried about how the look on her son's face would do an about-face when he began remem-bering more and more details about his past life?

The latter had to be the case. No decent mother would want to see her child in pain.

As I sat contemplating the thoughts I suspected were running through Candy's brain, Luke picked up the Sudoku book I'd given him and began thumbing through it again. "Huh," he said, sounding even more confused now than when he'd discovered the mistake his nurse had made with the IV.

"What?" I asked, curious.

"Oh, I don't know, it must be some typo or something. Either that or you somehow managed to time travel into the future and brought this book back with you." He laughed at the surely utterly preposterous thought.

"Wha-what is it?" I asked, stealing a glance back up at Candy, who, to the trained eye, appeared horrified, despite being a pro at attempting to mask it.

"The copyright says this book was published in 2016."

Oh, great. After all the meticulous care and attention to detail everyone had put into shielding Luke from all current events in order to allow his memory to return to him slowly, instead of rolling over him like a freight train, I had blown it all with a simple drugstore puzzle book.

"That's the problem with rushing something to print," Luke said, unfazed. "You make careless typographical errors."

"Yes," I sighed in relief, "a typographical error."

"Well, let's hope they learned from their mistake," Candy said, most likely directing that statement toward me.

"Knock, knock," Dr. Reid announced, entering the room.

When Luke looked up to greet him, I grabbed the puzzle book and threw it back into my purse. The copyright reference had been a close one, and I didn't want to take my chances with there being anything else contained within the book that would add to his confusion.

"Hannah tells me you caught an error she made setting up your antibiotics. Do you have some knowledge of IVs, Luke?"

"I'm in nursing school," Luke answered. "We probably touched on the subject and I'm just not remembering it."

"Well, it would seem you have a real knack for the medical profession." Dr. Reid smiled before turning his attention to the IV. "It seems everything is in order. Hopefully, your infection will have run its course and we can disconnect it tomorrow."

A young blonde, around my age in appearance, appeared behind Dr. Reid, briefly capturing his attention before he began talking again.

"Barring any complications, it's my hope that we can get you discharged some time next week, returning only as needed for rehabilitation.

"That would be great, Dr. Reid," Luke said, perking up.

"Of course, there are a lot of factors to consider before we make our final determination to discharge you. Any one of a number of things could hold up the process."

I couldn't be certain, but I felt as though Dr. Reid stole a quick glance at Candy when he made that last statement.

"I understand. I'll do whatever you need me to do if it means getting out of here."

"I know *you* will." Luke was probably the only person in the room who completely missed the doctor stressing the word you.

Dr. Reid knew that he could voice his opinions without rebuke in front of Luke without Candy being able to do a damn thing about it. He was an evil genius, that man. Hannah must have taken notes from him.

Not one to be outdone, Candy responded, "If he is well enough and it is in his best interest, he will be discharged."

"I hope so, Mrs. Hutchins." He turned around and waved the blonde into the room. "This is Lanie, an occupational therapist here. She'll be assisting you with mnemonics and other forms of memory training."

"Memory training?" Luke asked.

Oh, shit.

"You suffered a traumatic brain injury. We're just trying to assess whether and to what extent any cognitive deficits are present."

"Well, it would be nice to remember how I knew the IV was set up improperly."

"Yes, that would be nice to know." Dr Reid smiled as he turned around to leave the room, all while Candy shot daggers at his backside.

"If you wouldn't mind," Lanie spoke, "I would like to work with Luke alone."

"Of course," Candy said in a huff. "A little fresh air would do me some good, right about now."

"How long will the session be?" Luke asked, looking up at me.

"An hour, perhaps a few minutes over," Lanie answered.

"It's okay," I assured him. "I'll just head down to the cafeteria and read or something and come right back up."

Luke nodded, seemingly okay with that idea, as I turned Lanie over to him and left the room. With the way Candy had left, I figured it would be wise to let her be. Dr. Reid had thrown a brick through the hornet's nest, and I wasn't about to be the one to get stung. As I reached the elevator, a sudden vibration reverberated under my armpit from my cell phone inside my purse. I slid its straps down my arm and, using my other hand, reached into its depths, pulling out the still-vibrating device.

Mena was calling back, and I was fairly certain she would be pissed.

"I know, I know, I'm in hot water, but I can expla—"

"I was one more missed call away from disowning you and everything you stand for. How are you going to call me, leave some cryptic message, and then disappear off the face of this planet? I swear to god, Elle, you're going to drive me to drink even more than I already do. That's no small feat."

"Tell me about it."

"That wasn't open to commentary. Now, would you mind telling me what the hell is going on and whether or not I need to buy a plane ticket to come there and help you hide the body? Oh, hey, Carol."

"Geez, Mena, are you at work? Do you need to have this conversation elsewhere?"

"I'll be damned if I'm going to hang up now, just so you can ignore my calls later. Out with it."

I recounted the abridged version of the story to her, including in it the events of the day and my concerns for the future. For once in one of our telephone conversations, her end of the line remained largely silent, aside from the occasional smart ass, Mena-patented comment here and there.

"So that's it in a nutshell." I took a seat at an empty table in the hospital's cafeteria. "I'm stuck between a rock and a hard place without the slightest idea about what to do other than let the weight of it all crush me.

"Yikes," Mena said, baffled by the turn of events. "That's one hell of a way to get your ex back."

"Seriously? Mena, this isn't the time to crack jokes. I'm doing my best to keep it together with Luke and Candy, and ... and Monroe."

"Monroe?" she asked. If I hadn't captured her interest before, I certainly had now. "How is that pretentious prick doing nowadays?"

Even though she was able to convincingly muster up enough venom to spit out that last sentence, I could see through Mena, remembering the way she always looked at Monroe during one of their many banters back and forth. On the outside, they both projected an unwavering chill that, together, could freeze the depths of hades to its core. While on the inside, they were two loyal souls who lived life with a fierce intensity unparalleled by anyone, except for maybe each other. I'd fully expected that all the bickering and bantering between them would build up, eventually exploding into a night of unbridled passion. But when Luke and I broke up, Monroe and Mena steadfastly held onto their loyalty to the both of us and, in essence, broke up, too.

"He hates me, just as I suspected he would."

"Why that uncouth twat. Did he mention me at all?"

I laughed in spite of myself. "It was a brief encounter. We really didn't trade too many words, but I could tell that he doesn't want me here with the way he looked at me."

"Well, you did rip his best friend's heart out of his chest and stomp on it."

"I remember," I said, trying to shake the memory from my mind. "Do you think I made the right decision coming here?"

"I'm not certain whether there is a right or a wrong decision as far as this scenario is concerned, but if you're asking me whether I would have done the same thing ... leave my husband, my job, my life, to help a friend in their darkest hour? Yes, I would. With that said, however, I really think—for both your sake and his—that you shouldn't drag this out for too much longer. If Luke's memory hasn't returned to him in the next forty-eight hours, you need to tell him the truth."

Her last few words struck my ears as though they were being spoken from a mile away, reduced to nothing more than an echo. She was right, of course. Luke needed to know the truth, and I had to return to my life back home, yet the thought of it made every part of me want to scream.

"Unless," Mena continued after my end had remained silent for longer than she felt it should have been, "you don't want him to remember and you don't want to return to your life."

"That's ridiculous, Mena. Of course, I want to return home. I have a job, a life; I have Eric."

"Yeah, Eric," she sneered. Mena never kept her disdain for Eric a secret to either him or myself. From the moment she met him at our wedding, she'd found him arrogant and a bit self-serving. At first, she tried to grin and bear her visits with a clenched jaw and equally as clenched fists, which only relaxed when it was just the two of us. But then, her visits began to occur further and further apart, until before I knew it, one year had turned into two.

"He's my husband, Mena." I instinctively reached for my ring finger, remembering that I had removed my ring when all I felt was my own flesh beneath my fingertips. *Here you are defending him, all while pretending you're single.*

"He doesn't have to be," she muttered.

"Really? You're doing this right now?"

Mena sighed, finally relenting. "What are you going to tell Luke?"

"I'm not sure yet. I … I really haven't thought about that. Actually, I'm pretty certain I'm trying to avoid thinking about it altogether."

I looked up then to see Hannah walking through the line at the salad bar in the cafeteria. I hadn't had the opportunity to formulate exactly what I was going to say to her or how I was going to broach the subject of what I knew she had done with Luke's IV. Still, I didn't want to let the opportunity to have a one-on-one conversation with her pass me by.

"Elle?" Mena asked. "Did you hear me?"

"Huh?" I asked, trying not to let Hannah walk out of view.

"Do you need me to fly down there when you tell him? You know, for moral support."

"I appreciate the offer, but I think I'll be fine. I made my bed years ago; it's time I lay in it."

Hannah walked a styrofoam container over to the cashier. With any luck, after she paid for her lunch, she would walk it to one of the tables in the cafeteria, but that wasn't something I could necessarily count on.

"Are you sure, Elle? I could use a few days out of this shithole." A momentary pause ensued before I heard her speak again. "Oh, don't act like you couldn't either, Joe. This place isn't the fucking Taj Mahal."

"It's okay. Really, I got this." I watched Hannah walk away from the register with her container in hand, silently willing her take a seat in any of the many empty seats in the cafeteria. Instead, she curved around the seating area, heading to destinations unknown. "Listen, Mena, I have to let you go. Call you tomorrow?" In a frenzy, I sprung up from my chair, catching my foot on the leg of it, nearly falling on my face in the process.

"You'd better," Mena said. "Because if I don't hear from you in a timely manner, I'm flying down there."

"Noted. I'll take that as my warning." Hannah rounded a corner and disappeared out of sight. Not wanting to lose her, I all but ran through the cafeteria, stomach growling as if to remind me what I hadn't done while in the cafeteria. "I'll talk to you soon." Ending the call, I sped up and rounded the corner in the direction Hannah had just headed. In front of me was a wide vestibule lined on both sides with floor to ceiling windows. From the ceiling hung various marine life constructed out of paper mâché. With the way they were positioned, they appeared to be in various acts of swimming, some diving down to the depths of the vestibule, while others seemed to try to catch a glimpse of the world beyond the makeshift sea in which they were confined.

Up ahead, I saw Hannah walking to a glass door to exit out of the building. It felt strange, following her just to have five minutes alone with her to get a feel for what she may know about the life of the Luke I hadn't known in the better part of decade. How would I even approach her with it, and what would her motivation be to answer my questions? Her loyalty would be to Luke and to Candy. That combined with HIPPA laws were enough to keep her tight-lipped. Still, I felt compelled to know what she knew. It felt as though a piece of my mind had been asleep for the last few years and now that it had been awakened, it wouldn't rest again until it knew everything that had happened while it had been unconscious.

When I exited through the same glass door through which Hannah had, I was greeted by nothing but the front of the hospital.

Damn, she walks fast.

I walked down the sidewalk that lead out to the parking lot designated for the physicians and other staff. My hair whipped around my head, smacking me in the face as though trying to tell me to return to the building, that what I was doing was crossing some invisible line. The only reason why I was here was because Luke had asked for me to be and Candy thought perhaps seeing me again would trigger memories, ultimately leading to his recovery. It wasn't so that I could play detective, to find out the secrets of his life that had become none of my business the second I broke up with him. Yet, here I was, still walking down the sidewalk in the hope of running into Hannah.

An arch loomed up ahead, representing the end of the sidewalk and the beginning of the parking lot. I walked through it, casually observing the rows of vehicles ranging from Accords to Porsches. In none of the vehicles immediately in my line sight did I notice a petite, pixie of a girl. And if not for a split second later, I would have thought that my sighting of her in the vestibule had been nothing more than an apparition.

"I'm right here, although I wish I could say I was sitting behind the wheel of Dr. Reid's Porsche. Alas, that wasn't the hand I was dealt."

Embarrassed, I turned around to see Hannah leaning on the side of the arch with a cigarette in her hand. The styrofoam container with her salad was sitting on a picnic table, a part of the small staff-designated eating area that, aside from Hannah, remained empty. My eyes rested on the cigarette, watching the smoke being carried away by the wind.

"I know, I know, it will kill me," she said, putting the cigarette out underneath her shoe and then disposing of the butt inside of a nearby trashcan. "But so can stress, sugar, and alcohol, and since I'm unable to give up any of those, either, I may as well make my inevitable demise as satisfying as possible." Sitting down at the table, she opened the container. "Technically, I could be fired for smoking here."

"Why?" I asked, taking a seat at the opposite end of the picnic table. "Why do they care what you're doing to your own body?"

"It's not that they care, it's just that they don't want to look like humongous hypocrites when they tell patients that they really need to quit smoking for health reasons and are then themselves coming out here to light one up. We need to set an example, and if the patients were to see their own doctor smoking, what motivation would they have to listen to their recommendations?"

"I guess I never thought about it that way before." Hannah opened up a container of vinaigrette dressing and poured it over her salad. Watching her, I felt a little guilty about interrupting her lunch and what was probably the first chance she'd had to sit down since her shift started. "I'm Elle B— Sloan," I said. "Luke's ..."

"I know who you are," she said matter-of-factly, taking a bite from her salad. "Luke hasn't shut up about you since he woke up."

"I'm sorry," I said, embarrassed. "That must make for boring conversation."

"Actually, his stories are nice, a far departure from our usual conversation. It's been wonderful to see that side of him, jovial and full of life."

"You knew him then; Luke?"

She smiled at my inquiry, as though the answer should have been apparent and the question, unnecessary. "Yes," she answered, nonetheless. "I knew Luke ... I know Luke, I should say, very well."

"Oh." My response came out so quickly that I hadn't had the chance to filter out the element of surprise it contained.

"Don't worry, we weren't sleeping together," she said with a sly smile, responding to my obvious discomfort and the relief I was certain that followed. "We worked together. Hopefully, we'll be able to do so again." Her thoughts trailed away with her last sentence, like she hadn't meant to say it, but had meant to keep it bottled up inside of her head. I'd often shared the same coping technique, not allowing myself to vocalize a worry, as though doing so would breathe life into it.

"You worked together here?"

"Luke said you were a smart one."

Well, one thing's for sure, she's a snarky little bitch.

I wondered why Candy had failed to mention to me that Luke also worked here. Perhaps, it was so inconsequential that the thought hadn't occurred to her to tell me. Or maybe there was another reason ... like she just didn't trust me to know anything about Luke's life, knowing that I wasn't going to be a part of it anyway.

"So," I began, attempting to return to the reason why I'd followed her out here in the first place, "why did you do it?"

"Do what?" she asked far too innocently to legitimately be confused.

"I think you know what I'm talking about."

Hannah plunked a tomato into her mouth and stared off into the distance for a moment, politely allowing herself to finish chewing before she spoke again. "You know, it's a rookie mistake, leaving the IV clamped. A lot of nurses do it when they first start out, even some seasoned ones make careless mistakes."

"But not you. Just looking at you, I could tell that's not a mistake you would make, no matter how distracted you may be."

"You know, I'm starting to like you a little better already," she said with a chuckle. "You're right, though. I've never made that mistake, not on my first IV and not on the one I put in Luke today. But Luke, that was a different story." She smiled, remembering a moment I wish I had been there to share. "Poor Luke had never administered an IV before. It was during one of our first clinicals. We had an instructor who came straight from the bowels of hell itself. It was obvious that he was nervous, but he did it. He set it up perfectly, except for that one crucial detail, that one rookie mistake."

"He's a perfectionist," I said, interrupting her rumination. "And he's exceptionally hard on himself."

"That's for sure," Hannah agreed. "Anyway, the instructor, Professor Browning, read him the riot act right in front of the patient, basically verbally assaulting him in any way she could. But you know, I'll be damned if he ever made that mistake again."

"So by you doing that this morning, you'd hoped it would trigger that memory in him."

"I know he's in there somewhere," she answered, sullenly.

"It's funny because the only Luke I've ever known is the one in that hospital bed right now. This Luke you're trying to find, he'd be like a stranger to me."

"I think you'd be surprised. I didn't know Luke during the time you were together, but I'm sure there's shades of the same person in there. It was a breakup, not a lobotomy."

"I hope so," I murmured, my eyes trained out into the parking lot so as not to draw attention to the dampness in them. Our breakup had affected me in ways I hadn't expected. For the longest time afterwards, my senses had been numbed. Music was far less melodious, sugar downright bitter. Even my very sense of touch seemed to dull, and no amount of blankets could either warm or comfort me. *I* wasn't the same person I was ten years ago, so how could I expect Luke to be?

Hannah closed the lid to the lunch container. She'd eaten quickly, like the food had been just an unpleasant formality to her smoke break. As waif-like as she was, I wondered whether food was ever something she thought about much. "So why did the two of you break up, anyway?" she asked.

Either she was eager to compare my story to the one she'd heard from Luke, or he'd never spoken of me, a prospect that punched me in the gut in a way I couldn't have prepared myself for. "It's been almost ten years," I said, evasively. "All the details have blurred together to the point where they're indecipherable to me anymore."

"Well," Hannah said, standing up, "if you need help putting that puzzle together again, or if you just want to talk, you know where to find me."

I nodded, watching as she walked away from the table and disappeared around the arch, headed back inside to finish her shift. I waited a minute, allowing her to gain some ground before I stood up, so as not to make her feel like I was following her again. It was just past one hour since I'd left Luke, a perfect time to return to him."

* * * * **

I walked into Luke's room, finding him alone, his face red. That shade of crimson on Luke was, I knew, as a result of frustration. "Everything okay?" I asked, sensing his need for a soothing voice.

"It was," he sighed, "until Lanie started giving me all these memory tests—tests to recall the number of objects I could remember from a list. Tests to recall current and past events, names of family, friends, presidents."

"And how did it go?" I asked, cautiously sitting down on the side of his bed next to him. "How … how do you feel?"

"My head is throbbing and I wanted to throw that clipboard she had with her through the window. I wanted to scream, to break something, which I found both frightening and oddly satisfying at the same time." He shook his head. In his eyes were tears, something of an anomaly for Luke, and it ripped my heart in two to see them.

"I answered every single question correctly. I knew the answers. There was no doubt in my mind, but she feels I have memory issues, Elle. Even worse than I thought I had. What's wrong with me?

"Nothing is wrong with you," I comforted him, reaching my hand out to caress his cheek. The moment my hand met his skin, I was struck with a flood of memories that slapped my brain across the face with every flashback I had of me caressing his face before. All I wanted was to make his pain go away.

"I feel like I'm going crazy." He managed to blink back the tears as he spoke.

He deserves to know.

"You're not crazy," I said, moving my hand from his cheek to hold his hand. His hands had always dwarfed mine in comparison. Both of mine could have easily fit into one of his. "There's something you should know—"

"Elle," Candy called my name from the doorway, interrupting me. "May I see you in the hallway for a second?"

"Sure." I squeezed Luke's hand, as I stood up to meet Candy. "Be right back."

"What are you doing?" Impressively, Candy was able to pull off yelling all while maintaining her voice at the level of a whisper.

"Showing some compassion. Look at him, he's a wreck. I don't think I've ever seen him like this before."

"Yeah, well I have," she muttered.

"Touchè." Candy's words landed a blow that may as well have come from an actual physical assault.

"When he's told—if that's the way he has to find out—I'd rather he have us all here. Myself, Tom, Monroe. If you wanted to be there, you too, of course."

"So you want to host some sort of amnesiac intervention, then?" I asked, incensed to a degree.

"Luke's memory returning on its own would be the best case scenario, but if that isn't meant to be, I think surrounding him with the people he loves the most is the best way to break the news to him. It's what I would want done with me, if the roles were reversed. No matter how he's told, he's going to feel blindsided, hurt, betrayed even.

All I want is to minimize the blow to him. Have everyone there to answer any questions, fill in any of the gaps."

"And then there's me. His gaps are my gaps, too."

"You don't have to be here when it happens. None of us would fault you for that."

"No, I want to be. I need to be. My life has been spent running away from situations that make me uncomfortable, partly because I'd actually spent my entire life with someone who dealt with issues by avoiding them altogether, and partly because I'm a coward. I need to be a part of this, Candy. No matter what."

"Okay." She smiled, and I knew then that any issues the two of us may have had up to that point were gone.

"You had something to tell me, Elle?" Luke asked when Candy and I returned to the room.

"Oh," I said, stumbling over myself. With butterflies riding the corkscrew in my stomach, I managed to find a seat next to Luke's bed. "Just that you're not crazy, Luke. You suffered from a serious head injury. Things are naturally going to be confusing for you, especially at the beginning of your recovery. But it will work out. You have amazing people in your life that will make sure of that."

I only half believed what I had just said and hoped it would be enough to satisfy him for the time being. Candy seemed pleased; at least that's what her facial expression told me.

"If there's one thing getting me through all of this, it's all the support I have while I'm here and back at home."

"That's the Luke I remember," Candy said, taking a seat next to her son.

I sat, content to listen to Luke and Candy converse. Aside from a few of my friends in high school, their relationship had been the first dose of a normal, healthy parent/child relationship I'd ever been exposed to. They could talk to each other without judgment. Instead of utter deflation of the other's hopes and dreams, there was encouragement. Love never had to be earned, but instead came naturally without stipulations. Unlike me, Luke hadn't come from a broken home. Also, unlike me, he knew who his father was. And Candy and Tom were as close to perfect as any two parents could be.

They continued conversing with one another, laughing and discussing Luke's future treatments. Content, I sat there, listening to them talk about their day, as I closed my eyes and remembered the day I met Candy and Tom, a smile of my own spreading across my face.

CHAPTER SEVEN

2007

"Maybe he's a eunuch," Mena said quite seriously.

I rolled my eyes as I sat on my bed with my half-completed English Literature assignment sitting in my lap. "As much as I'd love to believe that the problem resides with Luke's manhood and not with him just not being interested in me in that respect, I sincerely doubt that his endowment or lack thereof has anything to do with it."

"Okay, then it's you," she said, returning back to the paper she was typing.

"Thanks."

"What do you want me to say? That you're completely doable and that he's crazy for not having tried to get into your pants by now? Because you are and he is. In fact, you're so doable that if I swung that way, I'd have done you by now. Christ, now I know how men must feel when we women ask them rhetorical questions. It's a wonder not more of them aren't gay."

It had been six months since our dinner at the Italian restaurant, and while we'd engaged in some pretty intense make-out sessions and some over the clothes, on the cusp of PG-13 action, he hadn't even so much as tried to make the attempt to take things further. During the first couple months, it was endearing. But now, I was beginning to wonder whether his interest in me was beginning to wane.

"Maybe," Mena began again, "he's waiting for you to make the first move."

"What?"

"Think about it, Elle. With your history and the incident at the bookstore, the man is probably scared shitless to touch you."

Mena, refusing to say the word 'rape,' had consistently referred to my assault as 'the incident,' partly because she didn't want to acknowledge what could have happened to me and partly because saying the word would make it more real than she was comfortable with.

"Luke doesn't know about my past," I said, "but you do have a point."

"Okay, problem solved. The next time you see him, jump his bones."

"You're always the dispenser of such profound wisdom."

"I try."

My cell phone pinged, notifying me that I had a message. Only three people ever really sent texts to me, and one of them was sitting in the room with me. Out of the remaining two, there was my mother, who usually only did so while drunk. Given that it was still early in the day, odds were it wasn't her, leaving only one other person.

"Huh," I said, perplexed.

"What?" Mena asked, more out of obligation than actual interest.

"Luke says he has a surprise for me. He says I need to pack my bags and that we're leaving tomorrow night."

"Maybe it's his penis," Mena said, only slightly more interested in the conversation than she had been before.

I sighed, attempting to make myself sound more annoyed with her response than I actually was, when in reality, I was hoping she was right.

* * * * *

My nerves were getting the better of me when I climbed into the passenger seat next to Luke after packing my suitcase away inside of his trunk. In contrast, he seemed just as cool as a cucumber, as always.

"I'm sorry if I seemed a little bossy in my text," he apologized. "It's just that the idea to do this occurred to me a second before I sent that message, and I was too excited not to text you."

"That's fine. Your message sounded, or read, rather, one hundred percent non-dictatorial."

"Good to know our relationship is still a democracy." He winked as he backed out of the parking lot at Cogsworth.

"So, if you don't mind me asking, where are we going on our overnight excursion?" I inquired, my mind brimming with all the possibilities.

"Yeah, I probably should have mentioned that to you," he said with a nervous laugh. "My parents complained that I never visit them anymore since starting school and moving in with Monroe, so I figured I'd come home for a visit."

Just then, I felt as though I were a balloon that had been poked with a pin. With the air steadily leaving me, I struggled to speak. "Home?" I squeaked. "Your ... your parents?"

"Yeah, is that okay?" He glanced over at me, his excitement becoming equally as deflated.

"Y-yeah," I answered, more to put him at ease than anything else. "I would love to meet your parents."

He chuckled to himself before speaking, "Are you sure? Because from the look of insurmountable terror in your eyes, I almost feel like I should be turning around."

"No, it's okay," I assured him. "I would be honored to meet your parents. I'm just such a compulsive planner that I was taken off guard, is all."

"That's good to hear, because my mom is chomping at the bit to meet you."

"They know about me, your parents?"

"I happened to mention you once to my mom in casual conversation. Ever since then, she often asks me about you—how you are, what you're like."

"Along with why you never visit her anymore."

"Oh, I already told her that it's totally all your fault," he said as calmly as he could, attempting not to smile and give himself away.

"As you should," I countered. "After all, she did raise you not to take responsibility for your actions."

"Exactly, and I wouldn't want to disappoint her, now would I?"

I laughed as I sought out Luke's free hand. Fingers interlocked, I held onto it as he pulled out of the Cogsworth campus and headed away from the city toward the suburbs.

Not much longer than twenty minutes later, Luke pulled into the driveway of a darling split-level home tucked in the middle of a quaint neighborhood at the top of a small hill. With it's simple, yet meticulous landscaping and the smoke rising from the chimney on the cool early spring day, it seemed positively cozy. Like something straight out of a fairy tale.

"This is where you grew up?" I asked Luke, already knowing the answer.

"I spent my entire life here, up until a year ago. After I moved, I became my parents' heathen only child, whom they fondly refer to as a deserter during casual conversation."

"They do not!" I exclaimed, laughing.

"You wouldn't think so, but just wait. I'm sure they'd love to recount that, as well as a multitude of other stories." He shivered at the thought, seemingly beginning to rethink our visit as he pulled into the driveway.

My breathing became shallower, and my heart began to beat a hole in my chest like a jackhammer. It had been quite some time since I'd met someone's parents, and I couldn't say as the last time even counted, because I had been a teenager in high school. Even then, I couldn't recall having been this nervous. I wanted Luke's parents to like me, to look me up and down and agree that I was a good fit for their son, to accept me as one of their own.

It was in that desire for acceptance that I realized just how much I really did care about him.

As Luke parked the car, the front door opened, and I saw a short woman step out onto the porch, followed by a very tall man who, by comparison, dwarfed her so badly that the two of them standing next to each other was quite humorous.

Now I know where Luke gets his height.

"Are you ready to be thrown into the lion's den?" he asked, doing nothing to calm my fragile nerves.

"Is this how you indoctrinate all your girlfriends? By throwing them off the deep end and telling them to swim?"

He laughed, taking my hand in his. "Only when I want to deflect attention from myself." With a smirk, he pressed his lips to the back of my hand.

"Just remember, paybacks are a bitch."

"I'm counting on it." Smirk still present, he unbuckled his seat belt and opened his door, heading to the trunk to retrieve my suitcase. Inhaling deeply, I followed suit, stepped out of the car, and met Luke on the driver's side of the vehicle. His steady hand found my clammy, slightly shaking one and entwined his fingers around mine as if to non-verbally tell me it was all going to be okay. Then, with a reassuring squeeze, he proceeded to walk up the cement walkway toward his ever-curious parents, while I remained about a step behind him, trying to conceal myself behind the bulk of his body.

"Your majesty has returned," his father declared in a voice one level deeper than Luke's. I couldn't be certain but I thought I detected a hint of sarcasm. "To what do we owe this honor?"

"I have laundry to do and need money," Luke joked. "And I wanted you to meet true royalty in the form of Lady Elle Sloan. Elle, these are my parents, Tom and Candy Hutchins."

Still nervous beyond belief, I managed to smile when Luke pulled me out from behind his back, finding myself only moderately comforted by the presence of Luke's hand on my shoulder. He was either preparing to catch me if I fainted or if I tried to make a break for it.

"Oh, honey," Candy exclaimed, throwing her arms around me. "It's so wonderful to finally meet you. I've heard so much about you from Luke, it's almost like I already know you."

"Is that a fact?" I asked, raising an eyebrow at Luke, whose face had deepened into a cherry red.

"She's not nearly as homely as you made her out to be," Tom said, fake whispering to him.

"I hate you," Luke fake whispered back.

With her arms still around me, Candy fired back, "Oh, Tom, stop getting him into trouble. He said no such thing, dear." Apparently, she felt compelled to assuage whatever fear I may have had of there being been even an ounce of truth to what Tom had said. "She's just as beautiful as Luke described her."

I wasn't used to a mom being a mom. Had we been coming home to my mother, in place of hugs, there would be judgmental stares, accompanied by a stream of cigarette smoke from the Marlboro in her hand, which she would flat-out refuse to put out, even when shaking hands. Instead of kind, articulate sentiments, there would be plenty of snark to go around, none of which would be in jest. Where my mother would most likely reek of stale cigarette smoke, vodka, and unrealized potential, Candy smelled of sugar cookies, fresh laundry, and sunshine. I was actually disappointed when her arms fell away from my body, as I wanted to take in her scent some more to commit it to memory.

"Let's not just stand here. Come in, come in." With her hand still on my back, she ushered us inside, as she described the pot roast she'd made for her prodigal son's homecoming. Once inside, Candy took my suitcase from Luke, despite his protests, and headed up a set of stairs with it to the upper level. Luke motioned for me to follow, which I did, finding myself taking in the Hutchins' residence with each step. It was just as cozy on the inside as it had been on the outside. With its country-themed decor and the fire roaring in the fireplace, coupled with the aroma of Candy's undoubtedly wonderful pot roast cooking in the kitchen on the main level, I found myself wanting to wrap myself in a blanket on the couch and never leave its confines again.

As we ascended the stairs, Luke started heading to a room to the left, while Candy continued straight on down the hall, prompting an uncharacteristic eye roll and sigh from Luke.

'What?' I mouthed to him.

"Have I mentioned how conservative my parents are?" he whispered, sighing as he stole a glance at the room he had been planning to enter before resigning to following his mother to the bedroom at the end of the hall.

"They're probably still convinced you're a virgin," I whispered back, elbowing him softly.

He released a nervous chuckle. "Yeah, probably."

"I'm sorry for the mess," Candy said, straightening the pillows on the bed of the otherwise immaculate guest bedroom. "I didn't have a chance to clean the room as much as I would have liked." She rested the suitcase down on the mattress, surveying the rest of the room with clear disdain. "I did, however, wash the sheets, so you will at least have a nice clean bed to sleep in."

"Thank you, Mrs. Hutchins," I said. "The entire room is perfect. In fact, I'm fairly certain there isn't a speck of dust to be found."

"That's very sweet of you to lie, dear. And it's Candy. Calling me Mrs. Hutchins makes me feel a lot older than I really am."

I nodded, watching as she walked back to the door, where Luke stood resting his body against the wall in the hallway right outside. He nodded at her, obviously in response to some nonverbal message she had sent to him.

"I'm going to check on the roast," Candy told us before heading back down the hall. "We should be ready to eat in about fifteen minutes."

"Okay, Mom," Luke called out to her, straightening his body back up to it's full height as he removed himself from the wall and entered the room. He sat down on the foot of the bed, where he watched me unpack the things I would need for the night and set them aside on the dresser near the bed.

"So," Luke began, clearly testing the waters, "do you like the surprise, or do I need to work on my surprise game some more?"

"Well, I certainly was surprised."

"Is this too much?" he asked, more concerned this time. "Elle, I'm sorry for having sprung this on you, but obviously my parents are an important part of my life and over the last six months, you have become an important part of it, too. I just wanted my two most important halves to finally meet and become a whole."

"When you put it that way ..." I took a seat on the bed next to him. "It's great, Luke, really." My hand found his cheek and turned his face toward me, leaving it there even when it became apparent that he had no intention of breaking eye contact with me. "It's just been a long time since I've been at this stage in a relationship. I'm a bit of a planner, always wanting to prepare myself for every last detail, and I would be lying if I said that my anxiety wasn't thrown into overdrive and my palms weren't sweating the closer we came to your parents' house."

"I would know that you were lying if you had said that, too. I'm still wiping my hand that was holding onto yours in the car across my jeans to get rid of the damp feeling." He chuckled.

More amused than incensed, I removed my hand from his cheek and playfully smacked his arm.

"But I'm happy you brought me here with you. Your parents seem like the wonderful people I pictured when you told me about them. And honestly, it's nice being in a household that seems somewhat normal. Your parents genuinely care about each other; there aren't beer cans strewn all over the place, and it would seem at least someone paid the electric bill this month." I laughed, stopping myself when I noticed the seriousness on Luke's face. "Your childhood must have been wonderful," I said, trying to lighten the mood again.

"It was," he confirmed. "It truly was." He paused, his eyes searching me like he was trying to decide whether to say the words that were so clearly on his mind. "Do you want to talk about it—your life back home?" he finally asked.

"No," I answered him without much hesitation, "at least, not tonight, anyway. I think we already made one giant leap in our relationship, but I don't think I could handle that particular one."

"You know that no matter what you tell me, it won't change my opinion of you, right?"

I nodded. "Oh, I don't know ... I may have some wicked skeletons in my closet."

"I wouldn't doubt that if you were Mena. I wouldn't be surprised if that girl has skeletons buried in her parents' backyard or tucked away in the trunk of a car submerged in the Shenandoah."

"Me either, actually," I confessed.

"But you? Not a chance. What you see is what you get, and that's truly—"

"Boring," I interceded.

"Refreshing," he corrected me. "There's no drama with you, no ulterior motives. You're as transparent as air. It's one of the reasons why I love you."

Stunned, I stared at him, speechless, attempting to process what he had just confessed to me. "You ... you love me?"

"I do," he all but whispered.

"When did you know?"

"For a while now. I've been wanting to say it, but it never seemed like the right time. I hadn't planned on doing it now, but it just came out, like my heart wouldn't let me hold it in any longer."

I grinned, soaking in his declaration, knowing that I had one to make of my own. One that I, too, had been holding back for a time yet to be determined for no good reason other than I had been too afraid to admit it—to both myself and to Luke. "Luke," I said, drawing out my confession by a few more seconds, attempting to shake the nerves free from my body.

"Yeah?"

"I love you, too."

I couldn't be certain, but I thought I detected him exhaling a breath I hadn't realized he'd been holding. Relief washed over his face. "Thank God, because it was about to get awkward in here." He leaned in and gently brushed his lips against mine for what he intended to be a brief, sweet kiss, fitting of the moment. But as he began to pull away from me, I felt a surge of desire overcome me, and I sought to return him to me, to physically capture everything I was feeling internally.

Surprised at first, Luke quickly recovered, matching me in both intensity and passion. His body leaned into mine, pushing me down on the bed with him, his mouth never leaving mine. "God I love you, Sloan," he murmured, sliding his lips down from my mouth to my neck. His breathing had become heavier; his own desire, evident.

"Dinner's ready," Candy called from downstairs.

Luke groaned in the space where my neck met my torso, tickling me. "Did I mention my mom has horrible timing?"

"That has to be her only negative attribute."

He sat up and ran his fingers through his hair to straighten out the few errant strands that had fallen out of place. Reluctantly, I followed suit, sitting up and straightening out my blouse. My body ached for Luke in every way possible. I hoped he ached for me, too, but with the ease at which he stopped, I wasn't quite certain.

"We'd better get down there before she sends a search party up here after us."

"Can't we just stay up here for a few more minutes?" As hard as I tried not to make it sound like I was whining, I ended up failing miserably.

"Unfortunately, not. My mother is one-quarter Italian. Trust me, she takes the dinner hour very seriously."

It was my turn to groan.

"My sentiments exactly," he said.

He stood up and offered his hand to me, which I took without much enthusiasm, walking with him as we made our way down to the dining room.

* * * * *

I lay in Luke's parent's spare bedroom, my eyes fixated on the ceiling fan directly above me. This day, this night, had gone better than I would have anticipated, had I been given the opportunity to anticipate it before Luke sprung it on me. Luke's parents were incredibly warm and inviting, making a point to ask me about my life at Cogsworth and my plans for the future, all the while having the good sense to listen to Luke's nonverbal cues and not pursue the topic of my family life when it naturally presented itself. After dinner, I'd helped Candy clear the table and wash the dishes, ignoring her insistence that I was a guest and shouldn't be lifting a finger. As Candy and I tidied up the kitchen, I listened to Luke and Tom engage in what I'd assumed to be their usual banter involving sports and Luke's class schedule for the fall. Later, I'd helped Candy with a crossword puzzle she'd been working on throughout the day, laughing as she regaled me with stories of Luke's younger, less formative years, including his penchant for running around the house naked up until he was six years old. Red-faced, Luke sat and listened, occasionally throwing in a correction where he deemed fit.

But there was one moment that had transpired this evening that stood out from the pack. One moment that brought an ache back into my body. I attempted to will myself to forget about it, to force my eyes to close and not open them until tomorrow morning, but I couldn't deny the invisible force beckoning me from down the hall. Was Luke asleep yet? Did he feel it, too? Luke's parents had gone to bed an hour before we had. Chances are they would be asleep by now and completely oblivious if I were to sneak into their son's bedroom.

As quietly as humanly possible, I rolled out of bed and crept across the room. Upon reaching the door, I turned the knob so slowly it probably took a good twenty seconds to actually open it. Once the door was open, I peeked my head out to survey the equally as pitch black hallway. I'd hoped to see some movement or light coming from Luke's room, but it was just as still as his parents'. Undeterred, I walked down the hall, thankful that the flooring was carpet and not wood.

When I reached Luke's door, I contemplated whether I should knock quietly or simply walk in. I put my ear to it to listen, not hearing so much as a snore. With the pull growing stronger, I opened his door in a more expedient fashion than I'd opened my own, quickly walking in and then gently closing it behind me.

"Elle?" Luke called my name from the darkness.

Without acknowledging him, I walked across his bedroom and crawled into his bed next to him, quickly finding his lips with my own. Shocked, it took him a moment to regain his bearings, but when he did, his enthusiasm was evident. He'd felt the ache, too; he just possessed more self-control than I did.

Not wanting to extricate myself from him, I awkwardly maneuvered my body underneath the sheets until there was nothing separating our bodies but our clothing. Luke's breaths became heavier when our lips briefly separated long enough for him to pull me on top of him.

Nope, definitely not a eunuch.

My hands ran up Luke's body, taking his shirt with me as I inched them upward. Following my lead, he pulled his shirt over his head and threw it aside. With his chest now bare, I found myself running my fingers down the length of his torso. He sat up to face me as I remained straddling him, taking my my head in his hands as he kissed me. His hands then fell slowly away from my face, as he guided them down to my waist. I raised my arms, allowing him to pull my tank top off. His breathing verged on labored, we sat facing each other half-naked, our bare chests practically touching.

I noticed then that, although the room had no source of light coming from the inside, the outside was a different story. Through the window a beam of moonlight shone through, highlighting perfectly, of all areas, my breasts, which were moving in time with Luke's own chest. Not particularly large, yet not particularly small, either, I always thought they were the better of my limited assets, and I was certain their unplanned spotlight would work in my favor.

"Is there any part of you that isn't perfect?" he asked, kissing me before I could answer him. His fingers, at first, had begun to eagerly venture their way up the length of my body, but had ceased their journey just under my breasts. He was stopping short for some reason, not allowing himself to push the limits and go further. I silently cursed his strength and my apparent weakness.

I parted my lips from Luke's just enough to speak. "Touch me, Luke." I'd hoped the desperation I heard in my appeal to him had lessened some once my request met his ears.

Luke paused, contemplating my request, until whatever willpower he had finally ran out. With our lips still hovering millimeters apart, Luke's hand moved slowly upwards, hesitating once more when he was no more than a finger's width away from their intended destination, making me wonder whether he was pausing for dramatic effect or whether he was legitimately nervous. Unlike the last one, this pause was mercifully short-lived, and I shuddered when I felt him lightly brush over me, a chill running up my spine that only subsided when his hold became firmer and his lips moved to my neck.

I groaned as his thumb brushed over my nipple. As much as I wanted to prolong this moment, I couldn't. My body wanted him more and more with each passing second, and before I could second guess what I was doing, I lowered myself on the bed and pulled him down on top me, wrapping my legs as far as they would go around his body.

My lips found their way to Luke's neck, while his stubble rubbed the base of my neck raw and the heat of his breaths set my skin on fire. He planted a series of kisses along my collarbone, but I still sensed a bit of hesitancy from him emotionally, even though between my legs, I could feel that he was anything but. It made me think back to my conversation with Mena and the night at the bookstore. Perhaps he was afraid. He had every reason to be.

I unwrapped my legs from his body. If he wanted me to take charge of the situation, I would. Taking my feet, I inserted my toes underneath the elastic of his flannel pajama bottoms and began to pull them down.

"Elle," Luke said, lifting his lips from my skin.

I inched his pants down once more, finding myself abruptly stopped by Luke's hand, as he balanced his body over me on his remaining arm. "Elle, stop."

Stunned, all I could do was lay there as he pushed himself back up to a sitting position on the bed. In the moonlight, I could see him running both hands through his hair as he let out a sigh.

"I'm … I'm sorry," I apologized, wanting to curl up into a ball in some desolate corner on the other side of the planet.

"No," Luke said, his voice softening. "You didn't do anything to apologize for. It's me, not you."

I'd heard the whole 'It's me, not you' spiel before and suddenly felt my chest begin to tighten. The room spun; the urge to throw up suddenly overcame me. "Why, Luke? I thought things were going well—wonderful, even?" I asked as I picked myself up from a prone position on the mattress and sat across from him on the bed.

"They are," he replied, scooting in closer to me. In the darkness, I felt his hand touch my cheek, his thumb running along my cheekbone the way it always did. "These last six months have been some of the best weeks of my life, and my parents both seem have become quite taken with you. My mom even mouthed 'Good job' when she walked out of your bedroom earlier today."

"But you haven't even tried to touch me, outside of the realm of a PG-13 rating since we've been together. I'm beginning to think that maybe you aren't …" I paused, gutted by the thought that he may end up confirming the ending to that sentence.

"That maybe I'm not attracted to you?" he asked incredulously.

"That maybe I don't want to have sex with you? Is that what's bothering you?"

I nodded, unable to vocalize my concern.

"I will never understand why you don't see how absolutely stunning you are. Everyone else does. When we're out together, I see the way other guys look at you. It's gotten to the point where I think I may have to start carrying a bat with me to keep them at bay. And as far as the sex concern, I'm pretty certain you could feel how badly I wanted you, too. Trust me, I'm paying for my decision now and will be for at least the next several minutes." He adjusted himself on the bed as though speaking of the issue had elicited a whole new wave of discomfort throughout his body.

"Would you like me to grab a bag of peas from the freezer for you?" I asked, only half-joking.

"That's actually not a bad idea," he said, chuckling at the thought of laying a frozen sack of vegetables on his crotch.

"Then why, Luke? You want to. I want to. What are you waiting for?"

He exhaled, hesitant to answer my question. "Well, for starters, we're at my parents' house, so I already have that strange mixture of excitement and unbridled terror to contend with."

"Yes, but that's not it, is it?" I asked, definitively.

Luke sighed. "I should have told you sooner, but I guess a part of me thinks that what I'm going to tell you would somehow make me seem like less of a man."

It was my turn to comfort him. Scooting in closer to him, so close that our legs were rubbing against each other, I placed my fingers along his jawline, stroking the cleft in his chin with my thumb. "Luke, you saved my life. I think that pretty much guarantees you a free pass to spill the dirty details on whatever weird, kinky shit you've been hiding from me without fear of judgment on my part."

He laughed, still clearly anxious. Pausing, he took a breath before he spoke again. "I'm a virgin, Elle."

I sat there, waiting for him to laugh, to say that he was joking, only to reveal what his secret truly was, but nothing besides silence came from his end.

"Elle?"

"How?"

"I've never had sex," he said, amused. "You see, I've never put my penis …"

"I know what being a virgin means," I snapped. "I just don't understand how you've made it this long. Surely, you've had other girlfriends. What about that Marg—Margie—Margarita girl?"

"How do you know about Margaret?"

"Monroe mentioned her the night I met him."

"Ah, yes, leave it to Monroe's big mouth."

"Was I not supposed to know about her?"

"Oh, no. No, it's fine that you know. I just wanted the first mention of her to come from me and not from my best friend, is all."

"She was special to you, Margaret?"

"At the time, yes. I thought the heavens themselves revolved around her. And so did she. Now I realize just how one-sided our relationship was. We were seniors in high school, and she was my first real girlfriend, so I didn't know at the time that relationships were supposed to be reciprocal."

"If you adored her so much, then what held you back?"

"Well, that's the thing, I wasn't holding back. We came close."

"How close?" I asked, suddenly finding myself jealous of a girl I'd never met before.

Even in the dark, I swore I could see the red glow on Luke's face. "Her parents went to the movies one night and Maggie called me to come over. I hadn't intended on us going any further than usual, but before I knew it, one thing led to another and we were both naked on the living room sofa with me hovering over her. Had I had ten more seconds, my virginity would have been shot to hell."

"But?"

"But then her parents walked through the front door. They'd

decided to see a different movie that was a half an hour shorter than the original one they were going to see."

"No!"

"Yup, Maggie's ultra-conservative, devoutly religious parents walked into their *Better Homes and Garden's* home in their *Leave It to Beaver* life just in time to see my bare ass sticking up in the air getting ready to defile their little princess."

Despite my best efforts, I couldn't hold back the giggle that had made its way to my throat.

"That's right, laugh at my misfortune." Luke began to chuckle himself.

"I'm sorry," I said, holding back my amusement.

"No, you're not. Besides, it is rather comical, now that some time has passed and I think about it."

"So what happened between you and Maggie?"

"Well, her parents thought I was Satan in the form of a teenage boy and forbade their daughter from ever seeing me again. I vowed to overcome that minor setback and communicated with Maggie through any method I could. We ended up making it through our first year of college, with me here and her down in Florida, until we finally broke it off for good about a year and a half ago when she dumped me and broke my heart."

"Oh, Luke, that's horrible," I remarked through a yawn.

"Come on, let's get some sleep." He pulled me down to the bed next to him, and I lay with my chest pressed against his and my nose wedged in the crook of his neck. My nostrils flared as they picked up the lingering scent of his cologne.

"Uh, Elle," he said, clearly in discomfort, "would you mind putting your shirt back on?"

"About ready to give up your vow of chastity, are you?"

"Very funny, Sloan."

I leaned over the bed and picked up my tank top from the floor, shrugged it over my shoulders, and laid back down with him.

"We're going to do it, Elle, I promise you. I've just waited this long, and I'd like it to be a tad more intimate and not twenty feet from my parents' bedroom when it happens."

"It's okay. We'll take our time. However long you need, just as long as it's before I turn thirty."

"How about twenty-nine and three-quarters?"

"Perfect." I smiled, winding my arm through his, while resting my hand on his shoulder.

"What about you?" he asked.

"What about me?"

"Your past relationships. Now that you know about mine, it's only fair. Is there someone I should know about?"

After he'd confessed his prior love life to me, I couldn't not talk to him about the one relationship I'd had, even though I'd sworn that no one but Mena would ever know the true hell I'd been through with Kyle and the victim he'd made of me. But there was something about Luke that was so calming that it made me believe I could talk to him about anything, and that he would find a way to somehow make it okay.

"There was one."

"That's a start," he joked.

"His name was Kyle, and he was the worst thing that ever happened to me." Luke's body stiffened underneath me. I waited for him to say something. When he didn't, I continued. "At first, things were great. He was my escape from my mother's blackouts, from having to be the adult because she had no idea how to be one herself. Kyle accomplished the one thing I'd been trying to do ever since I could remember: He made me forget about my life, if only for a moment. Because of that, I thought I was in love with him, but in hindsight, I think it was just a matter of being in love with the thought that someone could actually love me. And he was good at it, making me believe he loved me, when in reality, he never did."

"Why is it that you think he never loved you?" Luke spoke, alleviating my secret concern that he had fallen asleep as I was speaking.

"A narcissist is only capable of loving the person they see in the mirror and a psychopath isn't capable of loving anyone at all. Kyle was a combination of the two, which is quite a volatile combination. A man who loved himself, yet also hated himself at the same time. When I tried to leave him, the narcissist in him snapped, and began taking direction from his inner psychopath." I closed my eyes as the images from the day I broke up with Kyle, ones that I'd kept locked away in a vault in the deepest crevice of my mind, flashed before my eyes.

"We were at his house," I began again, clearly seeing Kyle standing in front of me. On that particular day, he'd worn his favorite red hoodie and distressed blue jeans with a mustard stain on the left thigh. "I explained to him that I'd been accepted into Cogsworth and that I would be moving away to live on campus. Kyle lost it, accusing me of abandoning him and questioning how I'd managed to be accepted at Cogsworth when my writing was crap in his words."

"What an asshole," Luke interjected.

"It gets worse. After he'd offended me, I got to thinking about all the passive aggressive comments I'd been subjected to at the hands of Kyle, and the inability to disagree with him without it causing him to question my intelligence. So I told him it was over between us, thinking that I would just walk out the door and never see him again. But as I turned to leave, he ran to the door, blocking it with his body. He had no intention of letting me leave."

Luke exhaled, causing me to say his name. "I'm listening," he said with an intensity in his voice that told me he was more distressed inwardly than he was allowing himself to express outwardly.

"Each time I tried to move past him, he would shove me back, eventually backing me into a corner. Kyle had a couple inches of height on me and probably about fifty pounds. There was no fighting back, and he knew it. He kept telling me that if I was going to leave him, he was going to ruin me. At first I didn't know what he meant by that, until he started ripping my clothes off me. Until he raped me and then beat me to drive his point home."

124

Luke had grown silent again, no doubt processing everything. I worried then that maybe Kyle had ruined me. What if Luke wouldn't want me now that he knew? I hadn't stopped to think just how much baggage I was carrying around before and waited for Luke to say something—anything. When the silence became too much for me to withstand, I broke it. "Kyle wanted to humiliate me in every possible way he could. He wanted to break me. And he did. For a while."

"He's a coward," Luke spoke, much to my relief, "and it's a damn good thing he isn't anywhere near here. Because if he were, I'd be going to jail tonight."

"He's not worth it."

"He's not worth the excrement he produces, but that doesn't mean it wouldn't make me feel better to beat the ever loving hell out of him. Really show him what a fair fight looks like."

"Trust me, it wouldn't be a fair fight. You're quite a bit larger than Kyle."

Luke wrapped an arm around me, pulling me in closer to him with his chest against my back. This celibacy thing wasn't going to be easy.

"Would you like me to go back to my room?" I asked, secretly worried that his answer would be in the affirmative.

"What?" he asked, almost pained. "No, of course not. Why?"

"Your parents. They clearly are not okay with us living in sin."

"Yes, but they forget that I'm an adult, and as such, we're going to handle this in an adult manner. I'm going to set my alarm to go off at five o' clock and kick you out of my room before they wake up."

"I must say your brilliance astounds me, Hutchins." I rubbed my fingers down the length of the hand he held against me before settling on winding my fingers through his.

"After everything you've been through, it's a miracle that you would even want another man to touch you again."

"That's just it, I don't want just any other man to touch me. I want you to touch me. Only you."

Luke's nose nuzzled the back of my neck while goosebumps

erupted down my arm, making me begin to question whether I should return to my room now before I was shot down by him again.

"I love you, Elle," he whispered next to my ear.

Despite having heard them earlier, I had to replay his words in my head over and over again for what felt like a thousand times before I was fully able to process them. For the first time in my life, I didn't have to question whether those three words were meant by the person who spoke them to me. I knew he meant them unequivocally.

"I love you, too," I whispered back, meaning those words even more now than I did when I first spoke them.

At first, I didn't think he'd heard me, but any doubt about that was erased when his arms held me against his body so tightly that our bodies felt more like an extension of one another than two separate beings. And it was like that, holding one another, that we fell asleep in pure, unbridled peace and contentment.

CHAPTER EIGHT

2018

I left the Hutchins' house before Candy the next morning, eager to see how Luke was doing after the minor setback he'd had the day before. Even though Dr. Reid had been largely optimistic that Luke would be back on the right track today, nothing could have prepared me for the bright-eyed, smiling vision I saw sitting upright in his hospital bed. His smile, the one I couldn't forget no matter how hard I'd forced myself to try over the years, greeted me when I entered the room. As did Hannah, who sat perched at the foot of the bed, an equally as big smile plastered on her face. I wondered then how close they had been and whether I was interrupting something by being there.

You're jealous. Why are you jealous? You're married, and it's not to Luke.

"Hey, beautiful," Luke said, snapping me out of my thoughts.

Hannah stood up from the bed, seemingly unaffected by Luke's greeting. "I'll be in to check on you later. If something comes up before then, you know the drill."

"Aye, aye, Ms. Hannah," Luke replied, never taking his eyes off me.

Hannah playfully rolled her eyes as she walked past me, leaving me alone with Luke. "You're looking leaps and bounds better today," I observed, taking a seat on the bed next to him. Without so much as a thought otherwise, I put my hand up to Luke's head and rendered my uneducated diagnosis. "Nope, no fever, either, and I see they removed the IV."

Luke grabbed my hand as I removed it from his forehead and held it in his lap. "Your motherly instincts are kicking in, I see."

"Which is amazing, all things considered."

"You're going to make a great mother one day, Elle."

I almost was. Smiling, I squeezed Luke's hand and stood up. "So, what do you want to do today, Hutchins? A little badminton or a lovely jog through the park, perhaps?"

"You're horrible, Sloan," he said with a laugh, staring forlornly down at his immobile legs.

"Surely, you can get out bed for a while and sit in a wheelchair. I could push you around."

"True. You can push me around anytime." He smiled wickedly. The shades of the Luke I remembered from my past had emerged once more. "I'm actually feeling somewhat healthy today for the first time since coming out of my coma, like maybe my body is starting to get its act together, or you're working your voodoo on me." He picked up his call button and squeezed the button just underneath the controls for the television. I wondered how tempted he'd been to turn on the TV, or whether Candy had found a way to disengage it entirely.

"Did you miss me already?" Hannah popped her head around the corner.

"Absence makes the heart grow fonder," Luke joked. "Is there even a snowball's chance in hell that Dr. Reid will let me get out of this room for a bit, if Ms. Sloan here promises to have me back by curfew?"

Hannah pursed her lips, her gaze bouncing from Luke to me and back again, finally resigning herself to a shrug. "I guess it doesn't hurt to ask, does it? I'll be right back with either a wheelchair and some able bodies, or a stern reprimand from Dr. Reid."

"I'm sure you must be bored out of your mind here," Luke said when Hannah had left the room.

"What? No!" I plopped back down next to him, grabbing his hand. "I just figured you would want to get out of this room for a little bit, but if you'd rather not, that's fine, too."

"It's a great idea. But I know that being in this place can't be the most exciting part of your day."

"Are you kidding me? There's no where else I'd rather be right now," I said, surprised by just how much I meant it.

"Now I know you're lying. Actually, I'm glad to be getting out of here. All I can think about when I'm alone is how far behind I'm going to be in my classes and how that's going to set me back from graduating on time."

"That should be the least of your concerns. You need to focus on your recovery, right now."

Luke's fingers traced around the outside of my hand, finding their way up my arm before stopping halfway up my forearm.

"My god, what happened to your arm?" Luke asked, concerned.

"Huh?"

I looked down the length of my arm to where his fingers had paused, noticing the long-since-healed, but still very much noticeable scar from a significant burn inflicted on me when I had attempted to hastily remove a casserole from the oven. The jagged white discoloration of the residual scar cut through my otherwise flawless complexion like a canyon that most certainly hadn't been there when I was with Luke.

"A burn," I said as confidently as I could. "Just a minor burn from a month ago, nothing to worry about."

"That wasn't just a minor burn," Luke observed. "It was probably at least a second degree burn to have left that kind of a scar. And a month ago, you said? It's remarkably well-healed for only having happened a month ago."

Of course, I would have had to have dated someone in the medical field.

I tried to form something intelligible in my head, a dead-on rebuttal in response to his observation, but before I was forced to pull a rabbit out of my hat like the magician I wasn't, the sound of footsteps entering the room commanded both of our attention.

"Good morning, Luke," Dr. Reid greeted him. "Ms.Sloan," he addressed me, nodding before returning his attention back to Luke. "I understand you'd like to see the world outside your room today."

"Very much so, Doctor," Luke answered.

"I think we can arrange that. How are you feeling? Any dizziness? Nausea?"

"None to speak of," Luke responded. "I'm actually starting to feel like myself again."

Dr. Reid smiled. "That's what we've all been waiting to hear."

Two figures appeared in the doorway, bigger men in stature than I'd seen in Luke's room before. Orderlies; big enough to lift a large, incapacitated man from a hospital bed. Beckoned to enter by a nod from Dr. Reid, they walked into the room, standing aside to allow Hannah and the wheelchair she was pushing to walk past them and park right next to Luke's bed. The orderlies then positioned themselves one at each end of Luke and lifted him so gingerly and in such an expert fashion, it was pure poetry in motion to watch them set him down in the chair.

"Elle," Hannah said softly, motioning for me to step out into the hallway with her. I followed her, looking back as Luke was being made comfortable in the wheelchair and prepped for our small excursion. "Take him to the third floor," Hannah said once we were out in the hall. "There's a small waiting area that's pretty dead this time of day. I had all of the magazines removed and the television turned off. There's some board games and plenty of windows."

"Thank you, Hannah. I really appreciate it, and I know he does, too."

"He'll have his call button on him, if you run into trouble." She smiled, but in her eyes, I could tell there was more she wanted to say.

"He deserves to have a good day. It's been far too long since he's had one."

That was part of it. There was far more than just that, I suspected. Again, it made me ponder just how close the two of them had been and just how much she knew about Luke.

* * * * *

"Checkmate." Luke's blue eyes peered up triumphantly from the board, where they had been fixated. He could have toned down his concentration level to next to nothing, and he still would have wiped the floor with me. "Let's see, that's five wins for me and ..."

"Zip for me," I said, rolling my eyes, a smile working its way across my lips.

"I can see all my weeks of training have greatly benefited you, either that or you're completely throwing the games." He seemed disappointed by the mere thought of the latter.

"Don't worry. I'm putting forth a legitimate effort here. It's sad, but true."

The irony wasn't lost on me that Luke's memory, dredging up events from, I guessed, 2007, was better than my own during that same time period. For me, over nine years of memories had taken over, clouding over past events and completely removing others to make room for only the most pivotal moments. Chess, apparently, hadn't been one of those moments. I dug down deep to retrieve the chess lessons Luke had given to me in his apartment, during the times when we were either too involved with studying or too poor to go out. They came surprisingly easy once they were unearthed. The frustration that had come with learning the game, the agony of defeat after defeat at the hands of Luke, and the sudden shock and accompanying impromptu dance party that occurred during the first—and only—time I'd managed to beat him.

"It's been a long month," I added to save face. "My brain has decided to check out for a while."

131

"This has been a lot to take in," Luke acknowledged, sadness returning to his eyes. "But if my recovery stays on the right track, I could be discharged out of here next week, and we can begin to put this behind us."

I tried to smile through the pain I felt creeping up on me. What would become of Luke next week? What kind of life awaited him back home?

"Elle? What's wrong?" Always able to see right through me, Luke's intuition hadn't been damaged in the accident.

I shook my head, afraid to open my mouth for fear of unleashing the tears I could feel percolating in the corners of my eyes.

"Okay," he said, unconvinced. "Well, don't worry. As soon as I get home, we're going to jump right back into lessons."

"That sounds fantastic."

"Now I know you're lying." Luke laughed. "Elle, I know you couldn't care less about chess and have only been humoring me. Right now, you're thinking to yourself 'Gee, I wonder where I can find a flight of stairs to push this bastard down to keep him here a little longer. Then he won't make me so much as touch one of those pieces I couldn't identify if my life depended on it.'"

I snapped my fingers. "Damn. Foiled again. Now I'm going to have to resort to Plan B." Giggling, I gathered the pieces of the chess set together and arranged them back inside of their box.

"You've come up with a Plan B? Impressive, Sloan. By chance, does this plan also include inflicting bodily injury upon me?"

"You'll find out soon enough." Pinching my thumb and index finger together, I mimicked the twirling of an invisible mustache, just like all the criminal masterminds did in every cartoon I used to watch as a child.

"Is it wrong that I found that somewhat hot just now?"

"What part? The implied facial hair or the emergence of my closet sociopath?"

"Strangely, both."

"Then I guess I'll just forgo all grooming and hygiene when I remove my moral compass from my pocket and promptly stomp it into the ground. In fact, why don't I just change my name to Monroe while I'm at it?

"On second thought, I retract my last statement."

I chuckled at the sight of Luke's pursed lips and his face contorted in disgust.

"You've always had the cutest laugh. Not too domineering, yet powerful enough to command attention. I swear I heard it in my dreams while I was unconscious. It made me fight that much harder whenever I felt myself slipping away—whenever my body wanted to succumb to the injuries."

"I honestly can't remember how long it's been since I genuinely laughed this much." My eyes stung in my attempts to stave off the tears that threatened to appear.

"It's probably been at least a good month," Luke said, particularly empathetic. "A month is a long time to go without laughter."

"Yeah, it is," I agreed, knowing damn well that it had really been much, much longer than that—so long, in fact, that I wouldn't have been able to pinpoint a ballpark date, even if someone had been holding a gun to my head.

Footsteps signaled the approach of others into the empty waiting area in which Hannah had directed us to stay. Given the location of the space and it being relatively tucked away as compared to the other community waiting areas, I was half-expecting to recognize those footsteps as belonging either to someone working at the hospital or someone Hannah had sent to visit Luke. Instead, a man and woman around our age came into view. They wore street clothes, but weren't anyone I recognized as being related to Luke or anyone I could recall him as ever hanging out with while we were together, a fact that was confirmed when they ended up taking a seat at the opposite end of the room. Yet, as the man sat down, his gaze traveled over to us, landing on Luke and remaining fixated on him for much longer than I thought normal. Still stealing casual glances over at Luke, the man turned to the woman with him and whispered something into her ear.

I turned my attention back to Luke, noticing that he, too, was stealing sideways glances at the man at the opposite end of the room. To my chagrin, in Luke's eyes, I found recognition. He knew the short, balding man, but couldn't place him. Most likely, the man in question knew exactly who Luke was, and could place him without any clues needed.

"We should probably start heading back to the room," I announced. "I'm pretty certain Dr. Reid didn't mean for you to be down here all day. If we're not back soon, he may sic Hannah on us."

"I don't know what it is," Luke stated, "but something tells me there's some bite underneath that soft exterior of hers. It's like she's waiting for the perfect moment to bare her teeth."

You don't know the half of it.

"Well, it was fun while it lasted," he said with a sigh. "I don't know how you do it, Sloan, but it feels like ever since you arrived, every day has become that much more bearable for me. There's actually a light at the end of this dark, foreboding tunnel, after all."

Relieved, I released the brakes on his wheelchair. Luke's words resonated in me in ways I wouldn't have been able to have fathomed two days ago, and I realized then that it wasn't just today I'd been looking forward to since waking up, but everyday I would get to spend in Roanoke. It was a thought that, in it's truth, made me feel guilty about what it's implications meant for Eric; my husband and a completely innocent party to everything that was transpiring here right now.

"What do you say, Elle?" Luke asked, inquisitively.

"About what?" I felt myself snapping back down to reality, as I grabbed the handles of his wheelchair and began pushing him across the room.

"Do you want to test our luck and make an escape attempt tomorrow? Maybe we'll even get lucky and be able to take a couple steps outside."

"Let's not get too crazy now. Unless you want to unleash the full fury that is Hannah and actually feel the teeth she keeps well-hidden sink into your flesh."

Out of the corner of my eye, I noticed the man who'd seemed to have noticed Luke stand up. My legs, sensing the potential for a rather uncomfortable encounter, sped up to put more distance between us and him. That, however, was all for naught.

"Luke? Luke Hutchins?" The balding man stood no more than ten feet from us, his eyes inspecting Luke, knowing without a doubt that he had made a positive identification.

"Yes, I'm Luke Hutchins. And you are?"

"Oh man, I knew it was you," the man said, suddenly excited. "It's me, Joe Markowitz." He unnecessarily pointed to himself to emphasize his own introduction. "Wow, I haven't see you in ages. What happened, man?"

I suddenly had a mental image of Robot B9 from *Lost in Space*, flailing his mechanical arms in the air, shouting, 'Danger, Will Robinson.' Fear sent shockwaves through my body, making my legs respond the only way they knew how: By walking away.

"Car accident," I answered Mr. Markowitz, as I attempted to steer the wheelchair in the opposite direction.

"Elle," Luke said, indignantly. "Wait. Stop walking away from him."

Reluctantly, I paused, all while my mind mentally prepared itself for whatever devastatingly confusing information Joe was about to spew to Luke.

"Joe Markowitz," Luke repeated his name almost accusingly, like he was unsure as to whether the information the man had given to us was accurate. "Wow, yeah, how long has it been now? Since our graduation, right?"

Oh, shit.

Luke graduated from high school in 2005. His last memory was from 2008. Joe, having chronologically aged by almost thirteen years, looked more like he'd aged by twenty and most definitely couldn't be confused with someone who had been a high school student three years ago.

Joe seemed as confused as Luke—not a good sign. "No, man, we saw each other at the reunion, remember?"

There wasn't time to be courteous. Looking down the hall, I feigned seeing a vision I knew wasn't there and called out to it as I proceeded to push Luke down it again. "We'll be right there, Hannah."

"Hannah?" Luke asked, sounding agitated and confused out of his mind. It was painful to hear him, knowing all too well the mess the tangled wires in his brain were in at the moment.

"It was good seeing you again, Luke," Joe called out behind us. "I wish you a speedy recovery."

Luke raised his hand, acknowledging him one last time before I pushed the wheelchair into an awaiting elevator car, letting out a sigh of relief when the door slid closed with a bang.

"That was a tad rude," Luke stated, recovering his bearings.

"I'm sorry, it's just I spotted Hannah in the hall, waving her arms and motioning for us to get back to the room." How I was going to keep this charade up when we returned to the room, I didn't know. "At least, I thought it was Hannah. It looked just like her. And I don't want to take my chances and make it so you won't be allowed to leave your room again."

"Still ..." Luke replied, his voice trailing off. "I honestly have no idea what he's talking about. Our ten year high school reunion isn't going to happen for like seven more years. And the way he looked. He's had it rough in the three years since we graduated. I hate to see what he's going to look like by the time we actually have the reunion. It's like ..."

"Like what?" I asked, his pause causing me more anxiety than I cared to admit.

"Like he's older than he should be. He's the Joe Markowitz from the future, but that's impossible." He paused, contemplating what he had just said. "It is impossible, isn't it, Elle? They didn't invent time travel while I was in a coma, did they?"

Pretty darn close.

"Of course not," I assured him. "He's probably just had a rough go of it. He's here, so who knows, maybe he sustained a head injury, striking his noggin hard enough that it jumbled some of the circuits in his brain."

"Possibly," Luke said, unconvinced.

He remained quiet for the rest of the short elevator ride, with his silence spilling over into the hallway as we made our way back down to his room. I couldn't blame him for his being quiet, for his brain was no doubt still processing everything that had transpired. And as much as I wanted to hear the carefree Luke speak again, I didn't feel it was my place to pull him away from whatever thoughts were going on inside of his head.

"Hey, man," Monroe greeted Luke when we entered his room. In true Monroe fashion, he sat in a chair next to Luke's hospital bed with his feet propped up on the mattress. In one hand was a small plastic container of Jell-O. In the other, a spoon. The rest of Luke's lunch lay untouched on a tray situated atop an overbed table. An unappetizing ham sandwich of sorts accompanied by an apple in dire need of medical attention itself awaited Luke's arrival. "It's cherry." Monroe held up the container in the event Luke needed confirmation. "You hate cherry, so I figured I'd save you the trouble."

"You're a real hero," Luke said. Even though it was an impossibility, I swore I could hear his eyes rolling. "I'll have my parents send you the bill. Even after insurance is applied, that's still going to be the most expensive cup of Jell-O you've ever eaten."

"It's a medical necessity. Worth every penny." Monroe licked the back of the spoon and threw the empty cup onto the overbed table, where it bounced twice before coming to rest next to the sandwich. "Besides, I'll take it out of your rent this month."

"Oh, you're back," Hannah announced, as she walked into the room.

"Why wouldn't we be?" Luke asked, slightly miffed. "Elle said she saw the frenzied hand gestures you made downstairs, beckoning us to return."

I whipped my head up to face a very confused looking Hannah, mouthing, 'Please just go with it,' while projecting what I was certain was a frantic plea in my eyes.

"Oh, yeah, silly me," she said with a laugh. "I swear some days I can be such an airhead. Too many patients, not enough brain capacity for memory retention, I suppose." She shot me a look as if demanding an explanation from me, but knowing that it wouldn't come right away. "Let me go get the orderlies to help you back into bed." With that, she bounded out the door.

"Hey," Luke said, addressing Monroe, "you remember Joe Markowitz, don't you?"

"Joe Markowitz." Monroe played with the name, drawing it out as if it would jog his memory.

"Geez, man, it's only been three years."

"Oh!" Monroe's eyes widened. I could almost visualize a light bulb lighting up over his head. "Joey. Yeah, I remember him."

"I ran into him downstairs. Man, he's looking rough, like he's been on every drug known to man and run over a few times. The last three years have beaten the hell out of him."

I glanced up at Monroe, briefly making eye contact with him. "Joey was always a bit of a wild man. It may all be catching up with him. Not everyone shares the stud gene that you and I have."

Hannah walked back into the room, her eyebrow raised as she heard the tail end of Monroe's reply. Following behind her were two larger men, one of the same orderlies who had assisted her earlier and a new one who reminded me of a tank. This orderly was thick and could probably run over just about anyone in his path without receiving so much as a scratch in the process. Yet as massive as he was, he was exceptionally gentle with Luke. Both he and his counterpart lifted him as gently as one would lift a cracked egg, careful not to incur anymore damage out of fear that it would break apart in their hands.

"Careful not to disturb his stud genes," Hannah said, amused. "I hear those are the one thing modern medicine can't put back together."

Monroe chuckled, Luke's face reddened. Absolutely nothing could faze Peter Monroe. I always believed that he was born without the capacity for embarrassment. Luke had been the same way, to a lesser extent, and if not for the feelings of emasculation that resulted from being unable to take care of himself, he probably still was. There was just only so much humiliation a person could handle before they fell apart.

"Could I get you anything?" Hannah asked. "Some more Jell-O, perhaps?" She eyed Monroe menacingly.

"Actually, if you have any orange flavored cups, that would be great," Luke replied, glaring at the sandwich and apple with disdain.

"And some more cherry, too, please," Monroe chimed in. "For later, of course."

Hannah rolled her eyes. "Don't press your luck there, stud." She placed a blanket over Luke's legs and helped him with positioning the pillows behind his back to make him more comfortable. "I'll see what I can find and be right back."

"Thanks, Hannah," Luke called after her.

"So," Monroe began, "you look like you had a pretty busy day today."

"Elle busted me out of here for a while." Currently, in a reclining position, it was evident that Luke was worn out from the sheer stimuli he'd encountered today. From what I had been able to gather from listening to Dr. Reid and Candy's hushed conversations, this was the expected result of the brain injury Luke had received in the car accident.

"And Dr. Reid authorized this?" Monroe asked, skeptically. Although he was addressing Luke, he was watching me with eyes that seemed to shoot daggers directly into me. He despised me; I could feel it even more evidently than before.

"Yeah," Luke replied, yawning.

"And he thought that was a good idea?"

"What do you think I should have done? Stayed in this bed for however god awful long it takes for my legs to heal and I become mobile again?"

"Of course not. It's just that, with your head injury, I know Dr. Reid mentioned to your mom that you could become easily over-whelmed out in public and that you should try to avoid that for now."

"I'm not overwhelmed, just a little tired."

"He also said it would make you fatigued."

"I'll take being dead tired from a day of freedom over wide awake and feeling like I'm in a prison cell any day of the week."

Monroe sighed, obviously wanting to say more in support of his side of the argument. Somewhere along the way, he resigned himself to the fact that he was going to have to pick his battles with Luke while Luke was in the state he was in. The old Monroe wouldn't have given up so easily. The old Monroe would have continued the fight until Luke conceded. It was a sign of maturity on his part, and probably the only thing about him that had changed from the person I used to know.

"Knock, knock," Candy called, entering the room, carrying a cup of orange Jell-O in one hand and a cup of cherry in the other.

"Thanks, Mom," Monroe said, catching the cup Candy tossed to him.

"Anything for my favorite son."

"Did you seriously just make that joke in front of your invalid son?" Luke asked. His voice came out as more of a croak, reminding me of frog on its death bed.

"Who's joking?" Candy asked. She was concerned. I could see it in her eyes, even though she wouldn't allow her mouth to betray it. She was trying her best to hold it together and be the glue the family needed her to be. "Elle, Monroe, would you mind excusing us for a moment?"

"Sure." I gave Luke's hand a squeeze as I walked past. Without saying a word, Monroe stood up and pocketed his cup of Jell-O inside of his jacket, which he left strewn across the chair next to Luke's bed. He knew what I had already sensed; that Candy was teetering on the edge of a cliff, only hanging on by the tips of her fingers.

"I think it's best if you plan on staying in bed for the remainder of your time here," she blurted out as soon as Monroe and I exited the room. I willed my feet to keep moving, despite wanting to hear what Luke's retort would be, and my desire to do something—anything—to fix things for Candy right now.

"That was a bad idea, you know," Monroe sneered, purposely turning to head in the opposite direction from me.

"I thought it would help him. Isn't that why I'm here, to help?"

Monroe paused with his back still turned to me. "If you want to help, you can do so by keeping your thoughts to yourself."

He recovered himself and commenced his walk down the hall, as I stood watching him, dumbfounded.

One of the less than desirable traits I'd inherited from my mother was the way she mismanaged her anger. Normally controlled and even, she had a way of storing her irritants away inside of a jar, just waiting for the day when that final straw came down like a hammer and all hell broke loose, culminating in one big ball of fury, comprised of the mild frustration and anger she should have expressed and gotten out of her system when each event occurred. When I was younger, I always felt like I had to walk on egg shells around her out of fear that her jar was one event away from overflowing.

With each step Monroe took away from me, I could hear my own glass jar cracking like thin ice under foot.

"Peter," I said, using his true first name to emphasize the anger I'd been keeping bottled up.

Monroe abruptly stopped in his tracks. Good, I'd gotten to him.

"What is it, Elle?" he asked, frustrated.

"Do you want to tell me exactly what it is that I've done to deserve the dirty looks you've been giving me since I arrived, or why you've been so short around me? Even though we haven't spoken to each other in years, we were friends once."

Monroe turned to face me, his expression unreadable. It didn't seem possible, but I could have sworn that he had grown taller since I'd last seen him, either that or I was shrinking under the judgment contained within his eyes, like a child anticipating a scolding.

"You're right. We were friends ... once. But it's hard to call someone that after you've found yourself caught up in the aftermath of the chaos they caused; after you've literally had to pick your friend up from the floor, only to find that he's only a hollow shell of the man you once knew. You killed him, Elle. A part of Luke died the day you left him without so much as an explanation."

"Monroe, I—"

"No," he interrupted, holding his hand out in front of him, "I neither need nor want to hear what you have to say. It's been ten years. The wounds have healed, the scars have faded as much as they can. Everyone has moved on. I've not been overly rude to you, only distant, like the strangers we are now, and that's the way it's going to be until you disappear from Luke's life again."

He turned to walk away, further fanning the flame that had ignited within me.

"I broke up with Luke. Granted, I could have handled it better, but there's no perfect way to break someone's heart, is there?" Monroe's shoulders slumped, and I thought I heard him sigh as he continued his quest to put distance between him and myself. "Besides, Candy and Tom have forgiven me and trust that I want to do right by Luke, why can't you?"

I expected him to keep on walking, to ignore me the same way he'd been doing, but to my consternation, he stopped and shook his head, chuckling.

"You think it was Candy's idea to call you, don't you?"

"Of course it was. Who else would have had the idea, you?"

"Yeah, actually, it was." With the way he said it, so firm and final, I knew he was telling the truth. "Candy is tolerating you for Luke's sake. We all are."

Stunned, all I could do was stand with my mouth agape, feeling like I'd taken a punch directly to the gut. "Why, then? If I'm such a horrible person and a burden to you all, wouldn't it have been easier to just tell Luke the truth?"

I couldn't be certain, but for a brief second, I swore I could feel a softening in Monroe's demeanor, like he had relaxed and could finally breathe again after at last being able to get out everything he'd kept bottled up over the years. Any hope I may have had that this kinder, gentler Monroe was here to stay, however, was fleeting.

"You know," he began after gathering his thoughts again, "the funny thing about trauma is that even as it's in the midst of wreaking utter devastation upon its victim, it has an odd way of spurring the body into action to counteract it. You may even say that trauma inadvertently brings its victim a sense of comfort. It's an exquisite contradiction. I mean, on the one hand, it's trauma, meaning that in order to exist, by definition, something awful must have happened. But on the other hand, our minds have such a beautiful way of responding to it that it almost makes it seem tolerable. Luke is the perfect example of that. He has no recollection of the car accident or of any of the more painful moments of his life preceding the accident. His mind has done everything in its power to shield him from pain by wiping his memory of everything that could possibly cause him to experience it. Which brings me to you."

"What about me?"

"To Luke's traumatized brain, you symbolize a lot of things; happiness, joy, comfort perhaps, but not pain. His brain doesn't associate you with anything negative. That's why you're here, Elle, and that's why no one wanted to tell Luke the truth. Now if you'll excuse me, I'm going to continue my hike to the pisser."

CHAPTER NINE

2007

"There she is," Mena proclaimed, making her way through the crowd at Magillicutty's with a drink in each hand, both of which she handed to Luke for safekeeping as she wrapped her arms around my shoulders. "Happy, happy birthday to you. Now let's get you sloppy drunk." She loosened her grip from around me and reached over to pluck one of the drinks out of Luke's hand. She then grabbed my hand with her free hand and wrapped my fingers around the glass that contained a mixture so strikingly blue, it reminded me of a picture I once saw of the Caribbean shoreline. Some of the mixture had spilled over the side of the glass and was making a slow descent down its stem. Not quite the drink connoisseur that Mena had become in the short time since her twenty-first birthday, the orange, pineapple, and cherry bits impaled by the skewer situated inside of the glass told me that it was most likely some sort of rum concoction. She was starting me out slow.

"I think you're sloppy enough for the both of us," I said, playfully rolling my eyes.

"Nope, not yet, this is my first one." She held up her own glass and showed off some sort of sickly-looking pink liquid, like its presence would be all the definitive proof I would need to verify her story as being true. For confirmation, I stole a glance up at Monroe, who nodded his head in corroboration. Both Monroe and Luke wore bright orange bands around their wrists that practically screamed "I'm underage." Luke would turn twenty-one in two months, while Monroe, the youngest of us all, had to wait a full half year before he could drink with the rest of us. It was part of the reason why I had resisted going out tonight, but Luke insisted that I celebrate my milestone birthday in the fashion the occasion was intended.

"There's a free table on the other side of the bar," Luke said, taking me by the hand. He guided us to the table, his large frame parting the crowd like an errant bull. Once seated, I took a sip of the drink Mena procured for me. The beverage, part slush, part liquid went down easily in an explosion of flavors so intense they drowned out the actual liquor. Before I knew it, I'd drained half the liquid from the glass, which would have normally given me pause, if not for the fact that Mena had already finished her drink and was in the midst of flagging down a waitress to order another round for the both of us.

"I'll take a cranberry vodka tonic and a sex on the beach for my friend here, since that's the only sex she's getting tonight."

Luke's eyes widened, Monroe suppressed a snicker and I, cheeks burning, found myself caught between wanting to run, laughing at my own expense, and all-out punching Mena in the arm. Clearly, there was more alcohol in the drink I had just finished than I had originally thought.

I reached into my purse and fished out money to hand to Mena, but was stopped short by Luke who dug into his own wallet and handed Mena a bill. "You're not paying for your own drinks on your birthday," he said, partially admonishing me.

"A twenty," Mena said, inspecting the bill. "This, coupled with the two drinks I bought, should be more than sufficient to get her nice and drunk."

As though on cue, the waitress returned with our drinks, setting an over-sized glass in front of me, the contents of which reminded me of a sunrise with its red, orange, and yellow hues. Gazing at it, I wondered whether this was how my mother's downslide had begun, sitting at the bar celebrating her birthday with a group of friends as drink after drink was placed in front of her for her consumption. Was it the first one that did her in, or did it take a few? How many had she consumed when she finally lost her ambition? Was it at the bottom of a Manhattan that she said screw it all?

"Elle?" Luke spoke my name, snapping me out of the trance I'd put myself under. "Are you all right?"

"I'm fine." I squeezed his hand. "Just thinking, is all."

"About what?"

"Nothing. Really, it's nothing important."

"I'm thinking she needs to get going on that drink, unless she wants me to leave her in the dust," Mena remarked. She'd already drained roughly three-quarters of her glass. Monroe's eyes widened, and I wasn't certain whether the expression that followed his obvious astonishment was one of disgust or admiration.

My mother, I knew, wouldn't have sat contemplating whether something she was about to do was right or wrong. She would have just done it. That in and of itself was enough for me to shove my intrusive thoughts back into the dark crevice from which they'd emerged. I was nothing like her, and I would never be like her.

With my renewed sense of self, I lifted my drink to Mena, who followed my lead by lifting hers, too, and the two of us clinked our glasses together as we celebrated my birthday the way it was meant to be.

* * * * **

Jackhammers. There were jackhammers breaking apart my skull. How many of them there were, I did not know, but it felt like millions. And I was certain that some of them had managed to carve their way to my brain. Even my eyes hurt when I opened them, like they were being stabbed by an army of tiny, dagger-wielding trolls. I didn't know where I was, and to my surprise, when the room came into focus, I found myself in my dorm room—without any recollection of how I'd gotten there. It was dark in the room, but not for lack of trying by the sun, the rays of which were desperately attempting to penetrate the blinds that had been pulled down over the window. Someone had drawn them to prevent them from entering the room and infiltrating my retinas. Someone knew that I would be in a sorry state when I regained consciousness.

I forced my eyes to move inside their sockets, feeling the pull of every muscle until I stopped them, at last allowing my pupils to focus on Mena's bed across the room. Empty. Meaning either it was much later than I suspected or she had never been in it at all. From the look of it, I would bet money on the latter. But if Mena hadn't brought me here …

Movement, slight but present, drew my attention to my desk in the corner of the room, where Luke sat thumbing through a notebook, oblivious to my return to the land of the living. I watched him, wondering whether he'd gotten any sleep at all last night and how we'd gotten here. Mena must have slept over at Luke's apartment, which made me wonder how she and Monroe could have fared the night together without killing each other. If one of them had been left standing, my money was on Mena.

Luke hadn't looked up from the desk yet. Instead, he sat intently turning the pages of the notebook after studying them. He seemed preoccupied, and I wondered what it was he was reading that had captured his unwavering attention.

"Hey," I managed to squeak out of my dryer-than-the-Sahara mouth.

"Good," Luke looked down at his watch, "early afternoon to you."

"How did we get here? How long have you been here?"

Luke stood up from the desk chair and walked over to my bed, where he carefully sat down next to me. He stroked my hair, withdrawing his hand when I shuddered from the pain. Who knew hair could hurt so much.

"Listen, my child, and you shall hear of the midnight fiasco involving Elle and beer."

"Very creative, Hutchins. You should have applied to Cogsworth with that kind of prose."

"Well, I would have, but it would appear as though I have the wrong equipment to apply."

"Yeah, you do." I smiled, finding even that act painful.

"Are you still drunk, Sloan? Because I think you're still drunk."

"I wish I were still drunk. Because maybe then the pain would go away." By now, my mouth was so dry that I could hardly form the words I spoke.

"Here." Luke helped me up to a sitting position on the bed and placed the glass of water he must have set on my nightstand into my hands.

"Thanks," I eked out, placing the glass to my chapped lips to take a drink. "Now, would you please regale me with the tale of my drunken shenanigans from last night?"

"Let's see," Luke began. "Where to begin, where to begin."

"That bad, huh?"

"Define bad. I mean, you're still alive, so it couldn't have been that bad, right?"

"Luke."

"Well, after about the fourth drink, you and Mena decided the table was holding you back from your true calling."

"I really don't like where this is going already."

"Oh, Sloan, you have no idea. Apparently, your true calling revolves around the ABBA song, 'Dancing Queen,' and oh my god, what a dancing queen you made."

"So I completely humiliated myself in front of the entire Roanoke college scene. Terrific."

"Don't worry, there were one hundred times just as many drunk people from said college scene on the floor with you, all doing the same thing."

"I'm so sorry you and Monroe had to sit through that without so much as a sip of alcohol to make it somewhat entertaining for you."

"We didn't need the alcohol to make it entertaining. You and Mena supplied all the entertainment we could have needed, especially when Mena began picking a fight with a coat rack. She even asked Monroe to hold her drink and had started rolling up her sleeves before I pulled her away from it. Monroe thought we should let her throw a punch first."

"And why was she in a scuffle with said coat rack?"

"She thought it had stolen her purse. Monroe had it the entire time."

"Okay, and then what?" I groaned.

"You kept telling me, Mena, and even Monroe, how much you loved us. Hell, you even told the bartender that a few times. In fact, you were full of love until the bartender called last call—you flipped her off then."

I closed my eyes and sighed, imagining my and Mena's pictures hanging up on the bulletin board of Magillicutty's with a caption that read *Deny Admittance To* above them.

"At that point, Monroe and I decided it was best if we left before things began to escalate."

"*Before* they began to escalate?"

"Before they began to escalate and become something other than completely hysterical. So we all but dragged you and Mena out of the bar and watched as you stumbled your way across the parking lot, trying to find my car while attempting to maintain your balance at the same time. Spoiler alert, it took you twenty minutes and Mena only fell twice before Monroe decided it was best if he walked behind her to catch her when she began stumbling."

"So we're leaving Magillicutty's, then what?"

"Everyone piled into the car, where it was decided that it

probably wasn't a good idea to drop off two extremely drunk women by themselves."

"So you came here with me and Mena went back to your apartment with Monroe?"

"Yup."

"Poor Monroe."

"My thoughts exactly. But if anyone can handle Mena, it's Monroe."

"Well, at least I didn't throw up all over myself,"

"You're right, you didn't throw up all over *yourself*."

Oh hell. "Where, Luke?"

"My car."

"Oh, no. Luke, I'm so sorry," I moaned.

"Don't worry about it," he said, all too understanding. "My floor mat can be cleaned."

"I blame, Mena."

"Under normal circumstances, I would, too, but I wanted you to go out, so I'm right up there with her."

I closed my eyes, envisioning how ridiculous I must have looked the night before, stumbling around, slurring my speech, making rude gestures at innocent strangers, and capping the night off by vomiting in Luke's vehicle, all of which I'd seen my mother do at one time or another. How many places had she awoken not knowing how she'd gotten there? How many strangers had she slept with before conceiving me? It was all too much, the thought of me going down the same path that she had.

"Whoa, Elle, baby," Luke said, wiping a tear from my cheek. "It's okay, seriously, my car can be cleaned."

"It's not that ... well, it is that, but it's not all that," I managed to blubber through tears.

"Then what is it?"

"It's my mom. I'm turning into my mother."

"One night isn't going to define who you are, Elle. I don't know much about your mom, but I'm certain her life consisted of more than just one night of irresponsibility."

"But it had to have started for her somewhere. She had her one night, too. You don't understand everything I've been through, everything I've seen."

"You're right, I don't," he said, lying down next to me on the bed. "But I want to. Would you please tell me about her, Elle?"

I wiped my eyes with my shirt sleeves, noticing that I had managed to change out of my clothes from last night into more suitable bed clothes. "Okay," I whimpered, drawing in a deep breath. "Here it goes."

Through occasional tears, I recounted my childhood, beginning with the fact that I was the product of a drunken, one-night stand and would probably never know who my real father was, and segueing from there into my life as the daughter of a high functioning alcoholic. All the evenings I was forced to fend for myself at dinnertime because my mother was either passed out or at a bar somewhere, coupled with the numerous trips to the emergency room for stomach pumps or other alcohol-induced injuries or illnesses. Not to mention the revolving door of men who had made their way in and out of our lives. All the while, Luke listened intently, quietly absorbing the tale of my childhood with the utmost of attention.

"I'll understand if you want to run away," I murmured after completing my tale with my eventual graduation from high school and my acceptance at Cogsworth.

"Run away?" he asked, perplexed. "Why would I want to do that?"

"Because I'm damaged goods. Because what if I turn into my mother? What if I already am my mother? Luke, you don't deserve that."

"For starters, you're nothing like your mother." His arm found its way across my body. "Do you know how I know that?"

"How?" I asked, genuinely curious.

"Because you're worried about becoming your mother. Do you think she ever worried about the consequences of her actions?" He paused long enough for me to respond with a shake of my head. "Besides that, Elle, look at you. You're talented and smart; you were awarded a scholarship to one of the most prestigious colleges in the country. They don't just hand those out. Their recipients have to earn them, and you did. You're making something of yourself, and from what I read this morning, you're going to have a very successful career ahead of you."

"Wait, what did you read this morning?" I asked, realizing that I already knew the answer. My journal of short stories and poetry was on my desk and must have been the notebook he was reading. "You read my journal?"

"I'm sorry," Luke apologized, his face reddening. "I didn't mean to, but after reading your first poem, I couldn't stop. Elle, you have an extraordinary talent. It's no wonder you were accepted here."

"Tell my mother that," I muttered. "She thinks a creative writing degree is a garbage degree and can't believe I'm wasting my time here."

Luke fell silent, but remained holding me. He was only the second person who knew everything about my life, after Mena. And even Mena didn't know all the details I'd shared with him. "Promise me something," he said more sternly than I was anticipating.

"Anything." My curiosity was piqued by the urgency in his voice.

"Promise me that you will take me to meet your mother one day, so that I can show her what a wonderful, well-rounded woman her daughter has become in spite of her. That, despite her best efforts to take you down with her in the sinking ship she's on, you've made something of yourself, and your talent will take you further in life than any of her empty beer cans will."

"I don't know," I interceded. "She has a shit ton of cans strewn across the house. She may be able to pay her mortgage off with them if Indiana ever institutes a bottle deposit."

"Promise me, Elle. Please."

With a sigh, I squeezed his hand, mulling over the inevitable ramifications that would come with agreeing to make this promise. Luke was too good for the train wreck that was my former life. And a part of me, the one that was consistently growing incrementally each day, had begun to feel like he was too good for me in my current life, too.

Until I met Luke, I'd wanted to live with my head buried in the sand, ignoring all the problems going on around me while I concentrated on my life as it was. Luke was making me face reality; he was trying to heal wounds that had long since become scars.

"Elle?"

"I promise."

CHAPTER TEN

2018

I sat on the couch, watching Candy in the kitchen preparing a roast for the night's meal. Tom stood next to her, steadying himself, every so often leaning against the counter. They spoke in hushed tones. Although Candy and I had made amends in the car on the way back to the Hutchins' home, I knew she was still a little miffed with me. Torn as I pretended to watch the news, I tossed around whether it would be better for me to pack up my bags and leave their home tonight, taking a gamble on whether or not I would find a decent hotel room for my last two days in Roanoke.

Only two more days.

My heart sank into my stomach with the thought of leaving Virginia and the Hutchins behind once again. It contrasted vastly with the guilt tugging at my brain, reminding me that I had a life, which included a husband, back in Indiana.

But, still, only two more days.

With my isolation threatening to take my thoughts to places I didn't want them to go, I stood up and ventured to join Tom and

Candy in the kitchen. Candy had already declined my offer of assistance. She had always been a firm believer that a guest in her home was just that, and it would speak ill of her to treat them otherwise. I always wondered if her inner control freak was using that excuse as a crutch to ensure that the task was completed to her specifications. It was hard for someone like me, someone who was used to doing everything for themselves at all times, to sit back while someone took care of my needs. It felt almost unnatural.

I shot Tom a sheepish smile, as I took a seat at the table. The conversation I'd had with Monroe earlier in the day replayed in my head. Candy, Tom, everyone I'd encountered with the exception of Luke were only tolerating my presence. At the time, it had been a tough pill to swallow, now I found it eating away at my insides like acid. His words were poisoning me, bringing about a slow, painful demise. Their rejection of me was even more painful than that of my biological mother's.

"Are you sure you aren't up to eating with us?" Candy asked Tom, concerned.

Tom, appearing paler by the second, had taken to bracing himself against the counter more than standing, practically sitting on it at times to keep himself upright. Seeing him in that state was devastating and made my heart shatter in two for Candy.

Candy moved from her position in front of the stove, where she'd been stirring her homemade mushroom gravy with a wooden spoon. She paused when Tom began mumbling something incoherent, wiped her hand on a dishrag, and felt his forehead.

"It doesn't feel like you have a fever," she offered. "Are you sure you don't want to try to stick it out?"

Tom shook his head and spoke, this time more audibly, "No, honey, I'm too tired."

"Let me help you upstairs, then," Candy insisted.

Tom moved to rebuff her offer, but stopped short, knowing that he was already defeated. I had never known Tom at his full capacity and could only imagine what an intimidating powerhouse he must have been in his youth. It was clear that the disease was defeating him now, and that it had gained remarkable ground since I'd last seen him. Even his spirit seemed defeated, but I wasn't certain whether that had more to do with his own deficits or with Luke.

"I'll take over," I offered, standing up from the table. "You just need me to keep stirring it, right?"

"That would be great, Elle, thank you," Candy answered without so much as an argument otherwise.

She placed her arm around Tom and shuffled with him up the stairs, headed to their room.

Spoon in hand, I picked up where Candy left off, stirring while trying to focus more intently on that, not Tom. My mind followed suit quickly, perhaps also wanting to focus on something mundane, instead of the emotional roller coaster it had been on over the last few days. Before I knew it, I had became so intent on what I was doing that I failed to hear the backdoor close.

"You made it," Candy announced.

Brought back down to reality, I glanced over my shoulder to see Monroe standing in the kitchen. He glanced briefly in my direction before turning his attention back to Candy.

"It's good to finally see you again outside of a hospital setting." She wrapped her arms around him, an embrace he faithfully reciprocated. I imagined all the tension, the tears, the heartache over the last month melting away from the both of them, if only for the moment.

"Don't get too excited, Ma, you know I'm only here for the food," he quipped.

"I figured as much," Candy replied with a smack to his back. She'd begun making her way back over to me, when I spoke.

"I can finish, if you want, so you and Monroe can talk." Even though I wasn't exactly known for my prowess in the kitchen, I figured it would be best if I kept my distance from Monroe tonight, considering the conversation we'd had earlier.

"No, no, honey. That won't be necessary." Candy recovered control of the spoon and shooed me out of the kitchen.

"Still the control freak, I see," Monroe remarked, pulling a chair out from the table to sit down.

"Still the big mouth, I see," Candy matched him in wit.

"It's one of my best qualities. After my heart-stopping good looks, of course."

Candy rolled her eyes, as the timer on the stove heralded the completion of the final component of our meal. Hungrier than I thought, my stomach growled as I took a seat at the opposite end of the table from Monroe.

* * * * *

I'd remained largely silent throughout the course of dinner, answering the occasional question from Candy and making the appropriate commentary where necessary. All the while, Monroe and Candy engaged in conversation. In between the lulls, I noticed Monroe would glance over at me as if he expected me to be speaking more. Or perhaps he wanted to speak to me, even though I couldn't imagine what else he'd have to say to me after today.

It was during Candy and Monroe's conversation that I was able to glean bits and pieces of the life Monroe had lived in my absence. He had a son in kindergarten. His name was Jackson, and it would seem as though Jackson was every bit as precocious as his father must have been. When talk of Jackson came up, I caught myself stealing a glance at Monroe's left hand, which was conspicuously unadorned. It wasn't long before I picked up on the name Amanda, Jackson's mother, and conversations that led me to believe the two had never tied the knot. In fact, it seemed like Monroe had been more or less a lone wolf for the better part of the last decade.

"So," Candy began, "I spoke with Dr. Reid today, and it would seem that they want to work toward a tentative discharge date for Luke."

"Really?" I asked. "When?"

"Wednesday."

"Wednesday, as in five days from now?" Monroe asked, echoing my thoughts.

"Yes." Candy seemed exhausted by the mere thought.

"That's ridiculous. He's in no condition to take care of himself yet," Monroe fumed.

"It's not about whether or not he can take care of himself. It's about whether there's anything more the doctors can do for him there. Luke's stable. He needs extensive rehabilitation, but that's no reason to keep him there as an inpatient. I'm surprised they're keeping him until Wednesday, to be honest." Candy sighed. I could envision the checklist she was preparing in her mind. So much to do, so little time.

"So when are you telling him, then?" I asked the moment the thought occurred to me.

"I was thinking this weekend. With you having to return home on Sunday, I figured it would give you an opportunity to be there, if you wanted to be."

I'd been offered three days of bereavement from work, but my conscience wouldn't allow me to take it, opting to burn vacation time, instead. As of now, I was scheduled to return to work on Monday. I wanted more time; I needed more time, and I didn't care how selfish that sounded. If Luke was going to be discharged on Wednesday, I needed to be there.

"What about Tuesday?" I asked.

Candy and Monroe looked up at me, confused. "What about Tuesday?" Candy asked.

"I'll call into work and tell them I've run into some complications and I need three more days. I have the vacation time to burn, anyway. That way I can be there on Wednesday when he's discharged—so maybe you can wait to tell him on Tuesday?"

Candy smiled, contemplating my request before turning back to Monroe. "Will you be able to be there Tuesday afternoon?"

Monroe nodded. "Yeah ... yeah, I'll be there."

"Thank you, Elle." Candy turned to me. "It means everything to me that you would be willing to interrupt your life once more to help us. But are you sure we wouldn't be putting you out?"

"Of course not, and even if you were, it doesn't matter. It's not about me, or you, or anyone else. It's all about Luke, right now. I owe this to him."

Candy opened her mouth to speak, but was swiftly cut off by the shrill ring of my phone. I looked down at the screen to see Eric calling. "I have to take this," I excused myself before standing up from the table.

Given the tone of our last conversation, I waited until I stepped outside before taking the call. "Hey," I answered cautiously.

"Elle Bell," Eric responded, far more enthusiastically than he had the last time we spoke.

"You seem chipper today. Good day at work?"

"Good? Try fanfuckingtastic. We won, Elle!"

I remembered that Eric had been preparing for a trial. With everything that had been going on with me, I'd completely neglected to consider anything important that may be going on in Eric's life.

"That's great! Wh-What case was this again? You said it was for a big deal client, or something?"

"It is now."

"What do you mean?"

"The son of the CEO of a local engineering firm was accused of rape—completely unsubstantiated allegations. Long story short, we were able to get the case dismissed on a technicality and the kid's father signed with our firm on the spot to handle all the legal work for their corporation. That's a huge acquisition and I'm going to get all the credit. I'll be sure to make partner this year."

Despite Eric's giddiness, I felt sick to my stomach. All I could focus on were the words 'rape' and 'dismissed on a technicality.'

"Elle, are you still there?"

"What about the girl?"

"What girl?"

"The girl who was raped."

"Allegedly raped."

"Okay, allegedly raped. What about her? I mean, do you think he did it, this CEO's son?"

Eric fell silent, as I took a seat on a purple flowered patio chair, suddenly finding myself ill.

"I don't know," Eric mustered. "He was drunk, she was drunk, you know how kids are. It was a he said, she said deal. It's just well-known around town that our client's family has money, so ..."

"So you're saying you think this girl was a gold digger, some kind of opportunist?"

"I'm not saying that, Elle, I thought you'd be happy for me— for us."

"You do realize that I was raped, right? I mean, of all the things about me for you to forget about, that couldn't possibly have been one of them."

"Shit," Eric sighed. "No, Elle, of course I didn't forget about that, but that girl wasn't you. It's an entirely different situation."

"That's where we'll just have to agree to disagree. Because I'm pretty sure I was that girl once and that she'll be me someday. My story is her story."

"All right. You're right. From now on, I will be more discriminatory when it comes to the clients I take on because in the Book of Elle, not everyone is entitled to fair and equal representation."

It was my turn to fall silent. Yet unlike Eric, no further retort from me was forthcoming. An awkward, deathly silence filled the void between us, until Eric spoke once more.

"I'm sorry, Elle. I should have been more sensitive. If I had known it was going to upset you like this, I never would have mentioned it to you."

"It's not about me. It's not me I'm worried about." I rubbed my temple with my free hand, taking in the mild spring breeze that carried with it the faint smell of lilacs. "How about we change the subject … start this conversation over? I really am happy for you. I know you've been working hard to get where you are."

"Thank you." He paused, carefully choosing his words to me before he spoke. "So, how are things going there? You're coming home on Sunday, right?"

Crap.

"About that," I began, unsure as to how to broach the decision I'd made with Eric and what kind of argument would ensue.

"You're staying longer, aren't you?"

"I was thinking about extending my stay until Wednesday," I said. "Luke is being discharged on Wednesday and they want to tell him on Tuesday." And by 'they,' I meant 'me.' "I figure I'll stay to help in any way that I can and then pack up and head home Wednesday morning."

Eric's reaction to this bit of news could have run the whole gamut of emotions. Despite not having a lot of time to brace myself for the inevitable fight when I informed him of the decision I'd made, I still felt like I was ready to plead my case in the same courtroom fashion in which he was accustomed. What I wasn't prepared for was how he actually did respond to this latest development.

"I understand and I think you should be there."

"Come again?" Clearly I hadn't heard him correctly.

"If you think you need more time, I will fully support your decision."

"That's really amazing of you. Thank you, and I promise you I won't be extending my stay any longer."

"You'd better not, or I'll hold you in contempt."

* * * * *

When I came back inside, I saw Monroe sitting alone at the kitchen table. He had his phone in his hand and appeared to be typing a text. The tension between Monroe and I at dinner had been so thick it was bordering on suffocating. It surprised me that he was still here. Surely, it must have been just as uncomfortable for him, too.

Feeling the air being sucked out of the room once more, I did an about face and diverted back to the kitchen, where I would try to make myself look busy, as I waited for Candy to come back. In my head, it sounded like a great idea. But, as it turned out, Candy had the same idea while I was outside, unwittingly thwarting my plan to try and completely avoid further conversation with Monroe. After I'd left the table, she'd cleared it, rinsed the dishes, and stuck them in the dishwasher, rendering any attempt by me to try to make myself look busy just that, an attempt to try to make myself look busy.

"She went to bed," Monroe announced.

"Oh." My reply came out more like I had been startled than anything else. On the counter sat a pot of coffee. Next to it was a small ceramic mug, inviting me to fill it. Monroe was already holding a cup of his own in his hand. I couldn't be sure, but something told me that Candy's early retirement had been deliberate. Uncertain as to what she thought this would accomplish, I acquiesced to her request and poured myself a cup of my own, taking a seat at the table with Monroe.

The four of us—Mena, Monroe, Luke, and I—had been so close at one time that it was surreal how much of a wedge the passing of time had been able to drive between us. Monroe and I didn't know each other anymore and were nothing more than strangers. Two people sharing an awkward cup of coffee.

Monroe, perhaps feeling as though the situation wasn't awkward enough, drew first blood. "Why did you break up with him, Elle?"

"Do we really want to do this now?" I couldn't look at him, instead opting to run my finger around the rim of my cup, wishing it would swallow me. I couldn't stand to see his snide countenance—not now, not tonight.

"When would be a good time for you? Tomorrow at noon? I could put it in my phone, set an appointment."

"Didn't you get everything out of your system earlier? Really, Monroe, I'm not up for another verbal beating right now." I scooted my chair away from the table and stood up.

"Elle, wait."

As I prepared to return fire, I noticed a complete change in his demeanor. He'd softened a bit, a side of him I hadn't recalled seeing since … ever.

"Please don't go."

Before I could process his request mentally, my body complied by sitting back down and scooting the chair in closer to the table.

"Look, I know it may seem like a first, but I'm really not trying to be a jerk. It's just that, your leaving and ending things with Luke the way you did didn't just affect him, it affected all of us. Candy, Tom, myself, anyone who even remotely had contact with Luke for several months afterwards—we all suffered. And I just want to understand why."

It was a fair request. Nevertheless, it hit me hard, even with almost a decade to prepare for it. Because admitting the why behind my breakup with Luke was akin to admitting my own weaknesses, opening up a Pandora's Box of psychological issues I'd acquired over the years, never to be closed again. Be that as it may, I owed it to him, just as I owed it to Luke.

"I know," Monroe began again, "I know the reason Luke gave me—that it stemmed from a tiff you'd gotten into with him over your mother. But I don't believe that was it. I never believed it, actually. Neither did Luke, but he was too heartbroken to pursue it. We all were. So I must know why. Was there someone else?"

"No, absolutely not," I protested. "There wasn't anyone for a very long time after Luke. There couldn't have been. He was one of a kind."

Monroe sat staring at me through occasional sips of coffee as if to say, *Go on.*

"I didn't want to be in a relationship when I met Luke. I'd fought against the idea of ever putting myself through what I'd been through in the past, knowing how much baggage I was carrying. Then I met him, and there was just something about him—a pull that I couldn't deny, like the pull of the moon on the tides. Everything was so natural with him. And then I was reminded of something."

I took a sip of my own coffee, which had begun to cool considerably, as I thought about how to word my explanation to Monroe without it sounding absolutely absurd. An impossible task.

"I was reminded that I came from nothing. The illegitimate daughter of an alcoholic, who had been abused and completely broken, had met and fallen in love with quite literally the most perfect person from the most perfect family with the most perfect life. What did I have to offer him? Nothing. I had nothing to offer Luke, the reality of which became all the more apparent when I took him home to meet my mother. He was appalled, and he should have been. She was every bit the mother I'd left when I went away to Cogsworth—blunt, uncaring. The complete opposite of Candy and Tom. I'd always been bitter about my lot in life, but I'd never allowed myself to feel ashamed. That all changed after Luke came into my life. I realized how ashamed I was of everything."

"But he didn't care about any of that. All Luke ever wanted was you. What you came from didn't matter to him."

"I think I realized that years later, but at the time, all I could think about was how much I didn't deserve this good thing that had been given to me—this rainfall in the midst of a drought. He was too good for me. That thought haunted me every day, lurking in the shadows to spring on me whenever I was at my most vulnerable, until I finally submitted to it. So when my mother became ill and needed me to take care of her, I knew I couldn't drag Luke into it. It wasn't the life for him—he deserved better. So I let him go, knowing he would be so much better off without me. I didn't want him to uproot his life, too. I didn't want to be responsible for him turning out like me."

Monroe remained silent, not quite looking at me, not quite looking at anything really, like he was searching the void for something he couldn't quite find. It was a lot to take in—I knew that. To anyone looking in on the outside, it may have sounded incredibly ridiculous, but it was my truth. One that I'd had to live with, regardless.

"Didn't you marry some lawyer, or something?" Monroe inquired.

"What was it about him that made you think he wasn't too good for you?"

"I was older and there were … circumstances."

Monroe raised his eyebrow, telling me that I wasn't going to get by without elaborating. Considering I'd gone this far, I decided to continue.

"I thought I was pregnant … I was pregnant, actually. Eric figured he was doing the right thing, even after we lost the baby."

"I'm sorry." Monroe sounded sincere and I responded with a nod.

"It's okay. Besides, it's not about the status, it's about the person. Eric may be an attorney, but he's no Luke. He has his own demons, many of which mirror my own. That put me on equal footing with him in my eyes."

"You're not your mother. You know that, right? You were better than that."

"Now you sound like Luke." I smiled. There was so much I wanted to ask him about Luke's life after I'd left—things I wanted to know, yet didn't at the same time. Of course there had been others, there had to have been.

"What about Luke?" I relented, psychologically preparing myself for whatever I was about to hear. "He had to have moved on and found happiness at some point."

"Sure," Monroe confirmed, "he moved on. He dated here and there, until …"

"Until what?"

"Nothing. Having someone in your bed is just that—having someone in your bed. Happiness is so much more than a warm body sharing a mattress with you."

"That's a very deep observation, Monroe," I said, chuckling.

"Just call me the Mid-Atlantic's answer to Plato." He yawned, despite the cup of coffee in his system. "Sadly, I'd like to say that observation was based upon wisdom and not solely on the kick in the balls my own life dealt to me, but alas, here I am."

"Tell me about it?"

He spoke in surprising detail about his life—more so than I would have thought I would have gotten out him. Like me, he'd dropped out of college, opting instead to join the workforce as a laborer in a plastics factory, a decision he regretted later when maturity set in. He'd made a decision to go back to pursue a degree in engineering, but then had met Amanda, the woman who would later become the mother of his son. Although he'd never married her, the thought had crossed his mind, but then left just as expediently as it had arrived. Instead, they split and shared custody of Jackson. Talking to Monroe, it seemed like old times again. The years that had separated us were falling away like we were somehow traveling back in time.

"How's Mena?" he asked meekly.

"She's good. Just as Mena-y as always. Working in New York still, hasn't gotten mugged yet. I think even the hardened criminals know to stay away from her."

"That's good to hear. I still think about her from time to time."

"I know you do." I looked up at the clock, just as my eyes had begun to grow heavy. "It's a quarter to eleven," I announced, mirroring his earlier yawn, "and I know Candy is going to be bright-eyed and bushy-tailed at six. I should probably get ready for bed."

"Same here," he conceded.

I grabbed my coffee cup, held out my hand to take Monroe's, and headed into the kitchen to dump the rest of the untouched pot of coffee down the drain. Behind me, I heard Monroe zipping up his coat and the heavy footfalls of his steel-toed work boots as he made his way to the back door.

"Hey, Elle," he said, stopping just shy of the door.

"Yeah?"

"For what it's worth, I really did miss you."

"I missed you, too, Monroe."

2007

It was mid-afternoon when we approached the sign welcoming

us to Jasper. With the ostentatious gold star in place of the usual dot over the 'j,' its green and silver exterior heralded the beginning of what would be an uncomfortable, at best, and disastrous, at worst, twenty-four hours.

"Look at you, hailing from the Nation's Wood Capital," Luke proclaimed, honing in on the proclamation proudly displayed underneath Jasper's obligatory salutation. "If I would have known I was going to be visiting such a land of prestige, I would have at least put on a clean pair of pants."

"That's all right," I countered, "you'll be forgiven. After all, you've been dating the town's former reigning Pulp Princess."

"Really?" he asked, impressed, skeptical, and a bit prideful at the same time. "Is that a thing?"

"It is now." I giggled for the first time in hours.

The closer we'd come to Jasper, the quieter I had become, just not from the fatigue of the several hour car ride. On the contrary, I was on edge. My adrenaline was on full blast. Luke sensed it, too, but held back from saying anything to me, knowing that I wouldn't want to talk about it.

Unfortunately, Jasper was small, which meant that we were within minutes of arriving at my mother's home. Mentally drained, I leaned back in the passenger seat and closed my eyes as though that would somehow pacify my concerns. Luke had offered to drive, primarily due to the questionable reliability of my five hundred dollar junkyard on wheels, but also because of his innate ability of picking up on the cues I displayed when my nerves were shot and I was close to going over the edge.

My mother lived in a small, two-bedroom, ranch style home in a rural area near the Patoka River. I'd driven the roads leading from town to her house countless times and was so familiar with their snake-like curves that I could tell exactly where we were with the passage of each sharp turn and bump without opening my eyes. Right now, Luke's sedan was rounding the curve by the small corner gas station less than two miles from my mother's home. At least once a week during the summer, I would ride my bike to that small, red brick building with the change I'd found in our couch cushions, or from selling lemonade and mowing lawns, to buy a pack of bubble gum and a pop for the ride home. Sometimes, after I'd had a particularly fruitful week, I would be able to buy one of the store's pre-made bags filled with assorted hard candies and the occasional chocolate. Those bags would last the majority of the week, if I could keep them away from my mother.

After taking the curve near the gas station, the road straightens out, revealing a field on each side of it. On even years the fields were home to soy beans; on odd years, corn. Sensing how close we were, I opened my eyes to see the healthy stalks, already well over a knee high, surrounding us like the road was but a mere path intruding through their field.

When I was little, I used to play hide and seek in the corn with the smattering of other children who lived nearby. It was easy to get lost if you weren't careful, especially for a small child whose head came nowhere near to being as tall as the tip of the stalks. And as we steadily approached my mother's house, the thought of jumping from the car to hide in the fields became more and more appealing.

"Here," I said, directing Luke down a long dirt drive.

You couldn't see the house from the road, as it was tucked behind several evergreen trees, each standing in attention like soldiers guarding a fort. If you didn't already know there was a house was there, it would be easy to miss it, but I knew it was still there. I could feel its presence looming at the end of the driveway—I could feel her presence. She'd be home, probably still hungover from last night, despite having known I'd be coming. That is, if she even remembered the conversation we'd had a week earlier. Her sobriety at that time had been questionable.

Luke emitted a grunt through gritted teeth when his car struck yet another rut in the driveway, jostling us and scraping the undercarriage of his car. The dirt drive had always been an annoyance, ensuring dirty shoes and vehicles, but it had never been so bad that you could barely drive down it.

"Must be her way of keeping solicitors away," I quipped to try and take Luke's mind off of the damage that was being done to his car.

"I imagine it's pretty effective," he said, grimacing as his tire struck yet another hole. "If my alignment survives this, I may consider taking her off-roading more often."

In a way, I was grateful that we encountered the rutted dirt road first. It lowered my expectations of what to expect when the house finally came into view. But even with those lowered expectations, I still found myself in for a shock.

"Oh my shit," I uttered, shocked and ashamed all rolled into one.

"I couldn't have said it better myself," Luke answered, forgetting about the state of the driveway and focusing, instead, on the place we'd be sleeping tonight.

When I'd left home, the house had been in decent shape, all things considered. Granted, it never would have been a Parade of Homes home, but it hadn't been a complete eye sore. Not like the unkempt structure we were steadily approaching. Its beige paint was chipping away from its exterior as though the house itself were weeping. The roof had been repaired in patches, clearly visible due to the repairs having been made using tan shingles, instead of the prevailing black shingles that comprised the rest of it. A window—the window to my old bedroom—was cracked. A piece of duct tape was secured over it from the inside.

So as not to be outdone, the lawn, mostly crabgrass from what I could tell, was mid-shin in height. A sign that it likely hadn't been mowed since last fall.

"Maybe she's been working more," Luke said, his optimism showing.

"I know her hours, they haven't changed in at least the better part of fifteen years. This is pure neglect."

"Well, maybe it all became so overwhelming to her that she can't do it all and can't afford to hire anyone."

"Stop giving her the benefit of the doubt," I said, more irritated than I meant to come across. "I've balanced her checkbook enough times to know what she pulls in each month. She makes decent money, enough to pay a kid to mow the lawn, and for a can of paint for the house. And she could easily save up for a new window. It's her priorities that are deficient, not her funds."

"Sorry," Luke muttered.

"No, I'm sorry." I squeezed his hand, which was resting on the center console. "I've been trying to make myself believe that she had bettered herself since I moved out, that she'd woken up, but clearly that's not the case. If anything, she's gotten worse, and it angers me. I shouldn't have taken it out on you."

Luke pulled up next to my mother's silver Jeep, where he parked the car. "If it's any consolation, I'd be somewhat of a train wreck if you left me, too. Maybe try cutting her some slack, until you know what the situation is with certainty. I know it's easy to jump to conclusions, but if you've convinced yourself that you already know the answer, then you won't be open to accepting that maybe there are other reasons for why things have gotten to this point."

I nodded. Luke was right, but he didn't have the years of history I had. A leopard doesn't change its spots. As much as I wanted to have faith in my mother, to think that she would be a complete one-eighty from what I remembered, it just didn't compute. All the data pointed to a different solution—the same one I'd arrived at time and time again after one heartbreak after another.

"Let's not go in there with any preconceived notions that will only ruin our time here. We'll be leaving tomorrow, just keep telling yourself that."

"Okay," I answered, managing to form just the slightest hint of a smile. "Let's just go and get this over with."

"That's the spirit."

We traipsed through the yard to the front porch, the boards of which were sunbleached and in the same amount of disrepair as the rest of the house. I maneuvered my body around a loose board at the top of the steps with Luke following my lead. I'd half expected to see the bodies of crumpled beer cans—fallen soldiers, or so my mother used to call them. To my surprise, she'd managed to at least keep the outside of the house free of their aluminum bodies. On the outside, she almost seemed sober.

With a glance back at Luke, and the thought that there was no turning back now, I opened the storm door and knocked on the front door. It was a strange feeling, knocking on the door of the house I'd let myself into time and time again. But in the years since I'd been away, I felt like I'd lost that privilege, not that I'd really wanted it in the first place. Even drunk off her gourd, my mother was light on her feet, like a cat stalking its prey. If alcoholics had superpowers, that was hers. As we waited, I wondered whether she was delaying answering the door for dramatic effect. Whether she'd seen us pull up, or whether she was already passed out on the couch. I'd begun to raise my hand to knock on it again, when I heard the jiggle of the doorknob on the other side.

Luke grabbed my hand in a show of solidarity while we awaited the opening of the door. The front door stuck, the result the house settling, and it took her a couple tugs before she was finally able to open it. My mom now in full view, I couldn't help but scrutinize her the same way I had done with the house. By comparison, the home was worse for wear, but she was not far behind it. Always youthful, my mother had steadily started looking her age of forty-three. Streaks of silver interwove themselves throughout her otherwise toffee hued hair. Her crows feet had deepened enough to become noticeable, but the most striking difference was her skin. Her usual alabaster complexion had taken on a dull yellow luster, one so subtle it wouldn't have been noticed by those standing only slightly farther from her than where we were standing now.

"Hi, Mom," I greeted her in a monotone voice that would put Ben Stein to shame.

"Will you look what the cat dragged in," she proclaimed. She grabbed me by the shoulders and planted a wet kiss on my cheek, leaving behind lipstick residue. The faintest hint of beer, Coors most likely, caught my nose. For once she didn't reek of alcohol, but it was still early. "My, look at you; you look healthy." As she spoke, she was clearly assessing my midsection. Behind me, Luke exhaled sharply, perhaps wanting to say something, but stopping himself when his better judgment caught up to his mouth.

"That's what happens when you're able to eat three meals a day like a normal human being."

"Oh, come on now, Ellie," my mother said, smacking me on the back, harder than I'm sure she meant to. "You know I didn't mean anything by that. I'm just so happy to have my little girl home for a visit. I was beginning to wonder whether I'd ever see you again. You and your big important college life; you've become too good for your old mother."

A light switched on just then, as though she'd just realized that I hadn't come alone, despite my having told her that I would be bringing my boyfriend with me.

"And who's this tall drink of water?" she asked, looking up at him in an exaggerated fashion.

"Mom, this is Luke; Luke, my mother, Betsy Sloan."

"What did you do, knock her up or something?" She stole an obvious glance back at my stomach.

Luke looked down at her in shock, his eyes flickering back and forth between me and her. There was a war brewing in his head. I could see the spark in his eyes, just waiting for that final straw to blow up into an all-out blaze.

"Oh, for crying out loud," my mother huffed. "Haven't they taught you how to have a sense of humor in college?" She turned to walk back into the house. "Come on inside, I feel rain coming."

As we walked into her home, I looked back at Luke as if to say, *You asked for this.*

172

When we entered the house, I was pleasantly surprised to see at least half of the living room was habitable. There was a clear distinction between where my mother had cleaned and where she'd probably said, "Screw it, it's good enough." At least, she'd had the common courtesy to pick up most of the beer cans, leaving only two as far as I could tell, one sitting on the coffee table and the other on the mantle above the fireplace. She frequently either forgot that she had already opened a can or where she'd put the can she remembered opening, so multiple cans sitting around with varying levels of alcohol in them were not uncommon.

I directed Luke to the newish-looking sofa, still miraculously free of stains, that had probably been recently cleaned off just for our visit. Taking a seat, Luke looked around the room, clearly taking in his surroundings, a far cry from the accommodations he had been accustomed to. I wondered what was going on inside of his head, whether his opinion of me was changing for the worse.

"Look what I made," my mom said, carrying in a plate and setting it down on the coffee table in front of us. "Your favorite. Just call me Betty Crockpot."

"It's Crocker." I inspected the oatmeal raisin cookies skeptically. "These are *your* favorite, Mom. I'm a peanut butter cookie person, remember?"

"A cookie's a fucking cookie," she answered like a true Thoreau, grabbing the can of Coors from the table.

"Just like a beer's a beer, huh?"

"Now don't you start with me, Ellie. I go to work every day. My bills are paid. I have my shit together when it needs to be together. I'm not the gigantic mess, living in a sea of beer cans, or whatever other hyperbole you like to spout about me." As she spoke, she noticed the forgotten can sitting on the mantle and all but skipped over to it. "Hot damn, I thought I'd lost this one. Who said God doesn't provide?" It was a rhetorical question, one she knew I wouldn't answer. I'd made my thoughts on her drinking clear to her years ago. Anything she said in defense of it was purely just to instigate me.

My mom flopped down on the same worn out recliner she'd been sitting in since I could remember, a can in each hand. She sat one can down on the end table next to her, only releasing it to grab the remote and flip on the television. She'd sprung for cable since I'd left.

"So, Luke," she began, not making eye contact with him in favor of the image of Jerry Seinfeld on the screen. "What are you going to school for?"

Shoot me now.

"Nursing," Luke answered her, his confidence unwavering.

"Come again?" My mother, undaunted by Luke's direct answer, asked, "You mean you're going to be a doctor, right?"

"No, I meant nurse. That's why I said nurse."

"Huh," my mom countered. "So is it because you're not, like, smart enough for medical school, or is it because you want to meet the ladies?"

"Mom!"

Luke put his arm around me to prevent me—I theorized—from jumping out of my seat. "It's okay, Elle. You see, Ms. Sloan, I'm more of a get to know the patients, get down in the trenches kind of a person, and although I think I could hack medical school, I'm content with my calling. And as far as meeting the ladies, there's only one I care knowing."

"Well, you haven't gotten out much, then," my mom quipped without missing a beat.

Luke opened his mouth to say something, only to restrain himself when I cleared my throat and began speaking.

"Come on, I'll show you around."

There wasn't much to show him. The house was small, but I would have cut out my own kidney and sold it on the black market if it would get me out of that room at that moment. Leaving my mother to her television and beer, I led Luke down the hallway to my former bedroom. The pine door, scratched from years of wear and tear, stood ajar, revealing a room in the same state it was when it was left behind.

I found myself overcome by nostalgia. My former room reflected

174

the story of a girl who'd hastily left her life in the dust, taking with her only the bare essentials. With the day I left as fresh in my mind as if it had happened yesterday, I walked into the room.

"I feel like I'm intruding on your life," Luke said. "It's like you were just here."

"Don't think for one moment that she intentionally left it this way because she missed me." I took a seat on the blue-striped comforter covering my former twin bed. "She was just too lazy to do anything else with the room. This was easy. She always took the easy road."

Luke smile, a sad smile that matched the rest of his face. "You know, she can say whatever she wants to about me—and I'm sure she would—but I won't tolerate her saying anything about you."

"There's nothing she can say to me she hasn't already said before. It's not your fight, Luke, it's mine." I laid back on my bed, scooting over to make room for him to sit down. "And this is why I wasn't too keen on running back here."

"You're here because of me," Luke lamented. "I'm sorry I made you come."

"Don't be. You're a part of my life now, and so is this. I'd rather you see all the pieces to the puzzle that put me together, rather than having to construct something abstract."

Luke nodded. This had to be a culture shock to him, considering the way he had been raised. My mother's life had probably been nothing but a cautionary tale told to him by his parents before he left home for college.

"I'm not my mother."

"That's the understatement of the century," Luke snorted.

"She was very smart ... is still, I suppose. She could have made so much more of herself. Somewhere along the way she gave up." A stain resembling tea accidentally spilled across a white tablecloth, graced the ceiling above me, directly underneath one of the the hastily patched areas on the roof. I wondered how long the rain had been allowed to infiltrate the house and drip inside my room before she noticed it.

175

"You don't think any less of me, do you?"

Luke shook his head. "Of course not." He stroked my hair, knowing just what to do to pull my thoughts away from the dark path they were traveling down. "If anything, seeing how you lived makes me that much more proud to call you my girlfriend. You're like a phoenix rising from the ashes. You could have easily taken the same road as your mom, but you didn't. You're choosing to fight. If that's not admirable, I don't know what is. But what does make me think less of you is that life-sized poster of Ashton Kutcher. Honestly, Elle, there's no excuse for that."

"Like you never had posters hanging up on your walls as a teenager."

"None of them were of Ashton Kutcher."

I laughed, feeling for the first time since we arrived like maybe, just maybe, we may survive this visit after all. And then it all came crashing down.

CHAPTER ELEVEN

"What was that?" Luke asked, startled.

"God only knows," I replied, concerned, but not as shaken as he was. Unlike him, I was used to random crashes erupting throughout the house, accompanied by swearing that could put Andrew Dice Clay to shame. He looked at me as if to ask, *Aren't you going to get up?*

"I guess we'd better find out." Resigned, I pushed myself off the bed.

"Son of a bitch," my mom moaned as we entered the living room.

She was on her knees on the floor next to the television. The cord had been pulled out of the wall by the sheer weight of it. Many people would wonder how it had fallen from its perch on the entertainment center. I wasn't one of them. The sway in her body was slight, yet noticeable to anyone looking for it. She'd been approaching three sheets to the wind when we'd arrived. Since then, the whole damn mast had blown away.

Luke picked the television up and placed it back on the stand, saving my inebriated mother from injuring herself.

"Damn!" she wailed upon seeing the crack traveling down the center of the screen.

"What happened?" Luke wondered, still oblivious to the obvious.

"The stupid screen kept going in and out, so I got up to adjust it and—"

"Oh, please," I said, snorting at the thought.

"What the hell is your problem?" My mom stood up, having to steady herself against the entertainment center halfway up. I noticed she kept her body weight propped against the piece of furniture.

"Do you seriously need to ask that, Mom? Geez, you're acting like I didn't grow up in the same household as you. Adjust my ass. You either kicked it or threw something at it because you're too far gone to use common sense."

"How dare you insult me in my own house. You go to school far away and you come back thinking you're all high and mighty."

"Yes, how dare your daughter strive to be something better than this." I gestured around the room, eventually landing on her.

"Give me a break. Don't act like you're any better than me or that you're going to be some famous author somewhere. For crying out loud, Elle, you're wasting your time. You're no Danielle Steel, and you never will be."

At this point, through her slurred speech and questionable mental state, I would have just walked away, knowing that it was no use arguing and using logic with her at that moment. Luke, however, did not possess the foresight I had.

"Wasting her time?" Luke asked, incredulous. "What kind of mother tells their child that they're wasting their time pursuing a degree in a field they're passionate about?"

"Luke," I attempted to intercede, but by then, he'd become so overcome with rage that not even God himself could stop it.

"She's trying to better herself—to do better than you. You wouldn't provide the life she deserved, so she's providing it for herself. Hell, Elle is a better mother to herself than you ever were." I gently rested my hand upon his shoulder, which seemed to act as a buffer, calming him enough to ease the trembling that had erupted throughout his body. "And just so you know, I've read her material. She's a damn fine writer, with a talent so raw and so beautiful that she brought tears to my eyes."

Barely able to keep her balance, my mother was fuming on the inside. I could tell by the crimson shade overspreading her cheeks. She was a hard boiled egg. On the outside, her shell remained unchanged, unable to reflect the rage brewing within. On the inside, however, all hell had broken loose.

"Elle, are you going to let this spoiled, pissant, behemoth … pissant talk to me like that?"

"Good-bye, Mother." I gestured to Luke to grab our bags, as I proceeded to turn toward the door.

"You're not leavin', I'm kicking you out," she fumed. "Now get the hell out of my house!"

"Whatever makes you feel better," I called back to her.

Luke positioned himself between us, a move I knew had to have been intentional. What he didn't know, though, was that my mother was only good at throwing verbal punches. Real ones took too much effort.

"And don't fucking come back, ya' hear!"

Without saying a word, Luke closed the door behind us before she could unleash more left hooks at our psyches. We sat in silence for the majority of the way home. Me out of utter humiliation. Him because, between processing the shit show that had just unfolded in front of us and wondering what was going on in my head, he genuinely didn't know what to say. Nonetheless, he spoke first.

"I'm sorry."

"It's not your fault. She's always been like that."

"I know, and you warned me about that, but I think a part of me wanted to see it for myself, like maybe I thought you'd been exaggerating this whole time. I believed you. Really, I did. I'm just sorry I subjected you to all that."

"Luke, it's fine. She doesn't bother me as much anymore. I've de-sensitized myself to her."

"Well, if I can help it, I don't care to ever be in the same room as that woman again."

2018

"So where's ol' Mena Straszewski?" Luke asked, sitting up in his hospital bed.

I glanced across the room at Monroe, who sat working on his third cup of Jell-O that evening. He shrugged at me, leaving me to carry on an explanation.

"Between studying and otherwise gracing the world with her presence, she's actually been taking a couple trips to New York, scouting out different publishing companies in preparation for graduation next year. She sends her love, though."

"Mena in New York. I didn't think it would be possible for that city to be any more dangerous."

"On the contrary," Monroe chimed in, "do you think anyone would dare mug her? I think she'd be a pretty effective deterrent."

"What about you?" Luke asked, turning his attention to Monroe.

Confused, Monroe stopped shoving spoonfuls of Jell-O in his mouth long enough to digest Luke's inquiry. "What do you mean, man? I've been here the entire time."

"I know that. I meant if Mena moves to New York. Are you going to follow her or stay in Roanoke?"

"Why would he follow Mena?" I asked, noticing that Monroe wouldn't even make eye contact with me.

"So she doesn't know?" Luke asked. "You mean Mena hasn't told you?"

"Told me what?" It was my turn to ask questions, even though the answer was right in front of me refusing to stare me in the face.

"We were— been sleeping together," Monroe answered, shoving another bite into his mouth to avoid going into detail.

"She's actually never mentioned it," I commented.

It made sense, Mena and Monroe. I figured I'd already known it, yet I felt like I'd gone crazy from time to time, imagining I'd see stolen glances here and there between them. How Mena would disappear, returning a little more chipper than when she'd left. Mena had never been particularly private, especially when it came to her dating life. And I wondered why she never thought to mention Monroe to me, and then it hit me. She'd loved him. He meant so much more to her than she wanted to admit because she didn't want to be perceived as being weak and vulnerable.

"Don't worry," Luke added. "Monroe didn't exactly tell me, either. I happened to come home from class early one day and saw things that I will never be able to unsee."

"Okay, that's enough reminiscing for one evening." Monroe threw the empty cup of Jell-O into the trash and stood up. "It's eight, Elle, I think we need to be heading out for the night."

"Stay," Luke, clearly fatigued, muttered as Monroe and I stood up.

Monroe continued to shrug his sweatshirt over his head. "I'm sorry, Luke, but we can't. I have class tomorrow."

"I wasn't talking to you, unless Mena has you into ménage à trois now."

"As much as I'd like to spoon you all night, buddy, it's really time for us to get going."

Monroe glanced back at me as if to say he had nothing else and it was up to me now.

"Um, I-I really don't think I can. It's against the rules, isn't it?" I asked.

"We'll find out." Luke pressed the call button near his bed, as I looked up at Monroe, wide-eyed.

"Everything okay in here, Mr. Hutchins?" a red-headed nurse I hadn't seen before asked upon entering the room.

"Everything's fine. I'm just trying to clear up a little debate here. Now I've been here for over a month and I'd really like my girlfriend over here to spend the night with me. But my friend over here says that's not possible. My question is, you wouldn't deny a seriously injured man his first and probably only wish during the rest of his stay here, would you?"

The young nurse looked between Luke and me, confused. "Well," she replied after some thought, "if she's the only person staying and it's only for one night, then I really don't see a problem with it."

"Thank you, Heidi, that's all I needed." Luke smirked. It was a small victory, but in that moment you would have thought he'd won the Superbowl.

"I guess that settles it," I conceded. "We're having a sleepover."

* * * * *

"You know, I think Monroe is onto something. This Jell-O is fabulous," I announced, sitting in the recliner that was brought in just for me for the night with my feet propped up.

Luke grinned. He'd been alternating between alert and lively to dozing off, struggling against the latter. A piece of me felt guilty every time I saw his eyelids covering those bright blue eyes of his. He was staying awake for me, willing himself back into consciousness. I wanted to tell him to sleep, to give into his body's plea, but just as he didn't want to drift away, neither did I. So I fought it with him; making conversation, making him laugh. But in the last hour, it was clear that all I was doing was delaying the inevitable.

Eyes closed, Luke spoke softly, "When I get out of here, I'll be sure to smuggle some out for you."

"They should give you a year's supply after all you've been through."

Luke yawned. By this point, him opening his eyes looked downright painful.

"Luke." He turned his head, forcing his eyes open to look at me. "It's okay; go to sleep."

Relief flooded over him, as his body seemed to relax upon receiving my blessing. Yet, despite his body relaxing, Luke's mind was still working. I wondered if it really ever shut off.

"Sleep with me, Sloan?"

"Of course, Hutchins. I'm staying with you tonight, remember?"

"No, that's not what I meant."

My heart sank. If a line had been drawn in the sand, agreeing to his proposal would certainly be crossing it.

"There's not enough room in there," I answered him, not necessarily shooting his offer down but not agreeing to it, either.

"Give yourself some credit, Sloan." He managed to slide his body ever so slightly over to the right side of the bed. He was right, there was ample room for the both of us.

Just get in bed with him and climb back out after he falls asleep.

If you do that, you'll only be leading him on.

But he thinks you're still his girlfriend, anyway.

A dizzying battle of wills was underway inside of my head. Was there ever a circumstance where doing something wrong was the right thing to do?

"Elle?" Luke asked again, his voice slipping further into the oblivion.

"Of course," I answered him. I would compromise. He'd fall asleep and I would sneak back into my chair.

I kicked my shoes off, peeling off my socks one by one before climbing in next to him. His hospital bed was stiff and not in the least bit comfortable. How he had lain here confined even after he'd woken up, I didn't know. I'd have completely lost my mind by now.

"What ... do I smell funny?" he asked, amused.

I had positioned myself on my side with my back facing him. It was the position I always slept in.

"No, no, I just sleep better on my left side." Rolling over, I realized that there was just enough room on the bed to accommodate the two of us without any space left between our bodies, and I found my hand coming to rest on Luke's chest. He stopped me as I tried to pull it away, an unspoken request for me to leave it where it was.

"I know you only sleep on your left side, and you can roll over again, but I want to see that beautiful face before I fall asleep."

"You always had a way of knowing just want to say to me to get your way."

"Have, Sloan. I'm still here, remember?"

"Yes, you are, and so am I."

"Did you hit your head, too?" He chuckled, which took all the remaining energy he had.

"It just feels like a lifetime since I've felt so at peace—since we laid in the same bed together."

"A month away from you was a lifetime for me, too."

With his breaths becoming more rhythmic, I knew he had fallen asleep. Now was my chance, to do the right thing and climb back into the recliner. He'd never know. He had always been a heavy sleeper without the added pain medication. If the tables had been turned and it was Eric in this situation, I would expect him to seize this opportunity. It was in our vows, after all, to honor one another.

To be faithful.

But I was being faithful. Nothing even remotely resembling cheap and tawdry had transpired between Luke and I. And it wouldn't. It couldn't.

Then why do I feel so guilty now?

Maybe my body was adjusting to the two-by-four underneath me and had indelibly become paralyzed in place, like it was being molded into the very fabric of the mattress itself. Maybe I felt like my presence was too calming to Luke—like he needed me here to get a restful night's sleep. The first in over a month for him. Or, maybe, it was because underneath my hand, I could feel his heart beating, and I didn't want to let it go. Not now. I needed more time.

And so that's how I fell asleep, peaceful and content, holding Luke's beating heart in the palm of my hand.

2007

I fanned myself with a paper napkin underneath the simplistic elegance of the vinyl tent that shielded some one hundred or so people from the rain. The late July heat, coupled with the moisture in the air, made our enclosure that much more miserable, but as etiquette dictated, we couldn't let our discomfort show. It could be worse, after all. We could be standing underneath the bright lights positioned at the head of the tent, where the bride and groom were dancing. The one saving grace was the fact that Luke had chosen seats at a table right next to the faux windows carved into the tent's sidewalls. The thin material provided a minuscule amount of relief whenever the occasional gust of wind graced us with its presence. Without that one solace, I doubt I could have made it through the evening.

"How did you meet the groom again?" I asked Luke.

He'd been unusually quiet all day. At first I thought he was sick and suggested we skip the wedding and the two hour drive to the venue hosting it, only to back away from that idea when he looked at me like I'd just run over his cat. Even still, he was much more fidgety than normal. So nervous, so unlike the Luke I'd come to know and love.

"Hmm?" he asked. It appeared my question had succeeded in breathing new life into him, like a sudden clap of thunder in an otherwise dead silence. I nodded to the groom, silently reiterating my inquiry. "Oh yeah, Adam. I met him in middle school during eighth grade. We then went on to play basketball together in high school and hung out here and there. We kept touch after graduation, occasionally working out at the gym together before he moved and met Rebecca."

I nodded, just thankful to hear his voice. That was probably the most he'd spoken all day, very much out of character for him. It made me uncomfortable, like he had something brewing in his mind that he was too afraid to share with me. Perhaps he wanted to let me go and didn't know what to say to not hurt me. The thought struck me in the gut like a battering ram. My pallor had to have been at least three shades lighter than even my usual pale ivory.

At our table were a couple of other people who Luke seemed to have known, though obviously not as well as Adam. They appeared to be about our age, and I guessed they were former classmates of Luke's, perhaps just a notch below acquaintances. The Luke I knew would have struck up a conversation with them, nonetheless, finding some sort of common denominator with them, until they were brought up to that acquaintance level with him. Yet there was nothing.

Instead of trying to make small talk with him, I sat in silence next to him, watching the happy couple twirling their way back to their seats at the conclusion of their dance.

"Do you want to dance?" Luke asked out the blue. It was my turn to be surprised by his voice.

"Come again?"

"Dance," he said, holding his index and middle finger on one hand down to signify a pair of legs, which he then made glide through the air. "You and me?" He pointed to me and then to himself. Amused, I had to laugh at his theatrics, even if I remained a bit nervous about where this night was heading and whether there would still be an us after it was over.

Luke held out his hand, which I eagerly took, grateful for the physical contact with him. Maintaining a firm grasp on his hand, I followed him down the aisles of tables that were so closely packed together I was beginning to feel claustrophobic. It was even worse on the dance floor.

Luke paused next to the cherry floor, constructed from interlocking portable tiles, searching for an opening—any opening—that would allow enough room for the both of us. There was none to be found, unless we wanted to dance practically on top of the other couples next to us. Just the thought of that was already making me dizzy.

"Come on," I said, guiding him around the floor to the side of the tent, where I discovered an opening that led to the yard outside.

"Elle?" Luke put up a resistance, stopping me in my tracks. I was neither strong nor big enough to pull the mass of his body any further. "You know it's still raining, right?"

"Really?" I asked sarcastically. "I hadn't noticed."

"So we're going out there, why?"

"Because we're going to be smothered to death if we stay in here, and you have to admit it feels much better out there, despite the water falling from the sky." I gave his arm a small tug. This time, his body relented a little and lurched forward as though I were a tugboat and he an ocean liner.

"What about your dress?"

"It's just a hunk of cotton."

"Well, if that's the case, then." Before I could stop him, he'd scooped me up into his arms and dipped me so that my head and chest curved outwards into the rain.

Even the raindrops were warm, but they were a welcoming sharp contrast to the slow cooker we'd just come from. My body shivered with relief, and I took in their comfort, seeking to wrap myself in each drop that fell upon me like a warm blanket.

"My god," Luke whispered, "I didn't think it was possible."

"What?" I asked, positioning myself upright and wiping the rain from my forehead.

"Every day I look at you and think to myself how lucky I am to have such a beautiful woman by my side. I think that you couldn't possibly be any more beautiful than you are in that moment, but here we are. Elle, you look so radiant right now that I had to catch my breath with each drop that fell on you."

"That's a relief," I whispered, running my hand through his thick, blond hair.

"A relief? Why's that?"

"You've been so distant today that I thought ..." I didn't want to finish that sentence, as to say it out loud may somehow validate it.

"You thought what?" Luke held onto me tightly, whether it was a conscious decision or simply a reaction, I didn't know.

187

"I thought for certain you were ending things with me tonight with the way you've been so quiet. It's so unlike you to be subdued, and I couldn't think of any other reason."

"No." Luke shook his head, his expression softening. "Elle, I love you." He kissed my forehead, allowing is lips to linger there. The touch of his velvety smooth mouth on my skin sent a shiver down my spine. "I'm afraid you're going to have me to kick around for as long as you like."

"I hope so." My body relaxed, like a weight had been lifted from my chest and I could finally breathe again. "Hutchins?"

"Sloan?"

"What is it, then? What has you so anxious?"

"Let's dance," he said, completely ignoring my question, as he whisked us both out from underneath the protection of the tent's awning and into the unforgiving elements.

A slow song had started playing inside; a new R&B number I'd heard played on the radio frequently lately. I wrapped my arms around Luke's shoulders. His own arms slipped around my waist, low enough that I thought I detected a slight hitch in his breathing, as our bodies slow-danced to the music, surrounded by the fresh, earthy smell of the rain mixed with the fresh cut grass.

"I always wanted to do this," I spoke softly, watching a drop of rain slide down a strand of his hair and drip down onto his shirt collar.

"Do what?"

"Dance in the rain. It's silly, I know. I've just seen it in so many movies that I wanted to try it myself, and I must say, I think those writers may be onto something here."

"It's a definite first for us," Luke said, a hesitation present in his voice. His mouth was so close to my ear that his words vibrated in my eardrum. "Elle?"

"Yes?"

"I reserved a room at a hotel for us to stay tonight. I just figured we'd be here late and neither of us would be up for the car ride back to Roanoke."

He wanted to say more—I could sense it—but he was clamming up again. With each passing minute, the rain was thoroughly soaking streaks down my blue dress, forming several small rivers, and my hair was rendered a sopping mess plastered to the side of my face and the back of my neck. Luke's hair and clothes had not fared any better. His blue shirt, one chosen to match my own attire, was blotchy from the rain.

"Good thinking." I held onto him tightly to affirm my grip, just as I had begun to feel my fingers slipping away when the rain began to compromise my grasp. Was this what all his nerves were about, sharing a bedroom? Something we've done numerous times before?

"Elle," Luke spoke again, almost too softly for me to hear.

"Hmm?"

"Speaking of firsts for us, I was hoping that maybe tonight could be the night."

2018

I awoke to a tickling sensation across my cheek. Like a crack in a windshield, it slowly spider-webbed, spreading out from its source. The sensation was so soft, so tender that I didn't want it to stop, and I kept my eyes closed in the hope of prolonging it. Because if I were to open them, the sensation would stop, as waking me up was his ultimate goal.

"I know you're awake, Sloan," he said, amused. "You can keep your eyes closed as long as you want, but the twitching corners of your lips give you away every time."

I opened my eyes to see Luke lying on his back, his head turned to the side, facing me. I'd slept through the night in the hospital bed; on my right side, no less, facing him. In the time I'd been with Eric, I hadn't been able to sleep face-to-face with him in our bed.

What would Eric think if he were to see me now? What should he think? He'd be right to be upset, to feel betrayed, and I would deserve whatever admonishments he launched at me. But as much as I knew I should be ashamed, as wrong as what I'd done was, I hadn't felt more at peace in a long time than I was right then.

"I was never known for my poker face," I replied, propping my head up with my hand.

"Now that's an understatement." Luke grabbed the bed's remote and pressed the button to raise the head of it upwards into a sitting position.

I adjusted myself next to him, concealing a yawn in the sleeve of my shirt. My watch slid down my wrist, dangling from it and reminding me for the thousandth time that I needed to have it re-sized. Eric had given it to me for Christmas two years ago. I remembered him getting a little irritated with me when I hadn't put it on right away. It wasn't because I hadn't liked it. I had. But just eyeballing it, I could tell it was going to be too loose, which would cause him even more distress that would somehow be my fault. Eventually that day, I'd humored him and put it on, pretending it was a perfect fit. Looking at it now, I saw that it was only a quarter after six in the morning. At least it was still too early for anyone to have dropped by to see the spectacle we must have made in Luke's hospital bed.

Luke grasped my arm just as I was positioning myself to get up out of bed. "Do you have to get up already?" By the tone of his voice, I sensed he was disappointed by the thought.

"I should probably clean myself up. I'm sure I look like something straight out of a Wes Craven film."

"You're far from *A Nightmare on Elm Street*." he answered, pulling me into his arms. For being otherwise an invalid, he was still as strong as I remembered.

"Ah," he groaned, sucking in air between his clenched teeth.

"What is it?" I pushed myself away from him, inspecting his body.

"My ribs." He exhaled and leaned back against the mattress. "They've healed well enough, but they're still tender from time to time."

"I'm so sorry," I exclaimed. "I should have been more careful."

"It's not your fault. I'm the one who pulled you, remember?"

"Still," I leaned back with him on the mattress, " I should have stopped you."

"Why do you do that?"

"Do what?'

"Blame yourself for things that are clearly not your fault."

"I don't know ... I've always done it. From an early age, my mom had me conditioned to believe that all the evils in her life were my fault. It just kind of stuck."

"How did I know your mother had something to do with this?"

"Well, she's d—" I caught myself right before I made the fatal error.

"Your mom's what?" Luke asked. He'd caught it, like I also knew he would.

"She's desperate, depressed, delusional, dreadful, take your pick."

"How about all of the above," he muttered. Gingerly, he put his arm around my shoulders. "Not to upset you, but we've been learning a little about diseases of the liver in class lately."

"What about them?"

Luke hesitated, possibly contemplating whether he should finish his thought. "One of the symptoms is jaundice. When we were out visiting your mom, I couldn't help but notice how yellow her complexion was. Maybe you should consider telling her to get her liver checked out."

You don't know the half of it.

"She won't listen to anyone who tells her to quit drinking, but I will mention it to her. Thank you."

I actually had mentioned it to her. Repeatedly. Over the course of several months, even. She never listened, not until the very end. When the pain had gotten so bad and her blackouts longer in duration. By then, it had been too late.

"I've told you this a million times before, and I'll tell you a million times more, you are the most amazing, talented, caring woman I've ever known. Life has thrown so much at you and you just keep on fighting. You're so incredible ..."

"I am not a superlative, Luke. I'm me. I'm Elle. I'm average. Just because I grew up under a shitty set of circumstances and didn't come out just as equally as shitty a person, doesn't make me any better than the rest of the world. I just have a much lower standard of comparison. There's nothing special about me. Trust me."

"Look at me," he said, his fingers lightly tracing my jawline. Listening to him, I turned my head to look at him, finding myself just as lost in the depths of his eyes as I'd been all those years before. "You, Ellen Rae Sloan, deserve every good thing that comes your way. You're smart, funny, kind-hearted, and even somewhat good looking."

I laughed, if only to keep the tears at bay. As Luke's fingers continued to caress the outline of my jaw, he smirked.

"I mean, you know, some people may even think you're beautiful, but that's just some people."

"The crazy ones."

"Oh certifiable, for sure." He leaned in closer to me. Unlike last time, instead of shirking away, I remained steadfast. "My point is that you deserve the world, Elle. Every good thing that comes your way, every opportunity is just a testament to how much you've worked your ass off—to how much you've overcome. And I promise you, if it's the last thing I do, I will make you believe that, too."

Before I could stop myself, before I could listen to my conscience screaming inside of my head, I closed the space between us, my lips finding his. His arms wrapped around me tightly. My hand found its way to his face, feeling every curve of his cheekbone. He opened his mouth ever so slightly, and I mine. With the touch of his skin against mine, I was transported back in time, recalling the chemistry Luke and I had shared as though it were yesterday. The memories that were fresh in his mind came flooding back into mine, so real, so vivid that I was almost able to forget the present and live in the past with him.

Almost.

I pulled myself away from him abruptly. My heart pounded inside of my chest; my head spun, bringing me back to the present and the harsh reality. The walls seemed to be closing in on me. I needed air and I needed it now.

"Elle?" Luke called my name just when my feet hit the floor. "Is something wrong?"

"No," I answered him, overcome by nausea as I crammed my bare feet into my shoes. "I'm okay, really. I just … I just need some air."

"Did I do something?" He seemed stunned, shaken even, by the prospect that he could have possibly have done something—anything to make me run away from him the way I was.

"No, no," I tried to reassure him. "You've done nothing wrong, Luke. It's me; it's all me."

Once out in the hall, dizziness overcame me, and I was only able to make it halfway across the wing before I all but collapsed against the window overlooking the courtyard. Tears cascaded down my cheeks. Every day I'd been here, my heart had broken little by little. Today it had finally shattered.

"Jesus, Elle, what happened?" I turned to see Hannah standing behind me. "Oh, shit, you're crying. Are you okay? Is-is Luke?"

"He's fine," I told her when it looked like she was ready to take off toward his room. "It's me who's not so great."

Her concern for Luke transferred itself onto me, as she leaned against the window.

"Do you want to talk about it?"

"He's the same Luke I remember, even better, if that's possible. And I thought I could handle this, that I could make amends for the past, but it's becoming too much."

Hannah reached inside of the pocket of her blue and green polka-dotted scrubs and handed me a tissue, which I took without even the slightest apprehension, even though I wondered why she had a single tissue stowed away inside the pocket of her pants.

"Things got a little out of hand this morning."

"You don't say," she replied, much to my surprise. She paused to look out the window, leaving me to briefly wonder how much she actually knew. "Making my rounds this morning, I saw you two together in Luke's bed. My first instinct was to wake you up."

"Why didn't you?"

"Because I knew what was happening was what Luke wanted. He seemed so at peace, so restful. It's probably the first restful sleep he's had since his accident. I didn't want to ruin it for him. So I stood and watched the two of you for a minute, smiling to myself. It was one of the sweetest things I've seen in quite some time around here."

"It shouldn't have happened, though. I let things go too far. It was up to me to stop it, but I didn't. I couldn't."

"You love him."

"Of course, I did. However, now I—"

"That wasn't a question, Elle."

CHAPTER TWELVE

2007

"I don't think I'll ever get warm again," I said, as we entered our room.

"I should have pulled you back inside the tent sooner." Luke closed the door behind us and then stuck the hotel's key card inside his wallet.

I'd caught a hint of the occasional shiver from him during our ride here and knew he was just as cold as I was. Although our clothes had dried substantially, they were still damp in spots, amplifying any and every draft that came our way.

"Wait a minute." I turned to Luke, wide-eyed. "I don't have any clothes."

"Yes, you do." Luke patted the duffle bag slung over his shoulder.

"You bought clothes for me?"

"Not exactly." He chuckled, setting the bag down on the floor next to the bed. "I had a little help from Mena."

My mouth dropped, unwilling to believe what I'd just heard. "You asked Mena to pack my clothes?"

"Yeah. I mean, I didn't want to just rummage through your things.

195

Being a woman and your best friend, I figured she'd know what to pack for you."

"I'm afraid to look," I lamented, opening the bag, my face crestfallen the second I saw the contents inside.

"Is it as bad as you thought it would be?"

"Did you actually see her pack anything in here?"

"No," he confessed. "I left the bag with her and went downstairs to grab a water out of the vending machine. By the time I returned, she had it packed."

"That was your second mistake. Your first one was asking Mena to pack the bag in the first place."

"Why? Oh shit, Sloan, please tell me there's something in the bag."

"Oh, there's something all right."

One by one, I pulled the half dozen towels Mena had packed out of the bag, until there was nothing left but a note at the bottom in her handwriting.

Don't come back with your virtue still intact.

"You have got to be kidding me," Luke said, flopping down on the bed, groaning. "I guess we're going to have to lay our clothes out to dry, but in the meantime ..."

"We'll just have to be naked," I finished his sentence.

We locked eyes with Luke looking away first. He was nervous. As was I, actually. And the purpose for us being here hadn't been broached since our dance in the rain. "I-I'm going to go to the bathroom to dry off some more."

Luke nodded. "Okay."

Taking care to close the door behind me, I sat down on the tub, my heart pounding so fiercely that I could feel it in my throat.

You've done this before. What the hell is wrong with you?

It's Luke. You haven't done it with Luke before, that's what's wrong.

It's his first time. He's going to remember this night for the rest of his life.

196

No pressure.

"Ah," I groaned, burying my head in my hands.

I sat balanced on the side of the tub with both legs outstretched in front of me, the left crossed over the right. It felt like I was a breath away from having a panic attack, which reminded me of Luke and the way he carried himself at the wedding. He was just as nervous then as I was now, to the point it had paralyzed him.

Get your shit together, Elle.

Heart pounding, I stood up and unzipped the back of my dress, watching as it slid down my body and landed on the floor. The blue fabric pooled at my feet like a puddle. As I stripped my undergarments away from my body, I wondered whether Luke was still fully clothed. Most of all, I wondered what he was thinking; what he expected of me when I emerged from the bathroom. Now completely naked, I picked up one of the neatly-folded white hotel towels from a rack above the toilet and commenced towel-drying my hair.

Still damp, my hair had begun to dry in waves, framing my otherwise terrified face. After drying it the best that I could, I wrapped the towel around my body. Thankfully, it was especially oversized and I was able to wrap it completely around me without a hint of skin showing on either side of my body.

Thanks to Mena, I had nothing—not even a tooth or hairbrush to ready myself for the night, let alone a shaver. What I wouldn't give to run a razor over my legs at least one more time today. Of course, Mena had known exactly what she was doing all along, making getting me laid a personal mission.

Hand trembling, I opened the door and stepped out into the room. At first I didn't see him, and I would have thought the room deserted if not for the duffel bag of towels on the bed and Luke's button down shirt on the floor nearby. Further inspection revealed his shoes neatly tucked underneath a small table next to the bed. A lump weighed heavily in my throat as I searched the floor for the rest of his clothing, ultimately coming up short. And as my cursory search of the room was coming to an end, I was startled by the grating sound of the sliding door to the balcony being opened. I looked up to see Luke entering the room, still wearing his khaki pants, but nothing else.

He hadn't been paying attention at first, and I went completely unnoticed by him until after he stepped into the room and slid the door closed behind him. He made a move to step forward, stopping dead in his tracks when he noticed me standing in front of the bed, clad in nothing but the towel.

"This is the best I could do because, you know, Mena."

"God bless, Mena," he proclaimed.

He strode to me with such confidence in his step that it made me second guess my original thinking, that he'd been a bundle of nerves all along. That thought, however, was laid to rest when he stopped several steps short of me, like he was afraid I'd shatter if he were to come any closer. He'd never shied away from touching me before.

"Nervous?" I asked, trying to get an idea of what was going on inside of his head.

He nodded before he could get the words out. "Terrified is more like it."

"We don't have to do this. It's okay if you don't want to," I said, despite the devil on my shoulder telling me to shut up.

"Elle." He took a step closer to me. "I want nothing more than this ... than to be with you in every conceivable way possible. When we were dancing and I watched the rain falling down your neck, only to disappear down your body and into your dress, it was all I could do to contain myself from ripping your clothes off and taking you right there."

"If anything, that would have made one hell of a story for the bride and groom to tell their grandchildren."

Luke smiled. I took that as my cue to take a step toward him.

"I may not be any good at this," he said, grimacing, as if admitting to it had caused him actual physical pain.

"Is that why you're so nervous, because you're afraid I won't enjoy myself?"

"Of course," he replied, like the fact should have already been apparent to me. "You've done this before and I haven't. As crazy as it may sound, there's a very small part of me that worries you'll be comparing me to him the entire time."

"Luke." I made the final move, closing the distance between us entirely. My hand found its way to his face, where it rested, my fingers lightly caressing the stubble that had appeared along his jawline. "For starters, I've only been with one person, and he was miserable, as you well know. So much so that sex was the last thing I wanted for quite some time. You're making it sound like I'm a pro at this when I'm just as petrified as you are."

"But that night at my parents' house, you were so sure of yourself. There was no hesitation."

"Because I love you, Luke. I loved you then and I love you even more now. I wasn't as nervous then because my heart was just becoming invested in our relationship. Before you, I didn't realize how special sex could be, or even how special it should be. And I'm scared shitless now because every ounce of me wants to be perfect for you. I'm worried that I'll let you down."

"Oh, Sloan." He placed his hand on top of mine, which rested on his face. "I can't fathom there ever being anything you could do to let me down."

"Even if I were to tell you that I think *Star Trek* is better than *Star Wars*?"

"Okay, well maybe you found the one thing you could do."

I laughed. "I love you so much, Hutchins."

"I love you, too, Sloan. So very much."

He moved his hand to my face, where he traced my lips with his fingers. "Are you cold?"

"No," I answered.

"You're trembling."

"I think I'll be okay." Unable to hold back any longer, I kissed him, harder and with less restraint than ever before, expecting him to pull away from me, preferring a more conservative approach. But instead, he met my passion with even more fervor of his own, showing me just how much he had been holding back himself. As difficult as waiting for this moment had been for me, it had been ten times harder for him.

My towel slipped down the length of my body and fell to the floor, joining Luke's shirt. With one arm already around me, Luke groaned when he felt my bare skin in his hands, instead of the cotton fabric. He pressed his body closer to mine, his bare chest against my own, our lips still firmly together. After spending the last several months conducting restraint, he was allowing every desire he'd had to come forth, feeling the length of my body as far as his hands would allow him.

I unfastened the button of his khakis and let them fall to the floor, much the same way my towel had done. There then remained only a thin layer of fabric separating us from what we both wanted. Luke parted his lips from mine long enough to guide me to the bed. Gently, he lowered me down onto the mattress with him, until I was resting with my back to the comforter and him hovering over me.

He brushed his nose against my forehead, placing feather-light kisses down the bridge of my nose and face, stopping when he reached my neck. I felt him move then, knowing that he was removing his boxer briefs. Both of us now completely naked, I parted my legs as Luke lowered himself down on top of me.

"It's not too late to back out now, Hutchins," I said, running my hand through the thick waves of his golden hair.

"I'm never going to back out with you, not now, not ever."

"I think I just may take you up on that."

In a moment, so rhythmic it felt like the very definition of poetry in motion, Luke entered me, shuddering ever so subtly as our bodies came together. He rested himself on top of me then, taking care not to put the full weight of his body on my own, as his warm breaths cascaded down my breasts. My own breathing growing just as heavy, I kissed his forehead, knowing that no matter what happened next, nothing would ever be as pivotal for us as this moment.

We moved together as though performing a dance routine, one that we had choreographed and spent months preparing for, our bodies remaining in sync, reaching their climax together as one.

2018

I'd been avoiding Luke since morning, making one excuse after another for my absence in his room. As far as he knew, I was under the weather, which wasn't entirely untrue. Since our kiss, my stomach had been in knots and my conscience was stomping around in my head so much it was causing a migraine. Every so often, it would allow pictures of Eric to filter through my head, further compounding matters, as if I didn't already feel badly enough.

I didn't know how I was going to explain what just happened to Eric. There really was no explaining it. What had happened had happened. He'd trusted me when it was obvious he shouldn't have. I was much weaker than I thought I was.

Was it weakness, though?

I closed my eyes, letting the rays of the sun warm my back. Clouds resembling giant cotton balls proliferated the sky, allowing for more and more intermittent breaks for the sun to peek through. Each time it disappeared again, I shivered. Despite it being an overall unseasonably warm March day, the disappearance of the sun was noticeable, even through my thick cable knit sweater.

"Didn't get much sleep last night?"

I opened my eyes to see Candy walking through the arch in the direction of the picnic table where I sat. The bags under her eyes told me she hadn't slept well herself.

"Actually, I slept better than I thought I was going to."

"Really? You must have a butt made of steel to have been able to withstand that recliner and actually find it comfortable enough to have gotten a decent night's sleep."

I didn't know how much she knew, whether Luke had said something or, perhaps, Hannah. Knowing Luke, it wasn't him. As close as he was to his parents, what went on or didn't go on between us behind closed doors would never have been up for discussion. Not to mention, there was nothing about the way Candy spoke to me that led me to believe she knew anything at all.

"Luke tells me you've been sick."

"I'm not feeling great, but it's not virus related."

Candy raised her eyebrow. She always did that when hearing something unexpected. Like me, a poker face she had not. "Was it something Luke did?"

"No," I answered, practically cutting her off before she could finish. "It was all me."

Now that I'd said this much, I figured I may as well finish it off. It would all come out sooner or later. It was better that it came from me, so she knew I hadn't been trying to hide anything.

"I slept in Luke's bed last night."

There goes the eyebrow again.

"I know it was crossing a line, but it wasn't intentional. After he fell asleep, I meant to sneak out of the bed and crawl back into the recliner, but I fell asleep, too. And the next thing I knew, it was morning."

"That would account for the rainbows and sunshine mood he was in this morning."

She tucked a stray strand of hair back behind her ear. I expected her to sound a little more relieved by the situation than than she did.

"There's more."

Candy perked up, sitting up and straightening her small frame to its full height. I noticed that, this time, her eyebrow remained firmly in place. Had she been expecting this?

"There's no easy way to say this, no way that I can justify it without making it seem like I was trying to make some kind of an excuse." I looked up at her, believing that no one had ever captivated her attention more than I had right then. "I'm not sick. I've been avoiding

202

seeing Luke because we shared a moment this morning that went so far over the line it's in another area code."

"Oh?"

"I kissed him, Candy. It was so sudden and spur of the moment, almost like I had been transported back in time right with him."

She stared at me, silent. So silent that I thought for a brief second that she may be having a stroke.

"I'm so sorry. If you want me to leave now, I'll completely understand. I know that my being here has been trying for you, that you're just tolerating me as it is."

"Tolerating you?" Candy asked, confused.

"Monroe told me that you didn't want me here, and it was all his idea to have me come. I can't say as I blame you. I'm sure you must hate me. You're justified in doing so, but please believe me when I tell you that I never meant to hurt Luke, or any of you. Not now, not ten years ago."

Candy's lips turned upward at the corners ever so slightly. She wanted to smile, perhaps even embrace what I just said as the truth and nothing but, yet I sensed reservation from her, like she was eyeing a stove, unsure of whether or not to touch it for fear of being burned again.

"While it's true that I was a bit hesitant to reach out to you, it's not anywhere close to being accurate to state that I'm merely tolerating you."

To my surprise, she reached across the table and rested her hand on my own.

"After you and Luke broke up, it wasn't only him who was devastated. We all were. Tom and I, we felt like we'd lost a daughter. So when Monroe located you online, we were hesitant to call you. We both thought we would be intruding on your life, and that you would tell us you weren't interested, thereby rejecting Luke again. Then there was a part of us that was afraid you would accept our cry for help."

"Why?"

"We didn't want to fall in love with you all over again, only to lose you."

"Oh, Candy." I wiped the corners of my eyes with the sleeve of my free arm. "I always thought of you as the mother I never really had. Since coming back here, I've come to realize just how badly the breakup really affected me. I've missed all of you so very much. It wasn't only Luke I'd been in love with, it was all of you, too."

Candy took her hand away from mine just long enough to reach inside of her purse and pull out a tissue, promptly dabbing her eyes in a much classier fashion than I had done.

"So," she said after balling up the used tissue and sticking it in the front pocket of her purse, "given what happened this morning, are you thinking you want to go back home?"

I shook my head. "No, I want to stay and be here when Luke finds out. That is, if you'll have me."

Candy squeezed my hand, her eyes lighting up the same way they always used to do when she was excited. "There's nothing I would want more."

2007

"I'm beginning to think you enjoy kidnapping me, Hutchins."

"If you get into the car willingly, it's not kidnapping, Sloan." He playfully rolled his eyes.

"Have you changed your major to pre-law without telling me?"

"Would you like me to let you out?" he asked, slowing the car down ever so slightly.

"My curiosity is piqued now, so you may as well carry on." I gazed out the window, noticing that he had turned down the familiar street leading to the heart of town. Wherever we were going, it was most likely a place we had been to before. I searched my head for clues, any clue that would point me to our potential destination.

And then it came to me as sure as the date on the calendar.

"The coffee shop," I blurted out. "That's where we're going."

"Congratulations," he said, a little too surprised for my liking.

"Where else would I take you on our anniversary? Bermuda? Paris? Venice? None of those places have anything on our Main Street coffee shop."

"Our anniversary?" I'd never been one for sentimentality, neither had Luke, or so I thought. Our first, sixth, and ten month anniversaries sailed by with barely an acknowledgement by either of us, but it had been my intent to acknowledge our one year anniversary, even going so far as to buy him tickets to a local indie rock band he swore would be the next big thing. I was going to give them to him on Saturday, the anniversary of our first date. It simply hadn't occurred to me that he would consider the day we first met as being that hallmark date.

"You didn't remember what today was?"

"Of course I remember what today is. It's the date we first met. I was just planning on celebrating with you Saturday on, you know, the anniversary of our first date."

"What can I say, Sloan, I don't half-ass anything."

"Nope, you throw your whole ass into it, that's for sure."

Luke angled the car into a parking spot in the lot in the back of the shop, near the same light pole we stood by the evening we'd met and Mena made the plans for our first date. As usual, the shop was packed with students, their faces illuminated by the screens to which they were glued. I'd wager that ninety percent of them hadn't even noticed our entrance, being too preoccupied with the paper they were working on.

We skirted carefully around the tables full of our attentive peers. Near the back, and only after fervent searching on our part, did we locate a table that had been recently vacated—as evidenced by abandoned coffee mugs and wadded up napkins. Ever the gentleman, Luke pulled a chair out for me before dutifully moving the mugs to the outer edge of the table, tucking the wadded napkins into them.

"I see some things never change," he observed sarcastically.

"It's a good thing, too," I stated, catching him off guard. "Because if this place wasn't the hell hole dive that it is and it was some swanky, hipster, overpriced coffee mecca, we probably would never have met."

"I'll drink to that," Luke said with a smile. "If I had a drink, of course."

"You will, in about half an hour or so." I caught sight of the haggard waitress, the only one on duty tonight, as she frantically made her way to each table.

"That's all right. No one comes here for the coffee, anyway."

He was right. Although the barista put forth a valiant effort, the coffee here always had a hint of day-old gym sock mixed in with its mocha espresso and caramel latte flavoring. A price to pay for the affordable price of the drinks themselves.

"While we may have to wait for our coffees, I can't wait any longer for this."

I looked up to see Luke remove a sizable square box from his coat pocket.

"A gift? You got me a gift for our unanniversary?"

"It's not much. Seriously, don't expect anything on our actual anniversary. Except my hot body, of course."

"And while we're on that topic, may I suggest going to your place on the night of our actual anniversary, lest you want to be subjected to Mena serenading us from the hallway with an impromptu poetry jam session again."

Luke blushed, remembering the day Mena came back to the dorm early from class, having the presence of mind to at least knock on the door before entering.

"I'm still impressed by how many phrases she was able to rhyme with penis. She has talent. It's unfortunate she doesn't have any interest in creative writing. She'd be perfect for satire."

"You're stalling," Luke remarked, still holding the box in his hand.

"Luke, I don't have anything to give to you until Saturday."

"You know I don't care about that. Since when have I ever cared?"

Never. Luke had never asked for a single thing from me in return for his love and acceptance. Much like death and taxes, I knew that would always be an absolute certainty in my life.

"Okay," I sighed, accepting the smooth, white box, "you win. It's not much and you promise you didn't spend much?"

"I'm not promising anything," he said with a sly smile.

"The truth comes out." I eyed him suspiciously as I untied the red ribbon that held the box closed. From the shape of it, I'd already guessed that it was some type of jewelry, and sincerely hoped that it hadn't set him back much and that the extra hours he'd been picking up at the hospital recently weren't to help pay for something for me. Yet, I couldn't help but feel my heart skip a beat as I saw the expression on his face, so full of anticipation, anxious for me to see what was inside. It was important to him that I like his gift.

I gasped as I removed the lid, revealing the sterling silver cuff bracelet inside. The lights reflected off its smooth, polished exterior, creating a kaleidoscope of color.

"Not much, eh?" I asked, instantly wishing I had something more than tickets to give to him.

"There's more," he said, obviously pleased with himself.

"More? You got me something else? Seriously, Luke, I didn't—"

"No, there's nothing else in addition to the bracelet," he interceded. "Read the bracelet."

Confused, I removed the cuff from the box and turned it over, noticing right away that it was engraved:

And though she may be broken, she is not defeated.
She will rise, unfettered, unbeaten, unimpeded.

"This is from my poem," I gasped in disbelief.

"It's one of my favorite lines." Luke spoke cautiously, as though for the first time, he was beginning to think that maybe it would upset me that he had used my work without my permission. "I actually can't think of a more fitting description of you."

"I … I don't know what to say." I was struggling to hold back tears out of fear they may wash away the words staring back at me. "I never thought I'd see anything I'd written displayed anywhere but in the pages of my notebook."

I remembered the morning I awoke hungover after my birthday, catching Luke reading through my notebook. That had been six months ago. Six months and he still had my poem—or at least part of it—memorized.

"You have no idea how talented you are, how inspiring your own story is. I just wanted to give you something to remind you of that when your mind begins to wander and you find yourself believing the dark seeds of doubt that become so easily implanted in our minds during our darkest hours. Most of all, I want you to know that I believe in you, now and forever. You are going to be great, Elle. No matter what you do, I know you'll be a success."

CHAPTER THIRTEEN

2018

I still had that bracelet. It was safely tucked away in a velvet pouch in the jewelry box on my vanity back home. I'd taken it out only a handful of times over the last decade. Seeing it each time had been painful, though the pain had lessened in small increments, dulling to the point where I could see the engraved words I'd written so many years ago without tearing up. It was progress, I suppose. Eric saw the bracelet once. It, along with half my earrings, fell out of the box and onto the floor when we were moving into our house. I remembered feeling a sharp tightening in my stomach seeing him picking it up from the ground, believing that he'd have an abundance of very awkward questions about why I still possessed a piece of jewelry given to me by an ex-boyfriend. To my amazement, all he did was turn the cuff over in his hands, read the inscription, and muttered something about how generic and uninspiring the script was before he tossed it back inside the box.

It was memories such as those that visited me today in the quiet solitude of Luke's room, as I watched him lay sleeping in his bed. I wondered why he hadn't asked me about the bracelet since I'd been here. I'd worn it every day after he'd given it to me, only missing a day here and there when I'd misplaced it. Surely, Luke would have remembered the bracelet. Perhaps he was afraid to ask about it out of fear that I'd lost it. Maybe—

"It's not real, this isn't real," Luke moaned.

His sleep had grown fitful, his frustration evident, as he attempted to move his legs but couldn't.

"That never happened." He came close to shouting this time, forcing me to make the quick decision to wake him.

"Luke." I shook him lightly at first, my touch becoming more firm when that failed to rouse him. "You're having a nightmare."

"What?"

He awoke, sitting bolt upright, almost striking me in the jaw in the process. He was breathing heavily, and it was clear that he had no idea where he was at until his eyes found me.

"Elle," he said, throwing his arms around me, holding me tightly to his chest. "Yes, it was a nightmare. A horrible, horrible nightmare."

"It's okay now," I murmured, holding his head in my hands. "Whatever it was, it's over. You're okay."

"And you're here. We're here together, never to be apart again."

"What exactly did you dream?" I'd withdrawn from his embrace with an idea as to what that may have been already forming in my head.

"You were gone." He laid back down in the bed. "And you had been for quite some time. I asked where you were. Everyone told me that we'd broken up—that we had been for a while. It were as though time was put on fast forward, and I was living in a world that I didn't understand, one that I never want to return to again. If that's the way the world is going to be, if that's my future, I want time to stand still. Elle, I don't want to lose you, not in my dreams, not ever."

"Luke, I—" Out of the corner of my eye, I saw a form entering the room, catching my attention. Candy smiled apologetically, like she was sorry for having interrupted this moment. Right behind her, another figure entered. Dr. Reid. I stood up from Luke's hospital bed, as he approached Luke's side.

"I heard—as well as the rest of the floor—that you had a nightmare. Would you mind telling me about it?"

I stood next to Candy, listening to Luke recount his dream in further detail in response to Dr. Reid's questioning. The more he spoke, the more I realized that his nightmare hadn't been a nightmare, after all. It had been a memory. The concern on Candy's face only confirmed that notion.

"That certainly is an interesting dream," Dr. Reid announced. "Extremely detailed."

"This isn't going to extend my stay here, is it?" Luke asked, panicked.

"On the contrary. If anything, it makes your discharge all but assured," Dr. Reid announced. His smile took up the majority of his face. Uncharacteristic of him, I assumed. "In fact, I'm going to talk to Candy about your impending departure. I'll be back later to check on you."

"Sounds outstanding, Doc." Luke seemed relieved, even excited.

I watched as Dr. Reid left the room with Candy, torn between following them and staying with Luke.

"Hear that, Sloan, they're going to be springing me from this joint soon."

"That's what they say. It's great, Luke, really. I'm so happy and grateful for your recovery and the progress you've made. The fact that you're still alive is just such a miracle."

"Then why are you crying?"

I hadn't realized I was doing it, until he pointed it out to me. "I'm just so ... so excited for you." With the back of my hand, I wiped away tears from both cheeks. He saw right through me, I know he did.

"For us," Luke corrected me. "You're excited for us."

I nodded. "Of course, that's what I meant."

Anxious, I tried to smile naturally, but I knew it probably looked just as forced as it actually was. My place was with Candy and Dr. Reid, finding out everything Dr. Reid knew.

"As much as I want to celebrate this news with you, do you mind if I go out and listen to what Dr. Reid has to say? Your mom has a lot going on, and I want to make sure I'm there for a second set of ears in case she has questions later."

"No, of course I don't mind. That's very thoughtful of you. I'm sure Mom would appreciate it, too."

I nodded, only beginning to take a step toward the door when Luke called out to me.

"Elle?"

"Yes?"

"See you later?"

I smiled, remembering our past exchanges. "See you later."

"This is a real breakthrough, Candy." I heard Dr. Reid declare when I approached him and Candy in the hallway. "That wasn't a dream, that was a flashback of sorts. He's remembering. This is astounding. It means he may begin to remember other details about his life."

"I know," Candy said. "It's wonderful, Gene. Everything we could have hoped for."

"So what is it, then? You're not exactly jumping for joy."

"Is there a chance he could remember everything before we all get the chance to tell him tomorrow?"

"That's highly unlikely," Dr. Reid confirmed. "I suspect what memories do come back will do so in bits and pieces like they did this morning. He'll begin to piece things together slowly. With any luck, it will eventually be enough to bring him back to the present."

I put my arm around Candy's shoulders, sensing her need for support. Her relief evident, I wasn't prepared to take on supporting her entire body—or so it felt. Candy was strong, but even the strongest of buildings can crack with the right amount of force. As much as she'd been through, it was amazing that she had been able to withstand everything so far.

"And you, Ms Sloan." Dr. Reid turned his attention to me. "I'm not saying that your presence did or didn't bring about this unexpected turn of events. Maybe it's a coincidence that he began having memories now, maybe it's not. But if anything, your being here has helped calm Luke, allowing him to heal. With that being the case, it would appear your work here will soon be over, and you can return home back to your own life soon."

"It would appear so," I replied. Next to me, I felt Candy's weight shift. She was now holding me up.

"Don't look so happy, you two. Cheer up, it's time to celebrate. This is the best possible scenario."

"We know," Candy answered. "We're just so shocked and overwhelmed that we don't know what to say."

"Then I suggest you think about it tonight, because Luke is being discharged in two days."

Candy and I watched Dr. Reid walk down the hall, both of us collapsing to the floor when we saw him round a corner and disappear out of sight. In silence, we sat, each of us processing what the events of today would mean. Dr. Reid was right. This was the best case scenario, but it came with a steep price. One that would be paid tomorrow by the both of us.

2008

By the time I'd reached the fourth page of my essay on Ayn Rand, my pencil lead had been worn down to a shadow of its former self. It had been rendered so dull that the words on the page had turned from having bold, sharp edges to becoming more bloated in nature. Such was the life of a creative writing student with a professor who rejected most modern technology. Only six more pages to go.

The library was relatively empty, literally quiet enough that you could hear a pin drop. So when my cell phone vibrated on the table, it created quite a the commotion, garnering irritated glances in my direction. Quickly, I retrieved the device and glanced at the number on the screen. A 317 area code. That was the area code in Indianapolis. With a sigh, I rejected the call, figuring that it was probably a telemarketer or a wrong number.

Now back to my paper. Dammit, where was I?

Right as I was about to catch up to my brain and hop aboard my train of thought, the vibration once again rocked my table, this time drawing sighs from a few others seated at the tables next to mine. With an apologetic grin, I hurriedly tucked my paper, pencil, and my excessively earmarked and highlighted copy of *The Fountainhead* inside of my bag and power-walked out the door, just in time to catch the call on the last ring.

"Yes," I answered, annoyed.

"Is this Ellen Sloan," an equally as unpleasant female voice replied at the other end.

"It is. Who is this?"

"My name is Tiffany. I'm a nurse at the Indianapolis Metropolitan Hospital. We're calling because you're listed as the emergency contact for your mother. Ma'am, she's very ill …"

* * * * *

Liver failure. I couldn't say that I was shocked with the diagnosis. I'd half expected it, actually. Especially after observations Luke made a few months prior, all of which my mother brushed off. After all, he was a nurse, not a doctor. Doogie Howser wannabe she'd slurred right before I'd hung up the phone. Besides, she was still young. She'd have years before her body enacted its revenge on her for the way she'd treated it.

Such were the lies we tell ourselves to cope with reality.

Luke teetered between supportive and concerned for my well-being—notably not my mother's—and then ventured somewhere in the realm of irritated that I hadn't called him before I'd left. I'd reminded him of the disaster that ensued during our last visit, which for the moment, made him back down in that respect. Regardless, I could sense his disappointment in me when we spoke. The fact that I had left without saying a word hadn't set well with him.

It had been several years since I'd been to Indianapolis. The last time I was here, was when I went prom dress shopping with a few high school friends. I always appreciated larger cities. The more people around you, the less you stood out; the more privacy you had. In that way, I was like my mother. Just existing and unremarkable in every way.

"Excuse me," I said to the receptionist at the front desk, "Could you tell me what room Betsy Sloan is in?"

With her eyes still glued to the screen in front of her, the redheaded woman couldn't be bothered to even acknowledge my existence. Kind of like my mother.

"I'm Ellen Sloan," I said as though it mattered. "Her daughter."

"Room 413," she answered, seemingly bored. If need be, she couldn't have picked me out of a lineup.

"Have good day," I called back to her, as I attempted to navigate myself around the hospital. I wasn't going to bother asking her for directions. Room 413—the fourth floor. That should be easy enough.

When the elevator opened to the fourth floor, it revealed the first break I'd gotten that day. Directly across the hall was room 410, three doors to the right, was 413. I should have been upset, drying tears from my eyes before I entered the room. But my tear ducts were bone dry and I wasn't sad, I was angry. Angry that once again, my mother wasn't the mother she should have been. Angry because this disease could have been completely preventable, if not for her demons. But she chose not to care about me, about herself, about anyone, and it was up to me to pick up her pieces.

"Took you long enough." My mother's voice startled me when I entered the room. From the nurse's description of how sick she was, I hadn't expected her to be as awake and as relatively alert as she was.

215

"Really?" I asked, the bottle holding in my anger suddenly becoming uncorked. "You're joking with me right now? I just drove seven hours to get here. I'm missing class, and for what? God, Mom, they made it sound like you were dying on the phone."

"I am dying, Ellie."

I was standing, but I couldn't feel my legs anymore. In fact, I actually had to look down to make sure they were even still attached to my body. Speechless, I searched her face for some sign that she was making some kind of sick joke, but there wasn't one there. She was serious, a first for my mother.

"No," I said, "you're too young. You … you can't be dying."

"That's what I said, but those damn doctors disagreed with me. They say my liver's shot. Pretty soon, my other organs will begin to shut down, too."

"Pretty soon? Like what, a year, two years?"

"Weeks, months, they aren't sure; but years, that wasn't mentioned."

I attempted to walk to the corner of the room, where a chair sat next to my mother's bed, but couldn't quite get there. Instead, I collapsed onto the foot of her bed.

"A liver transplant," I blurted out the moment the thought crossed my mind. "Why can't they do a liver transplant? Take out the bad liver, insert a new one. Boom, problem solved, right?"

"All right, Ellen Sloan, M.D., cool your jets. You've been talking to your nurse boyfriend too much. It doesn't work that way."

"And why doesn't it?" I asked, ignoring her slight at Luke. "Transplants take place all the time. They save lives every day."

"Not mine they won't. Given my history, my doctor said I probably wouldn't be considered a viable candidate, not to mention they don't exactly have a warehouse full of livers awaiting a warm body. There's a list where patients can wait months, even years before they reach the top and become next in line to receive a transplant. Right now, I'm at the very bottom of said list, and as I just told you, I don't have months, let alone years."

"So what now? What kind of treatments are they going to do for you?"

"They're not."

"Excuse me?"

"I'm going to be discharged from here. I'll be sent home with hospice care, where eventually, I'll die."

I shook my head in disbelief. My ears had taken in everything she'd just said, but my brain was having one hell of a time trying to process it all. My mother was going to die, and she was going to die soon. It was a punch in the gut I hadn't been expecting. Despite her having been a shit parental figure, I was still a part of her. And in her own messed up way, she had tried. Granted, she could have tried harder, but she still had tried.

"Ellen," my mother spoke my name softly. I turned to look at her, noticing her eyes were glassy, further blowing my mind. My mother was crying. I'd assumed I'd see the Apocalypse before I'd ever see her shed a single, sincere tear, yet here we were. "I really don't want to die alone."

"What are you saying?"

"Move back to Jasper."

Stunned to say the least, all I could do was stare, speechless. If I would have had to guess how this visit was going to go, this scenario wouldn't have even approached my radar.

"You may want to close your mouth before something flies in there, Ellie."

I shook my head, hoping it would magically bring about some form of clarity, or that an answer would pop up inside of my brain like a Magic 8 Ball. No such luck.

"Do you have any idea what you're asking me to do?" I asked. "I have a life at Cogsworth. I'm pursuing a degree, building my future."

"An English degree," my mom scoffed. "Do you have any idea what you're going to do with that degree once you graduate? Any jobs lined up? A book deal, perhaps?"

"I know how you feel about the degree, Mom, and I'm not going to get into it with you right now."

"I'm just looking out for you. Do you know how many people actually make it as writers? It's a hard profession to break into, and unless—"

"Unless I have talent. Is that what you're trying to say, that I'm not good enough to make it?" The fumes left behind by my mother's harsh words to me from my childhood ignited once more.

"No," she said, stopping me in the midst of saying exactly what I should have said years ago. "I worry about you, Elle. You have no idea what you really want to do, no direction. You don't want to be an editor, you don't want to be a librarian or a journalist, you have no desire to one day teach English. All you want to do is be a writer, and it's great to have those kinds of dreams and goals, but you're an adult now and you need to be realistic. I know it's hard for you to believe, but I do want what's best for you."

"You've had a funny way of showing it."

"I know, believe me, I know. And I know you're going to need some time to think about my request, but I at least wanted to give you something to think about. There's no telling how much time I have left, but I know it isn't going to be long. And as much as I may deserve it, I can't stop myself from thinking about how much I don't want to die alone or spend my final days being taken care of by strangers at hospice when I could spend them with my daughter."

"Thinking about it is exactly what I need to do," I said, dizzy from all the possibilities swirling around inside of my head. "It may make me sound selfish, but I have a lot to lose now. I have friends who care about me and Luke."

"About Luke …"

"Oh, Mother, don't even start on Luke. Just because you two didn't exactly hit it off, doesn't make him a loser, or—"

"He's too good for you."

"I'm sorry?" I asked in disbelief.

"Luke is driven. He knows exactly what he wants and pursues it to the fullest extent. He needs someone equally as driven. That's not you, Elle. You're a free spirit, like me. Luke, he may seem great now, but the honeymoon period won't last forever. When it fades, you'll realize that you're not good for each other. He'll want one thing, you'll want another. If he wins, you'll be miserable, hiding in his shadow as you struggle to accomplish something that will make you feel like you deserve him. And if you win ... well, you'll ruin him. You're oil and water, two beings from different sides of the tracks."

"I can't do this." I stood up from the bed.

"Elle," she called after me. "Please, I don't mean to hurt you."

"Seriously, Mother? Did you hear what you just said to me? Can't you even comprehend your own words?"

"I need you, please," she pleaded. "I don't want to be alone, not now."

"I'll think about it. After all, I wouldn't want to ruin you, too, now would I?"

* * * * *

"So when is she punching on out of here?" Mena asked me, her attention having turned away from her laptop and redirected to me as soon as I returned to our dorm.

"Would it seriously kill you to show an ounce of decorum? She's my mother and she's dying."

"O-kay," she said, drawing out the first syllable. "When is that lovely woman who put forth a piss poor effort at raising you slated to kick the bucket?"

"I suppose that's a slight improvement." I opened my suitcase, pulled out my dirty clothes, and stuffed them inside of my laundry bag. "The answer is I don't know, but soon—very soon, from the sound of it."

"Hmm ... I guess it's not only the good who die young."

"Mena!"

"Okay, okay. I'm sorry." She adjusted herself so that she was sitting Indian-style in her chair, a sign that I had her undivided attention. Whether I wanted it or not. "It's just, considering all you've told me, I honestly didn't believe you would be as sentimental as you are."

"I'm not sentimental. I have compassion. There's a difference." With sigh, I threw my bag onto the floor and flopped down on my bed. The drive from Jasper to Roanoke was exhausting, no matter how many times I made it. "She's different, more reflective."

"You mean she's sober."

Becoming exasperated, I raised my eyebrow at Mena, hoping she would understand I wasn't in the mood. "She's never admitted she was anything less than the perfect mother. Since her hospitalization, I believe she's had to face the naked truth. There was guilt in her eyes. Honest to god guilt. And then, there were hints of the mother I've always known, like she can't apologize to me without also completely deflating me at the same time."

"What did she say to you?"

I didn't want to tell Mena what my mother had said about Luke. It would only infuriate her as it had me. Mena's fury was something I didn't want to deal with right now. Not while I was busy reconciling my own feelings.

"She wants me to drop out of school and move back home to take care of her."

"Is she smoking crack now, too?" Mena quipped, letting out an exasperated laugh. "Did you tell her that perhaps if she hadn't been such a shit mother that maybe you would've considered her request, or better yet, maybe that only a shit mother would make such a request from their child to begin with?"

Saying nothing, all I could do was stare down at my comforter and count the stitches around the quilted square in my line of sight.

"No. Ellen, for fuck's sake, you are not honestly considering her request?" Mena sputtered, like my mom's old Taurus used to do when it was on the verge of a breakdown. For the first and only time since I'd known her, she was flabbergasted, agitated to the core.

"I don't know yet."

"What do you mean you don't know yet?" No longer in a sitting position, Mena had jumped out of her chair and was pacing the floor. "How can you possibly not know? What is there to think about? She's asking you to flush your entire future down the toilet. A future you created despite her stellar influence."

"You think I don't already know that? Why do you think I came back? I didn't exactly jump at the opportunity."

"Yet you haven't completely disregarded her request, either." Mena scowled.

"She's my mother, Mena, and I can't very well allow her to die alone."

"So return to Jasper periodically."

"She's going to need around the clock care, which she wants provided by me and not a stranger. Honestly, I can't say as I blame her."

"You're right." Mena had paused her pacing long enough to face me. "I don't blame your mother. She's a crap human and always has been. Nothing new there. I blame you for enabling her; for allowing her to still get inside of your head."

"Oh, it's my fault?" My blood had reached it's boiling point, restraint was becoming harder and harder to maintain. "You know what, Mena? Why don't you remove that silver spoon from your mouth and take a moment to look around and realize that not everyone has the same opportunities as you. Some of us have to make the tough decisions in life."

"Since when did you become such a pious bitch?" Behind the angry mask she was wearing, I could see the pain in Mena's eyes. It hurt her to say that to me, despite feeling as though she needed to, given that I'd so obviously hurt her, too. "Fine. Leave, then. Just don't expect me to ever accept your decision, and don't even try to come crying to me when you regret it."

"I can't regret a decision I haven't made yet."

"But you have made that decision, Elle. I see it in your eyes. Don't even try to deny it."

Defeated, Mena walked out of our dorm, slamming the door shut behind her. After she left, I stared at the door for several minutes, waiting for her to come through it again. When that happened, I'd allow her to yell expletives at me, tell me how irresponsible I was being, chide me for a decision I honestly hadn't yet made, and then we'd hug each other, make up, and realize that this wouldn't be the end of the world for our friendship.

That wasn't what happened.

Mena never came through that door again that night. Where she went, I never did find out, nor did I ask her later for of fear of dredging up the past, invariably unearthing the hard feelings that were created between the two of us that night.

Instead, in our room, I sat alone, thinking. In hindsight, I suppose that was the best thing Mena could have done for me, leaving and not coming back. She was giving me time to reflect upon my choices. And she ended up being right in the end. She seemed to always be right, even though I, myself, didn't know it. Of course, I was going to choose to leave Cogsworth to take care of my mother, despite the person she was. Of course, I would do that, not only because I felt it was the right thing to do, but deep down, I felt as though she had been right about everything she'd said in the hospital.

To kill time and because I couldn't sleep otherwise, I washed my clothes at our campus laundromat, returning to our room just as the digital clock on my nightstand registered eleven after four in the morning. Still not tired enough to sleep, I fired up my laptop and shot an email to admissions at Cogsworth, along with my guidance counselor. In my email, I thanked the staff at Cogsworth for their support through the years and apologized for my sudden departure, insinuating that maybe I would return, even though I knew that to be rather unlikely. They would be upset that I hadn't had the lady balls to do this in person. But I had been balancing so precariously on the fence already that I was afraid that between the two departments, one of them would manage to pull me back over to the other side. Emails sent, I managed to fall asleep, hoping that Mena would come back the next morning in time for me to say good-bye.

She didn't.

Despite only managing to get three hours of sleep, I was still wide awake at about a quarter to eight the next morning. As soon as my eyes opened, I eagerly glanced at Mena's bed, dismayed to see it still as perfectly made as it had been the night before. I'd never seen her this upset about something before.

Spotting my duffle bag on the floor, I rolled over on the bed, allowed my feet to hit the ground, and gathered up the bag in my arms. I hadn't brought much with me when I came here, as I hadn't owned very much, anyway. For that, right now, I was thankful, as virtually everything I had brought fit nicely into that one bag, save for a few clothes, which I was able to pack away in another smaller bag I'd kept stuffed underneath my bed after I moved into the dorm.

Ready to leave, and still with no sign of Mena, I decided I would write her a letter, telling her everything I wanted to say to her. Things she wouldn't want to listen to me say to her right now, due to the anger and hurt feelings she harbored in her heart for me. And so, in the drawer of her desk, I rummaged around until I found one of her spare notebooks. Removing a pen from the ceramic holder on her desk, I penned a letter to her, close to three pages long, stating everything I wanted her to know. Basically, that I cherished every last second of our friendship, even though she exasperated me from time to time, that I was sorry for leaving the way I was leaving, and encouraging her to pursue a job in the publishing field. Finally, I asked her to one day find it in her heart to forgive me, ending the letter with my hope that we could move past this and that we would see each other again.

Then there was Luke. He knew nothing, other than my mother was gravely ill and that I was back in town. I'd neglected to tell him about my mother's request. We hadn't talked much while I was in Jasper, mostly communicating via text. He'd be in class right now— biology, I believed. I couldn't just interrupt his class to see him. Not only that, what would happen if I did? Surely he'd try to talk me out of my decision, much like Mena had tried to do. I would tell him it was useless and that my mind was already made up, that I was returning to Jasper tonight to meet with representatives of hospice, of whom I would be assisting with coordinating my mother's care. That would probably escalate into an argument.

No, I couldn't do that.

I would have to call Luke to explain what I was doing, hoping that he would understand why it was important to me that I do this, and also why I may not be returning to Cogsworth anytime soon.

Why I wouldn't be returning to him.

Without further thought on the matter, I sent a text to him, asking him to call me when he could, but letting him know that it wasn't an emergency. His phone was off in class, as it was a lab day. He'd be in labs until noon and would receive the message when he turned his phone back on. The first thing he would do was check it, as he'd be leaving directly from class for his shift at the hospital where he would have to shut it off again. This meant I should expect a call from him around ten after twelve. He'd be in his car, and I would be thoroughly enveloped by the mountains of West Virginia, well on my way back to Jasper.

Bags slung securely over my shoulder, I opened the door to our dorm room one last time, taking a final look around at the place where I'd met my best friend, where I'd spent the best years of my life. Not usually one for sentimentality, I couldn't help but be overcome by it as I looked at Mena's Panic! at the Disco and Red Hot Chili Peppers posters hanging on the wall, her well-organized desk with everything in its place, and meticulously made bed.

The only thing out of place on Mena's side of the room was the letter I left for her on her pillow. She'd notice it right away. Mena always had a habit of recognizing when things were out of place, and I had always told her that she'd make one hell of a detective, save for the whole interaction with people thing.

* * * * *

As predicted, I was almost through West Virginia when Luke called. It took me a moment to gather myself when the call came in and, thankfully, I was close to a rest stop when it did. While angling my car off the highway, my finger hit the button to accept his call, just as I'd found a parking spot in an isolated part of the parking lot.

"Hey," I answered, sick to my stomach already.

"Hey back," he answered. "What's going on? Aren't you back in Roanoke?"

"I was."

"What do you mean you were? You mean you drove all the way back to Roanoke just to drive back to Indiana again? Why ... oh my gosh, Elle, is your mom ... Did she—"

"My mom is still alive. I mean, she's dying, but she's not on death's door yet."

"Then why are you heading back?"

No matter how hard I tried to mentally prepare myself for this conversation, the truth was no amount of preparation was ever going to be enough.

"Is everything okay?" Fear permeated his voice.

"Yeah ... no. No, Luke, it's not okay."

"What is it? What happened? When are you coming back?"

"I'm not."

"Wh-What do you mean you're not?"

"My mother needs me right now. She doesn't want to die surrounded by strangers. She wants her daughter next to her."

"She wants her daughter to give up her future for her is what she means. Elle, it's not up to the child to be a soldier in their parent's battles. I know she's dying, and I'm really trying to be sympathetic considering the situation, but she had every opportunity in the past to have you in her life and she turned down every single one of them. Don't give up your future because she's trying to make up for her past."

"I've made my choice, Luke. I want to do this for her. I need to do this for her."

"Couldn't you have finished up school, first? You only have a couple weeks left in this semester and less than two years until your degree."

"And my mother has a couple weeks or months at best."

Luke fell silent, save for the muffled sound of his car rolling down the road. Just as I had predicted, he was in his car on the way to the hospital. "Okay, then, give me until the end of the week to get my affairs in order and I'll come out there."

"You'll come out where?"

"To Jasper."

My mother's words replayed inside of my head, and I finally understood what she meant. I would ruin Luke because Luke would do anything for me, including giving up his dreams to be by my side. He'd literally give up his entire life for me, quit school in Roanoke, leave his family and friends behind, and for what? To live a life of mediocrity, forever wondering what could have been? No, I couldn't allow him to do that. He deserved so much better.

"No," I said, cutting him off as he began to muse over how he was going to break the news to Monroe.

"No what?"

"I don't what you to come to Jasper." It took everything I had in me to hold in my pain, to be assertive when all I wanted to do was fall apart. I was a leaf in autumn, brittle and dead on the inside, ready to fall at any moment and crumble under the slightest pressure.

"It's not that big of a deal. I'll finish up my year here, transfer to a school in Indiana if I need to, and—"

"No. I said no."

Audibly shaken, Luke asked, "But why?"

My heart was breaking, shattering like a mirror dropped from a ten-story building. There would be too many pieces to ever find them all, let alone put them back together again, yet I had to do it. I had to respond to his question, even if my answer was a complete lie.

"Because I'm not in love with you anymore, Luke," I answered in as cold and unfeeling a tone as I could muster.

Luke inhaled sharply, as though he'd just regained his breath after having been socked in the gut. It killed me to hear him in such pain. If this call didn't end soon, there was no way I was going to be able to keep up this charade.

"H-How long have you felt this way?"

"A little while now. A few months, maybe."

"Months?" It was bad enough feeling my own heart break, but to actually hear his breaking in sync with mine was downright agony. "So, everything we've done over the last couple months—everything we've been through—you've been having your doubts about us, so much so that you wanted out of our relationship?"

"Yes." It was getting harder and harder to talk, to remain afloat in this storm.

"You're lying. You're not serious, Elle. You can't be. I would have known if you had been faking our relationship for that long. You've been yourself the entire time."

"Well, maybe you can't read people as well as you thought you could," I answered him, sounding more like my mother than myself. "Listen, Luke I wish you the best, I really do, but I have to go. I'm sorry it had to end like this, but it does. I'm not in love with you anymore … I never will be again."

"Well, I'm in love with you, and I always will be. I think all you need is time to think, time away for a while. Time to—"

"Good-bye, Luke."

If the finality of our breakup hadn't already struck him before then, it certainly had now. His heart, only just cracked up until then, had broken in half with a single word.

"Elle, no."

"Good-bye."

I ended the call then, turning off my phone to prevent me from calling him right back to tell him that I hadn't meant any of what I'd just said to him, that I really did love him, that there was no way I wanted to live my life without him there. But the damage had already been done. There was no turning back.

Over the next several weeks, Luke would call me periodically. All of his calls were sent straight to voice mail, his messages deleted instead of listened to. I couldn't hear his voice out of fear that I would beg him to come back into my life. Luke would do great things, but not here. Not with me. After about six weeks, the calls began to dwindle down to just once a week, eventually stopping altogether at the nine week mark, both a blessing and a curse.

My mother passed away on a cool crisp day in mid fall. The sun was shining brightly, providing some much needed warmth while I, and a handful of her former co-workers, stood around her grave site. I'd never met any of them, but they all seemed to know who I was. Much to my chagrin, they'd all arrived at the consensus that I looked exactly like her. I knew that was true, but I still didn't like hearing it because I only wanted to see myself when I looked in the mirror. Not my mother; never my mother.

"I'm sorry, Elle," a familiar voice spoke next to me, saving me from the darkness into which I had wandered.

"Mena?"

"There's no fooling you, is there?"

With tears in my eyes—the only ones I'd cried that day—I flung my arms around my best friend, grateful that our estrangement had ended.

"I'm so sorry," she said, just as choked up as I was.

"Me too," I replied, knowing that our exchange had nothing to do with my mother's death.

CHAPTER FOURTEEN

2018

Although I'd made my peace with my mother before and after her death, I still look back from time to time and think about how much she'd actually been able to manipulate me. She knew I was vulnerable and that my sense of self-worth had been non-existent. She knew that I would let Luke go no questions asked if I knew it would ensure his happiness, and she glommed onto that fact, using it to her advantage to capitalize on my insecurities.

It worked. She'd won. At least she'd had one victory in her life before she died, even if it had relied squarely upon her own daughter's misfortune.

Once again, I would be facing the consequences of my actions I'd taken at the behest of my mother. Not that it was entirely her fault. I was an adult, I could have made my own decisions. The decision to let Luke go had inevitably been my own. And now was the time to face the music.

Finding myself wide awake at six in the morning, I forced myself to get out of bed and prepared for the day, quietly packing my clothes and toiletries away in my suitcase. Even though I wasn't leaving until tomorrow, I figured I should at least pack my things in my car so that Candy and Tom wouldn't think I was trying to move in. Not only that, barring any unforeseen circumstances, Luke would be discharged tomorrow. Most likely he'd come here for at least a few days to continue his recovery. There should be no trace left of me when he arrived. Most certainly, he wouldn't want there to be.

The persistent silence in the house told me that neither Tom nor Candy had woken up. I glanced at the digital clock on the nightstand, which read twenty to seven. Candy was usually awake by now. She'd seemed exhausted lately, and I'd theorize that she was probably catching up on her lack of sleep.

Yawning, I climbed back on the freshly made bed and laid down on my side, allowing myself to take in every crack and crevice of the walls surrounding me. I closed my eyes, imagining the way the room looked when Luke was in it, every vivid detail coming back to me, like the dam that had been holding that information back had been breached, allowing the memories contained behind it to come flooding back in one enormous tidal wave of sensory overload. When Luke saw this room, he wouldn't recognize it. Perhaps he'd grow agitated by how much it had changed, how much it failed to resemble the room in which he'd spent his more formidable years. It had been somewhat jarring to me, and I had been anticipating the change.

Then again, after everything he was going to be told today, I was fairly confident that the aesthetics of Luke's room would be the least of his concerns.

* * * * *

Candy and I arrived at the hospital separately, three hours later. This time, she brought Tom with her, who looked almost as nervous as I felt. Not having children myself, I could only assume what it had been like for Tom as a father to see the horror and confusion in his son's eyes when he looked at him. Tom had felt like his presence was

230

a hindrance, as if he had been a source of his son's pain. This whole experience had to have torn him up.

We would all be meeting in a private conference room soon—the 'we' being myself, Candy, Tom, Monroe, Hannah, and Dr. Reid, the latter two of which would be present solely for support and to answer any questions Luke was going to have. I was certain there would be plenty of those, but I wasn't entirely convinced that they wouldn't be directed at me.

Movement nearby caught my attention. Monroe had entered the waiting area where we sat. The usually calm, cool, and a bit cocky man of which I'd become reacquainted, appeared downright disconcerted. Perhaps even a little nervous. The dark circles etched underneath his eyes were thick, as was the stubble accumulating on his chin. We locked eyes, and I couldn't resist grinning at the complete mess walking my way. He forced himself to smile back at me, as he settled down in the chair next to mine, nodding politely at Candy and Tom, who'd been quiet save for a few whispers every now and then.

"You look as bad as I feel," he said as an icebreaker when normal, polite conversation failed to materialize between us.

"Funny, I was just going to say the same thing about you," I replied.

In my peripheral vision, I caught the faintest hint of a smirk from him.

"At least I know I'm not alone," he replied, somberly.

I began to wring my hands, which were on my lap, together. "How do you think he's going to take it?"

"I don't know, honestly. He's going to be really confused, but I can't read Luke right now. Not the way I used to. Actually, I haven't been able to read him for quite some time."

My brow furrowed. "But you're his best friend? What happened between the two of you?"

"You know … life. We're still friends. We just aren't as close as we once were. Haven't been for about two years now."

"What happened two years ago?"

231

His face fell, like he'd just admitted something he shouldn't have. I imagined I could see the gears turning inside of his head, trying to figure out a way to backtrack.

"People just grow apart. It doesn't mean there's hard feelings, only that their lives are moving in two different directions."

He seemed remorseful when he spoke, saddening me. Monroe and Luke had been so close that I couldn't begin to imagine there having been something powerful enough to have pulled them apart.

"It would appear the gang's all here," Dr. Reid announced, his unnoticed entrance startling both Monroe and I. "Hannah's setting up the conference room and will meet us in there. Are we all set, or do you all need a few minutes?"

"Yes, Doctor," Candy said, standing up to greet him. "I do believe we're ready."

Speak for yourself.

Dr. Reid nodded. "Very well, then."

I stood up along with the rest of them. When I first arrived here, all I could think about was doing what I'd come here to do and leaving again to resume my life. A week later, all I wanted to do was prolong my time with Luke, if only for a moment.

"Unless I'm needed, I'd like to sit with Luke and keep him company while the rest of you are meeting. I mean, there isn't much I can contribute about his past, anyway," I announced so unexpectedly I even surprised myself.

Candy nodded her agreement before the words could escape her mouth. "I think that would be great, Elle. Luke would want that."

Casting one last glance at Monroe, I split from the group, turning in the direction of Luke's room. This was the last opportunity I would have to spend time with him before both his world and mine would fall apart, irreparably. If I didn't capitalize on the chance to spend these last few minutes together, I would regret it for the rest of my life. As I'd come to realize after I arrived here, I already had a mountain of regrets I would be forced to live with in that regard, anyway.

I walked into Luke's room, stopping short when I saw him in his bed. He was staring out the window at the sapphire sky. There was a peace surrounding him. He looked so serene, and I felt like I may be intruding for a brief moment, until I remembered the last precious seconds I had with him were falling away, like sand in an hour glass.

"Knock, knock," I said, as I walked into the room and sat in the chair next to his bed.

He smiled, appearing relieved to see me. "No matter how much Dr. Reid reminds me, I still can't believe I'm being discharged tomorrow. I was beginning to think I was living in some version of *The Twilight Zone.*"

"What makes you say that?"

"It's just the strangest thing, but lately I feel like I'm living two different lives. Events keep flashing through my mind that I normally would think may be memories, but they're of a life that I can't believe I've lived. Just before you walked in, I was wondering whether maybe the real life was the one being played out in these weird flashbacks, that I was really still in a coma and the images replaying in my head are part of the life I left behind. But then you walked in." Luke reached over and grabbed my hand. "And you're real. I can feel you, I can converse with you. What if I'm actually losing my mind, Elle?"

"But you're not," I said, squeezing his hand.

"How can you know that?"

"You sustained a pretty severe head injury. Your brain is rewiring itself. The images you're seeing, the confusion, are all part of your brain healing."

He nodded, having accepted my explanation for the time being. He wouldn't have long to wait to know the truth.

"Are we … are we together?" he asked, unexpectedly.

"Sure, we're together. I'm right here, aren't I?" I'd hoped my deflection wouldn't be noticed by him. I wasn't so lucky.

"I know we're in the same room as each other, goofball. What I'm asking is whether you and I are together still, as in a couple?"

233

"Why are you asking me that?"

"I know it's a strange question, but in the images I keep seeing, you are never there in person, just in memory. Those memories of you are both wonderful and painful all at once. I haven't been able to figure out why that would be. The only reason I can think of is that we aren't together anymore."

I couldn't think of a response, as blindsided by this revelation as I was. Shaken, I knew I should answer him, come clean. It was going to be laid out before him soon, anyway. But I couldn't. Be it cowardice or compassion, my lips just wouldn't form the words to answer his question.

As it turned out, I didn't have to.

Luke looked up to see Dr. Reid and Hannah entering the room, followed by Candy and Monroe. Dr. Reid positioned himself next to Luke on the opposite side of the bed, while Hannah stood next to where I was sitting. It gave me some comfort to have her next to me. A moment later, Luke's hand tensed as Tom entered, moving as best he could to stand next to Candy. Seeing Tom was a constant a shock to me, and I could only guess what kind of tortured thoughts were going on inside of Luke's head. Tom smiled at his son, clearly just as shaken as he was.

"What is this, an intervention?" Luke asked jokingly, although I still sensed his tension. He had a death grip on his bed sheet, probably an involuntary one.

"I wouldn't necessarily call it an intervention," Candy said, unable to suppress her nervous laugh. "Just call it a family meeting."

"With my doctors included?" he asked skeptically.

"Haven't they been like family to you? We just didn't want to leave anyone out."

"If that were the case, you would have invited me." A woman's voice, beginning in the hallway, slowly made its way inside Luke's room.

The expression on Candy's face was enough to sicken me. Her mouth had dropped open, as she gazed at the figure entering the room, a figure that remained unseen by those at the head of Luke's bed. Her kind eyes took on an almost reddish hue, aflame as they were. She shook, like a part of her wanted to pounce, as though she were a lioness preparing to defend her cub, but the more reserved part of her was holding herself back. The internal struggle, obvious. Next to her, Tom seemed to stumble a bit, his normally cool composure was also being challenged by the woman entering the room.

"Shit," Monroe verbally contributed his own feelings.

I looked up at him inquisitively, but was met by a stare that said, 'Brace yourself.'

"That voice," Luke said, just as confused as I was. "It sounds so familiar."

"I would hope I sound familiar to you." The woman behind the voice came into view. Tall with the slender build of a runway model, she was breathtaking. Her long, blonde hair was perfectly parted down the middle, framing her porcelain face. Her pale complexion enhanced her ice blue eyes; eyes so sharp they could cut glass. Draped over her body was a form-fitting sheath dress, blood red in color. The only thing out of place on her otherwise perfect image was her beak of a nose, which looked to have been the subject of at least one botched rhinoplasty.

"Margaret?" Luke asked, clearly stunned. "What are you doing here?"

Margaret? This was Luke's ex-girlfriend?

"Despite your mother's best efforts to keep me from seeing you, I figured as your wife, it's my duty to make sure my husband is on the road to recovery."

Wife?

My stomach sank to the floor. All I wanted to do was vomit right then and there. Between Monroe and Candy, how could neither one of them have mentioned to me that Luke was married?

"Married?" Luke asked just as confused as I was. "What are you talking about, Maggie? We haven't seen each other in years."

"I think it's time for you to be going," Candy stated, making a move to remove the much larger in stature woman. "I'll be happy to explain everything to you out in the hallway."

"Oh, I don't think so, Candy." Margaret pushed Candy's outstretched arm away. "I've been trying to do this the nice way for the last month, only get the brush off from you every time I called. We're going to do this my way."

Is Margaret the person whom Candy was speaking to that morning? Did she lie to me then, too?

I hadn't noticed them in her hand when she came in, but Margaret had been holding papers, which she unceremoniously plopped down on Luke's lap. "Now sign these, so we can be done with this already."

"Seriously, Maggie," Monroe said, making a mad dive for the papers before Luke could pick them up. "He's in no state to sign anything, right now."

"Oh really? He seems perfectly fine to me." Her gaze traveled from Luke, down his arm and to his hand, where my own hand still rested. Narrowing her eyes, she gave me the once-over. If a stare could shoot flames, I would be deep fried. "It looks like he's already shacking up with this one."

"You're one to talk, Margaret," Candy interceded, enraged like a mother bear protecting her much larger cub, "considering you're the one who's been sleeping with Dr. Vasquez for the better part of a year, remember?"

"Ladies, please," Dr. Reid interrupted what could have been an impending altercation. "Remember why we're here, Candy."

"Could everyone just stop talking for a moment?" Luke asked, beyond shaken. "First of all, Maggie, you will not speak to Elle that way. She's my girlfriend, and a hell of a lot better one than you ever were."

Oh, shit.

"Second, you and I were never married. I've been with Elle for the past eighteen months. Third, could someone please tell me what the hell is going on here?"

"So this is the infamous Elle Sloan?" Margaret said my name like it literally left a bad taste in her mouth. "The ex-girlfriend who dumped you over the phone and never spoke with you again for no reason at all?"

Luke diverted his attention from Margaret to me as if to ask, "Is this true?"

"Didn't you say she got married?"

I closed my eyes, knowing that I would have to tell him the truth this time.

"Elle?" he more or less plead. "Is this true … any of it?"

I opened my eyes, enabling a single tear to trickle down my face. Within the depths of Luke's stare, I could tell he wanted me to tell him this was nothing more than a fabrication, that he was dreaming again, and that none of this was real.

"Yes." I nodded my head, shaking loose another tear. "It's true."

Luke withdrew his hand from underneath mine and ran it through his hair, something he always did whenever he was stressed. "Let me get this straight, you're married?"

"Yes," I answered.

"But, we—"

"I know."

"I guess that explains some things." His body became rigid, and I noticed that he'd turned himself sideways, like he couldn't even bring himself to face me anymore. "So what, do I have amnesia or something?" He'd asked the question as a joke, but our silence ultimately confirmed to him it was anything but.

"Dr. Hutchins," Dr. Reid addressed Luke, completely taking both him and I off guard once more.

Doctor? Luke's a doctor? Why was this information kept from me?

"What? I'm a doctor?" Luke asked in total disbelief. "H-how much time have I lost?"

"Ten years, give or take a couple months," Hannah answered him.

"Wait, he has amnesia?" Margaret scoffed, throwing her hands up into the air. "And you didn't think this information was in the least bit important enough to tell me?"

Candy moved to say something in her defense, but was cut off by Margaret. If not for the fact that I was in shock, I would have seen what Candy had been about to start a couple minutes ago through to completion.

"At least it all makes sense now," Margaret continued, directing her verbal assault in my direction. "Luke would have never wanted anything to do with you if he had been in his right mind."

"Screw you, Margaret," Monroe blurted out.

"In your dreams, Peter. Listen, I'll give Luke, his attorney, or whoever one week to read over that Judgment. If it's not signed in a week, I'll have my attorney schedule a hearing and we'll see him in court, amnesia or not."

With an exasperated sigh, Margaret turned on her heels and click-clacked out of the room, leaving utter devastation in her wake.

"I always disliked that woman," Tom grumbled, carefully making his way to a chair with Candy's assistance.

Luke watched his father with tears in his eyes. Although, with the way he clenched his jaw and held his hands in tight fists, I sensed any sadness he was feeling was quickly dissipating, leaving only room for anger and betrayal.

"I want those papers, Monroe," he demanded.

"No, man, not right now. Give it some time to take this all in, first."

"Take what all in? The fact that my parents, best friend, my colleagues, and, I guess, my ex-girlfriend have all been lying to me for the last several days? I want to know the truth, all of it. So, please, be the friend you say you are and give me the papers."

Defeated, Monroe handed the documents over to Luke, who looked at them, intently flipping through the pages.

"It's true," he conceded. "I am married. To Maggie no less, and not to you." Still turned away, he glanced over his shoulder at me with so much pain on his face that I would have dropped off the face of the Earth if it meant taking it all away from him. "I would have married you, Elle. In a heartbeat. Just so you know."

I nodded, opening my mouth to say something, but stopping short when Luke addressed Dr. Reid.

"Am I ever going to remember the rest of my life again?"

Dr. Reid seemed relieved to finally have a chance to get a word in edgewise. He was probably the only one in the room who felt any form of relief. "If you would have asked me that a week ago, I wouldn't have been as optimistic as I am now. The dreams you've been reporting lately, I believe they may be memories very slowly making their way back. Will you make a full recovery? I don't know. Will you remember every last detail of your former life? Probably not. Will you be able to return to practicing medicine alongside myself and Hannah? I sincerely hope so. One thing's for certain, though. You are making progress. Without progress, you have nothing."

"Those were memories," Luke mused. "I knew it. A part of me knew I wasn't going crazy, but not a single one of you thought it best to tell me the truth after you saw me struggling? When you knew I was confused and I legitimately thought I was losing my mind? Seriously, Mom and Dad, not even you?"

"Luke," I spoke to the back of his head, "don't be angry with them. We all wanted to tell you. We just wanted to do it together, so you knew we were all here for you."

"Here for me?" Luke chuckled. "Are you shitting me right now, Elle? From the sounds of it, you haven't been here for me for a number of years. Actually, I have no idea why you decided to show up now, unless it was only to torment me further. You should leave. It would appear you had no problem doing that before."

"Luke, come on," Monroe interceded. "This isn't her fault. She didn't have to come, but she wanted to help you."

"I don't want her help."

I'd never heard him speak so coldly before. It hit me hard, like a smack across the face.

"Luke, I'm so sorry—" I began, but didn't get much further.

"If you want to apologize to me, you can leave. Leave now and don't come back."

My mind separated itself from the rest of my body when I stood up. My legs turned to Jell-O as I moved to the door, broken, exactly how Luke must have felt after our final phone call.

"Christ, if you're going to keep being a raging asshole during your recovery, I'm going to ask to be assigned to a different doctor," Hannah scolded as I left the room.

"Elle, please." Candy hurried after me. By the time she caught up to me, I was already halfway down the hall. All I wanted to do was get the hell out of Virginia and cuddle up and cry myself to sleep in my own bed. "Elle, I'm so sorry. He doesn't mean it. He's just so confused."

"But he does mean it." I only stopped long enough to address her. "And I deserved to hear it. What I didn't deserve was to be lied to."

Candy's face fell, knowing full well what I meant by that. "We just didn't know whether you were going to stick around or ..."

"Or whether I could be trusted," I finished her sentence. "I get it. Really, I do. All I can say is I'm sorry that I destroyed the respect you once had for me. And I'm sorry that I couldn't have done a better job with Luke while I was here."

"You were wonderful, Elle, and I'm sorry to have made you think otherwise. Please stay. None of us want you to go."

"None of you except the person I want to want me to be here the most. Good-bye, Candy."

I didn't look back again, but I knew she stood there, watching me walking away until at least the very second I was out of view, and most likely even thereafter.

The tension holding a death grip over my entire body dissipated the second I stepped out of the hospital. My shoulders slumped, and before I knew what I was doing, I found myself slumped over with my back against the glass walls of the catwalk. Even though he didn't want me anywhere near him, even though he despised me, it did nothing to silence the part of me that wanted to go running back inside of that hospital to be by his side. The unimaginable confusion and grief over the time he lost must be overwhelming. All I wanted was to take his pain away, to help him weed through the months, the years, he lost, just as he would have done for me. Luke had always stopped my ship from sinking when it was taking on water. Now I couldn't even return the favor.

So I left.

I peeled myself away from the wall, stood up, and walked the rest of the length of the catwalk to the parking structure. My purse strap slowly crept down my shoulder with each step, reminding me that I should probably fish my keys out of it. Allowing the bag to slide the rest of the way down my arm, I caught its straps and promptly opened it, digging through the black void for what should be a relatively easy find. As I approached my car, my fingers grazed the ridges of my key, finding the ring on which it was attached, and tugged at it until I was able to loosen it from whatever it was that had a hold on it.

As my keys emerged, a flash caught my eye, followed by the *ting, ting* sound of whatever it was that had fallen out of my purse hitting the ground. I bent down to find that my keys had dislodged my wedding ring, flinging it to the ground. The gold band stared back at me, begging me to pick it up and return it to the safety of my finger, but all I could do was stare, thinking of how my actions had been a betrayal to Eric. Strangely, though, that didn't bother me as much as the thought of the agony Luke was going through at that moment.

After a much longer than necessary amount of time went by, my fingers finally reached to pick up the symbol of the commitment I had made to another man and unlocked my car. The ring was still situated in the palm of my hand as I stepped into my vehicle. I didn't want to unfurl my fingers to look at it, even though I knew I had to sooner rather than later. Like hand washing the dishes as a child, it was a task I was going to delay doing until it was absolutely necessary. Unfortunately, that absolutely necessary moment was upon me, and I opened my hand to take in the simple piece of jewelry once more.

"Dammit," I lamented, allowing my emotions to overcome me for the first time since leaving Luke's room. "Dammit," I bellowed,

241

slightly louder than before. "Dammit! Dammit! Dammit! Dammit!" The last dammit in that series of dammits was an all-out scream, accompanied by the palm of my hand striking the outside edge of my steering wheel.

I'd done it. I'd been able to forget about him almost completely, except for a few fleeting moments here and there. For practically a decade, I'd kept his memory buried inside of a box in a remote corner of my brain. Now that the box had been opened, there was no denying why I'd done everything I could to keep from opening it. It was its own Pandora's Box, once opened, it had been destined to rain havoc down on my life.

I loved Luke. I still loved Luke. I'd only been trying to love Eric, convincing myself that my feelings for him were just as genuine and as real as they had been with Luke. That was a fact I couldn't keep buried away anymore. Once seen, it couldn't be unseen.

The ring fell back into my purse, as I shifted my hand to drop it in. I may never have Luke back, but that didn't mean I had to settle. It didn't mean I had to give up all my dreams and live my life to help build up the dreams of someone else. Luke had made me see my self-worth. He'd spent our last telephone conversation trying to make me realize that I deserved better. And for that, I was truly thankful.

CHAPTER FIFTEEN

By the time I arrived back in Indiana that evening, I was exhausted, mentally even more so than physically. Eric would be home by now, probably working intently in his office on a last minute brief, or preparing for a deposition, all of which kept him burning the midnight oil while I lay sound asleep in our bed. My hope was that I could sneak in without him realizing I was home. He wasn't expecting me to return until tomorrow, and I needed at least until then to mold my thoughts and feelings into something cohesive enough for me to articulate to him—to help him understand the unfathomable.

Our residential working-class neighborhood was already preparing to shut down for the night, as it was the middle of the week and days began early around here. Since moving in, I'd found that we mostly all left at the same time each morning, creating something of the appearance of an apocalyptic mass exodus from the neighborhood each day. It was particularly annoying if you happened to be in more of a rush in the morning than usual.

Our house was situated at the end of a cul-de-sac at the top of a hill, isolated from the rest of the homes just enough to afford us some privacy, yet close enough to keep us within the confines of the neighborhood's topography. With the sky steadily darkening, I pulled up the incline into our driveway. The house was ensconced between a virtual forest of maple trees, with only peeks of the front exterior visible from the road. Our driveway sloped up the hill and zigzagged around a couple of wayward pines, eventually straightening itself out near the entrance to the garage. And it was, just as I rounded the final curve, that I saw the small SUV parked in front of Eric's half of the garage.

Did he get another car without telling me? I thought, inspecting the foreign vehicle as I pulled my own into my side of the garage.

It was an older model Tahoe, one that could have been picked up for a relatively good price at an auction. A vehicle more desirable for winter driving than Eric's convertible, which would make sense if not for the fact that it was early spring. Eric also didn't strike me as an SUV guy, or one who would throw money away willy-nilly, for that matter, considering he was the one who encouraged me to use coupons when grocery shopping.

Tired from the drive and considering it inconsequential in the long run, I'd all but forgotten about the mystery vehicle when I walked inside of our house. It was dark, save for the light above the stove. Even Eric's office was dark, a shocker considering it was never that way unless he was out of town, which meant only one thing. He was in bed already. I'd have to settle on Plan B and hope that he was sound asleep and that I could just sneak into bed with him without having to answer any of his questions about how things went and the inevitable 'I told you so,' when he found out everything had ultimately been torn asunder.

Without bothering to hang my coat up, I threw it, along with my purse and keys onto the living room chair. I hadn't bothered to bring my luggage in yet. It probably still smelled like Candy and Tom's house; vanilla and cinnamon. Emotionally, I wasn't prepared to smell those scents yet. Perhaps, I would be stronger in the morning.

My hand covered my mouth to stifle a yawn, as I prepared to ascend the stairs, stopping short when I initially heard the noise. Soft and muffled, it was definitely of a vocal tone of sorts. Eric didn't normally sleep with the television on, then again, he didn't usually go out and buy new vehicles without consulting me first. There was a first for everything, apparently. Listening and hearing nothing further, I climbed a handful more stairs, pausing again when the sound was emitted once more.

Was that a moan? Not only that, was that a woman?

I tilted my head to the side, as though doing so would somehow help me hear better than I normally would. It seemed to work, though it was most likely because I was actually listening specifically for what I was hearing so clearly now. Yes, that was most definitely a moan, and it was most definitely from a woman.

Son of a bitch.

I'm not sure how I continued my climb up the stairs, or even why I continued for that matter. Our bedroom was located at the end of the hall, giving me ample time to change my mind, to turn back and leave, but continue on I did. I'd always been a firm believer of needing to see something with my own eyes before readily believing it. And it was because of that belief that the image I saw will forever be burned into my cerebral cortex.

The door to our bedroom was ajar, enough for me to see in without actually having to open it. Although the lighting wasn't the greatest, there was enough natural light remaining from outside for me to see Eric's naked rear end rocking back and forth on top of a woman whose face I couldn't make out, but of whom was having way more fun than I'd ever had when intimate with him.

I should have been angry, hurt, betrayed. All of the above. At the very least, I should have felt something. Strangely, and maybe even thankfully, I didn't. Indifferent; I was completely and utterly indifferent, numb to all pain.

Should I let them finish before I make my presence known? I mean, that would be the polite thing to do, wouldn't it? Screw polite ... heaven knows Eric probably already had.

My give a damn officially broken, I opened the door the rest of the way and flipped the switch, illuminating the inside of the room.

"What the hell!" Eric exclaimed at the same time the woman he was with let out a piercing shriek.

"Hi, honey, I'm home!" I announced in my best nineteen-fifties sing-song voice. "Oh, I'm sorry, I didn't know we were expecting company." The woman, my bed sheet wrapped around her naked body, attempted to hide her face, but I suspected I already knew who she was. She was larger, not exactly the type of woman I would have pegged Eric to be boinking behind my back, but she was young— twenty-five if I remembered what he'd told me about her correctly. "Why, darling, is that your new secretary? You've told me such wonderful things about her."

Like she isn't the best looking woman, but she does one hell of a job.

"Elle, baby, I thought you weren't coming home until tomorrow." He was trying to remain calm, cool, and collected, but I detected the waver in his voice.

"You're right, husband, that was the plan, but plans change, much, I see, like marriage vows. Now how about we get dressed so we can have a little talk downstairs? Nice to finally meet you in person, Charlotte." I waved at the woman, for whom I honestly felt more remorse than contempt. The poor girl had been used and would most likely end up discarded, just like I had been by Eric during the entirety of our union.

Not certain whether to shit or wind her watch, Charlotte slowly returned my wave, murmuring, "Nice to meet you, too, Mrs. Bell."

I sat on the couch in the living room, waiting for the two of them to get dressed and come downstairs. Occasionally I would hear an expletive erupt from Eric, who was probably pacing the room while poor Charlotte got dressed. His lawyer brain was turning, trying to formulate an argument or a way to spin what I'd seen with my own two eyes into something I knew it wasn't—a mistake, for instance. For the most part, Charlotte said nothing from what I could hear and was probably more or less terrified to walk down those stairs. When she finally did, I stood up to meet her.

Her arms were crossed in a defensive stance, and she went out of her way to avoid making eye contact with me. She was nervous, so nervous that I couldn't help but stifle a laugh, which only brought forth an extremely confused look from her.

"Come here," I said to her. Terror was clearly evident on her face as she attempted to process my request. Her eyes screamed indecision, torn whether to run for her life or comply with my request. "Seriously, Charlotte, I'm not going to do anything to you. If anything, you've done me a solid tonight."

Ashamed, she walked over to me, stopping short, just out of arm's length. Rolling my eyes, I bridged the gap and wrapped my arms around her in an embrace. "You deserve better than him, please always remember that," I said before letting her go.

Bewildered, she nodded and continued her walk to the door, where she freed her purse from the hall tree before making her way outside. The tears in her eyes as she left gave me hope that she may someday listen to my words and, with any luck, actually believe them.

"Elle?"

I closed my eyes, summoning all the strength I could muster to handle this the way it needed to be handled and not fly into a tangent like I wanted to.

"Eric," I responded, turning to face him. He stood behind me in the living room, his robe secured around his body.

"Elle, I don't know what to say. It's just that, you know you and I have been a little distant lately, and then you left to see your ex and—"

"Yes, I saw my ex in the hospital and, guess what, I didn't fuck him, Eric."

He was on the verge of blaming me for his having slept with another woman, deflecting the blame from himself and placing it squarely on my shoulders to try to make his actions seem reasonable. Something, I realized just then, he'd done throughout our time together.

"You don't have to be so crass. I'm sorry, really."

It was probably one of the most insincere apologies I'd ever heard.

He'd felt entitled to venture outside our marriage. I could read it all over his face, and as much as I wanted to smack the smugness from it, it wouldn't solve anything. Eric was what Eric was. That wasn't going to change. I'd known that going into the marriage. I'd just chosen not to see it.

"I should be mad at you," I said, continuing before he could cut me off like I could tell he wanted to do, "but I'm not. If anything, I should be thanking you for setting me free, for making me finally see that I do in fact deserve so much better in life. I've been selling myself short, letting go of relationships because I felt inferior. Because I believed all the people who told me I was nothing. It cost me my passion; it cost me the love of my life. But not anymore. So good-bye, Eric. I truly hope you find happiness, including someone to whom you deem worthy enough to stay faithful."

"Elle, wait," he called after me, as I grabbed my purse, keys, and coat and turned to leave. "Please, we can work this out."

"Yes, we could, but I don't want to."

He called after me a few more times without actually making a move to prevent me from leaving. Eric was nothing but lip service, and that evening was the last time I heard his voice again outside of a courtroom.

* * * * *

I hadn't brought much into the marriage as far as personal effects were concerned, but what I had brought had been significant enough for me to start my life over in the months that followed our expedited divorce. Upon her death, I'd learned that my mother had a sizeable 401k from her years of steady employment. And although it hadn't been the most desirable of living accommodations, she'd owned her home free and clear, meaning that I pocketed most of its meager sale price when I sold it a few months later.

When I met Eric, he seemed rather putout by the prospect of me supporting him in any way, since he had prided himself on having built a successful career. So my inheritance was placed into a trust, not to be touched throughout the entirety of our union and completely mine after the death of our marriage. Eric attempted to make a claim for it in the divorce, but I fought for what was mine—the only good thing my mother had ever given to me—reminding him that the partners in the firm were still completely in the dark about his extracurricular activities with one of their employees, a subordinate no less. In the end, we settled. I kept what was mine and he kept our home, including the equity and all the furniture in it.

A fair enough trade that would allow me to take my life back.

I'd found myself laughing at the irony that it was because of my mother that I could pursue my happiness again. And that's exactly what I intended to do. My inheritance from her wasn't close to being enough to allow me to sit around, but it was adequate enough to help pay the rent for my apartment long enough for me to be able to complete my degree at a local college. It also allowed me to quit my job at the call center so that I could focus solely on school. Some of the credits I'd obtained from Cogsworth were accepted by a local university and were transferable even after all this time. Two years and I would finally have the degree I should have had a decade prior.

All the while, I thought of Luke. How was his recovery coming along? Did he remember anything more about his past? Would he be able to return to practicing medicine? Those questions played through my head every night before I fell asleep. Sometimes they would be answered in my dreams and I would awaken satisfied for a time before they invariably came back to haunt me throughout the day.

Candy called me once since I left the hospital, but I hadn't answered her call. The last thing I wanted to hear was what a horrible idea it had been for me to have come there and how much Luke despised me. As painful as it was, some things were better left remaining unknown. At least then, I could draw my own conclusions and give Luke's story the happy ending it deserved. Besides, not only would my heart have been unable to take the truth, but it would skew the progress I was making in doing what I should have done a long time ago: Working on myself.

For once in my life, I would focus on me. Because I am strong. I am smart. I am Elle Sloan, and I'm worth it.

* * * * *

I fixed my makeup in the mirror of my visor, using an ample amount of powder to conceal the sweat beading along my hairline. The late summer heat had been exceptionally brutal this year and had been made all the more worse by my rushing from class to my car. From the university to the bistro was a distance of only three miles, not nearly long enough for my body to have thoroughly cooled down by the time I parked the car in the bistro's cramped parking lot.

I hadn't seen her in quite a while, yet it didn't matter. No matter how much time went by between visits, Mena always stood out from the crowd. Thankfully, the crowd at the bistro was particularly thin.

She sat at a small table on the patio, her long, espresso-hued hair fell just below her shoulders, stick straight and perfect, like the models in shampoo commercials. A pair of aviator glasses sat firmly on her nose, practically larger than her face. Despite the heat, she failed to display an ounce of sweat, looking perfect and svelte in her flowered sundress.

"There's my girl," she announced, standing up to greet me as soon as she saw me approaching her table. She wrapped her long, slender arms around me, holding me in an embrace that was firmer than I would have imagined, considering how petite she was. "Good god, woman." She drew back, giving me the once over. "I didn't need another bath today."

"Your candor is spot-on as always," I said, hoping the shade would lessen my perspiration. "In the sea of change, it's nice knowing there's at least one constant."

"I'm there for you, babe." Mena took a seat across from me, removing her sunglasses. "Besides, who said nothing has changed with me?"

"What? Have you grown even more quick-witted in your old age?"

"Let's just say I give less of a damn about what people think."

"May God help us all," I said, laughing at the thought of Mena being even more direct than she already was.

"Sometimes change isn't all that bad." Mena smiled. "It seemed to have served you well."

"It has. It will. Eventually." I ordered a latte from the waitress who stopped by our table just then. "The time it's taken to arrive at the destination I'm at now has been drawn out. I'm exhausted, but it takes time for a ship to begin changing course once the wheel has been turned."

"Have you spoken to him at all?"

"Eric? No, and the funny thing is I haven't even had the desire to speak with him. Most days, I forget he even exists."

"That makes two of us." Mena, smiled, raising her mug, before putting it to her lips. "So about this whole change thing. It's funny how it takes you in directions you never saw coming."

Confused, I could feel my eyebrow involuntarily raise. "I'm not sure whether I should be intrigued or afraid."

"That's funny, because neither can I." Mena motioned for someone behind me to approach.

Turning around, I found myself excited to recognize the tall, gangly, ruggedly handsome man walking toward us.

"Monroe!" I jumped up from the table to greet him.

"It's nice to see you, too, Elle," he greeted me without hesitation.

"I honestly never thought I'd see you again."

"Forever the optimist, I'd hoped we'd meet again." He smiled.

"If you're an optimist, then I'm Mr. Fucking Rogers," Mena proclaimed much to the displeasure of the couple at the next table.

"Always so eloquent," Monroe groaned, lightly pressing his lips to Mena's forehead.

"So, you two," I said, moving a finger from left to right.

"Don't say it out loud," Mena admonished. "I don't need other people to know."

"Know what, Mena?" Monroe asked, his voice raised. "That we're K-I-S-S-I-N-G."

Mena covered her face with her hands. "I hate you so much."

"No you don't," he corrected her.

"Dammit, no I don't," she conceded.

"How did you two get together?"

"Well, after you got back from Roanoke and told me what happened, I looked this one up online and gave him quite the keyboard lashing, which lead to a phone call, and a visit some time later."

"Which reminds me," Monroe chimed in. "I'm sorry we kept certain some things from you, Elle. Luke being a doctor, Margaret. We just weren't sure how things were going to go, and didn't—"

"You didn't feel like it was any of my business," I finished. "It's fine, Monroe. Your loyalty was to Luke, not to me, just how any good friend's would be."

"Still, we should have told you about Margaret. I'm sure seeing her was quite the shock."

"To say the least."

"Their divorce was finalized."

"Good to hear. It sounds like Luke can finally move on."

"What about you?" he asked.

"Let's see. I'm divorced after having devoted a couple years of my life to a loveless marriage. I live on my own and I'm the oldest student in any of my classes. But I'm doing what I want to, and I'm living my life for me, so there's that."

"Hear, hear," Mena announced, raising her mug once more. "I'm pretending this is wine, by the way."

"So I take it you're not dating?"

I waited for the punch line or some other Monroesque comment, realizing rather quickly that his question had been completely serious.

"No, I'm not dating. It may come as some surprise, but I've recently come to the conclusion that life isn't an Ed Sheeran song. There may be hope when it comes to the rest of my life, but when it comes to my love life, any hope of that being anything other than a train wreck was lost the day I left Roanoke ten years ago."

"Oh, I don't know, I think things could turn out 'Perfect' for you, after all," Mena pronounced, smiling slyly.

"I mean, maybe things will be okay for me in the end, but I don't know about—"

"You know, I'm just 'Thinking Out Loud,' but I predict more than just 'Supermarket Flowers' in your future."

My eyes shifted from Mena to Monroe, looking at him as if to ask, 'Has she completely lost her mind?'

"He'll really get to know the 'Shape of You,' if you know what I mean." At this point, she was giggling at her self-perceived wit. "Just don't ever let him take a nude 'Photograph.' I learned that the hard way."

Monroe and I shook our heads in unison, though I suspected it was because of entirely different reasons.

"For Christ's sake, Elle, just turn around," Mena sighed.

More confused than ever, I turned with a little prompting from a beaming Monroe.

"Hello, Sloan."

If it were possible for a person's jaw to actually drop to the floor, mine would have been scraping the bricks on the patio. On unsteady legs, I stood to face him, amazed that he was standing at all. Despite the seven months that had gone by since his accident, because his legs had been so badly broken, I'd questioned whether they would ever again be able to bear the weight of his body.

"Hello yourself, Hutchins."

He took a step forward with a pronounced limp to his gait, and that's when I noticed the cane in one hand and the bouquet of lilies situated in the other. Other than the limp, he resembled the Luke I'd met so many years ago. His hair had grown out, covering his surgical scars, and he bore a healthier rosy complexion.

"Psst ..." Mena interrupted my reverie. "Now would be the time for one of you to say something."

"Thanks, Mena," Luke replied sarcastically. He closed the distance between us, taking great care with each step. I wasn't positive whether this was the way he had to walk now or whether he was just being extra cautious around the other tables and chairs on the patio. When he came within a foot of me, he stopped and stared down into my eyes once more. "I know that I may be the last person you want to see right now, but I couldn't keep myself from coming to see you and tell you that I'm truly sorry for everything I said to you back at the hospital. I was—"

"A real dick," Monroe chimed in. From the sound of the slap behind me, a high five was shared between him and Mena.

"Thanks, bud, but I got this," Luke called out to him, annoyed. "I was a dick to you, and you didn't deserve it. What you did for my family, for me, was remarkable, and I owe you my thanks."

"Hey," Mena whispered loudly, "how about giving her the flowers."

Luke sighed as Mena muttered something to Monroe about this being the last time she would be bailing us out.

"This doesn't come anywhere near to making up for my behavior, but I hope it's a start."

He handed me the bouquet, which I took and held up to my nose to take in their scent, as I always did when around lilies. Luke smiled, clearly remembering that fact.

"I just got struck by a sense of déjà vu."

"That makes two of us, because I've had one for the last six months." I set the flowers down on the table and turned to face him again. "Luke, you don't have to apologize to me. With the way I ended our relationship, I felt like I owed it to you, and I really don't blame you for being upset. I can't begin to comprehend the confusion you were going through when Margaret came and blew your world as you knew it apart. We were all there and were going to tell you ourselves before she showed up."

"I know. Mom told me everything."

"I wanted to tell you. There were a couple times when I almost did. You deserved to hear it that way. I'm sorry that's not how it happened."

Luke nodded. "Th-There is something you could tell me, something I still don't know."

"Of course. Anything."

"I'll understand if it makes you too uncomfortable and you don't want to answer it." He paused, and I could sense he was having second thoughts about even asking me at all. "Why did you leave me, Elle? All these years, I wondered what I did, what I said. For my own sanity, I need to know, because something tells me it wasn't because you fell out of love with me. Maybe it was, but I never really believed that."

"No, I never fell out of love with you, Luke. The truth is, I'd fallen out of love with myself. Or maybe I'd never been in love with myself to begin with. I came from nothing, you came from everything. It was embarrassing bringing you back to my mom's house. If we would have stayed together, I would have brought you down. You would have followed me back home to take care of my mother, giving up your dreams. Luke, I wasn't worth that. You deserved better. I mean, look at you, you're a doctor."

He seemed bewildered, if not somewhat relieved before he spoke again. "So you think I deserved a woman from a happy family, one who was perfect in every conceivable way. One who was on my level?"

"Well, you and Margaret found each other again."

"And I was miserable every second I was with her. I spent so much time telling myself that things would be better, that I would have the same feelings for her that I had for you. But I never did. Margaret came back into my life at the peak of my loneliness. She knew it and took advantage of both that and the fact that I was on the verge of completing my residency. She was an opportunist. Different from you in every way. Elle, I didn't care where you came from, that your family life was less than ideal, or that you weren't perfect by your definition of the word. To me, you were the most spectacular woman I'd ever met. And yes, I would have followed you back to Indiana. Hell, I would have followed you to Timbuktu if you would have let me. But you know what? I would have found a way to continue my education. Where there's a will there's a way, and I had the will."

"So you remember your life between our breakup and the accident?"

"I remember enough to piece together the important events. Most everything I learned in medical school came back fairly quickly. I've been practicing under intense supervision, which I hope will dwindle away with time. As it is, I feel like I'm a toddler taking his first steps while the other physicians stand at the opposite end of the room saying, 'Attaboy, you can do it.' It's all been extremely ... humbling."

"That has to be incredibly frustrating for you," I said, stifling a laugh.

"I'm happy to see my plights are so entertaining to you, Sloan." He adjusted his weight on his cane, his legs obviously in discomfort.

I gestured toward a chair. "Do you want to sit down?"

"No, it's good to stand on them for a bit. I sat for quite a while on the plane ride here and then on the car ride from hell with that one over there." He nodded at Mena, shuddering at the recollection.

"You're still alive, aren't you?" she asked, unfazed.

"Yes, but not without my fair share of near heart attacks. But in the end, it was all worth it to see you again and to tell you what I needed to tell you. I'm just happy that you were able to find happiness in your life again, Elle. That's always what I wanted for you."

I looked back at Mena and Monroe, who both answered my silent inquiry with a shrug, as I turned back to Luke. "I'm sorry?" I asked.

"You're married," he proclaimed as though the answer should have been obvious to me.

No one told him.

I looked back to Mena for confirmation and was met with a smirk. All the confirmation I needed.

"So, I think I need to use the restroom," Monroe announced, scooting his chair away from the table.

"And I think I need to go help him," Mena stated, sliding out of her own chair to follow him.

"I don't think I want to know." Luke watched them disappear inside the building. He took a few steps forward to the empty chair next to where I had been sitting.

"I'm not married," I blurted out, unable to contain the truth any longer.

He stopped short so quickly that he had to steady himself on the table. Remaining there with his back turned, I started to wonder whether his misstep had been more of stumble rather than as a result of hearing what I'd said.

Still steadying himself against the table, he maneuvered his body back around to face me again.

"What?" he asked, his voice trembling.

"I was married, but I realized I wasn't in love with him, and I don't believe he was ever really ever in love with me, either."

"When … When did you realize you weren't in love with him?"

"When I was with you."

"I think I need to sit down now." Luke reached for the chair behind him and sat, wincing a bit when his knees began to bend.

"Did your ex do something to you while you were with me to change how you felt?"

I sat down next to him, running my finger across the smooth petal of one of the lilies from his bouquet. "No— I mean, yeah, he did cheat on me, but I didn't know that until after I returned home."

"He sounds like a real idiot."

I gave him a small smile, which probably looked more like a grimace. "I'm not going to argue with you there."

"So, when you were with me?"

"I realized that all I had done was tuck my feelings for you away somewhere. I'd been ignoring them because I didn't want to accept that I had lost the love of my life. I love you, Luke. No amount of time, no other person has been able to change that."

I lifted my head to meet his eyes, glassy from the pools forming in them.

"I'm sorry if I'm speaking out of turn. If you've moved on—"

"Moved on?" Luke asked incredulously. "Sloan, I was married and never moved on. I love you. I've always loved you. Hell, even when

I couldn't remember literally anything else, I still remembered that I loved you. God help me, it's become apparent that I'm never going to stop loving you."

"For crying out loud, kiss her already." Mena reappeared at the table and picked up a pack of cigarettes Monroe had left there. "Forgot his smokes," she said, unnecessarily holding up the box as she walked away again.

The touch of Luke's hand on my cheek brought me back to him. "As much as I hate to say it, I agree with Mena," he murmured, drawing himself in closer to me.

"That makes two of us."

As our lips touched for what I'd hoped would be the first of many more times to come, I, at last, found myself able to put my past behind me and focus squarely on the journey that was yet to be, knowing that no matter what, our love would make sure we always found our way back to each other.

About the Author

Sara "Furlong" Burr was born and raised in Michigan and currently still lives there with her husband, two daughters, a high-strung Lab, and three judgmental cats. When she's not writing, Sara enjoys reading, camping, spending time with her family, and attempting to paint while consuming more amaretto sours than she cares to admit.

You can learn more about Sara at http://sarafurlongburr.blogspot.com, follow her on Twitter via @Sarafurlong, and read more of her ramblings via Facebook at https://www.facebook.com/EnigmaBlackKindle.

Other works by Sara include the *Enigma Black* trilogy (*Enigma Black, Vendetta Nation, Redemption*) and *The Living and The Dead*.

Made in the USA
Middletown, DE
11 August 2022

70681970R00146